Deadlines and Valentines

Deadlines and Valentines

A JULES KEENE GLAMPING MYSTERY

Heather Weidner

Stan, thanks for all the love and support.
Dawn, thanks for all the encouragement. I miss you.

Praise for Deadlines and Valentines

"I devoured each and every page."—Mariam Mulla, Book Reviewer

"I just finished reading this book. I loved it. I'm looking forward to the next one!"—The Book Decoder, Book Reviewer

"I thought the interactions of the diva authors was hilarious, and really added to the story, we don't normally get funny moments in the true crime genre so it was really a treat."—Terah MacInnes, NetGalley Reviewer

"I liked this book a lot and the animosity among all the authors made this book fun to read. Everyone had a motive, but who is the real killer?"—Lisa Currier, NetGalley Reviewer

"The mystery was really good. I loved the Scooby Doo vibes. I would definitely check out more books by this author!"—Shaina Burris, NetGalley Reviewer

"Weidner's writing is crisp and keeps the story moving at a good pace."—Jennie Bishop, NetGalley Reviewer

"This was a really cute cozy read. Gave me Scooby Doo and the Mystery Machine vibes! I'll definitely have to pick up and read the other books to this series!"—Grace Lee, NetGalley Reviewer

"Loved this book, very interesting and keeps you hooked until the very end."—Rachel Phillips, NetGalley Reviewer

Praise for Christmas Lights and Cat Fights

"A resort owner starts solving the murder of the ex-wife of one of her guests. This book literally made me so jealous that I wasn't in a cabin near the mountains with fresh snow and a murder to investigate. The plot is very refreshing and enticing. The writing is sensational, I could envision everything so perfectly."—Shannon Coe, NetGalley Reviewer

"This book reminded of the mysteries I read when I was younger, good clean and fun! I like the author's writing style and she seemed to have a good knowledge of police procedurals without over doing it for this fun styled book. There's some good clean, budding romance, sleuthing and mystery that you won't want to miss!"—Angela Hodge, NetGalley Reviewer

"This was a delightful and suspenseful holiday mystery that will keep you hooked from the very first page. This book combines the festive spirit of Christmas with a thrilling murder mystery, creating a unique and captivating story."—E. A. Andrews, NetGalley Reviewer

"I really am looking forward to the next book! I highly recommend *Christmas Lights and Cat Fights* (and the other Jules Keene books!) for its amazing characters, delightful setting, and puzzling mystery! I think cozy mystery lovers will enjoy it as much as I did."—Christy's Cozy Corners, Book Blogger

"Such a cozy, festive mystery! I binged this in one sitting! Definitely need to pick up a trophy copy. I can't wait to read more by Heather in the future!"—Megan Moore, NetGalley Reviewer

"I thoroughly enjoyed this story, and if you enjoy cozies, I think you will too. Plus, there are cats, and it's Christmas. What's not to like? It's a nice addition to this series by Heather Weidner!"—Jackie Layton, mystery author

"Absolutely loved this book! The author's writing style is amazing! I look forward to reading more from them!"—Rebecca May, NetGalley Reviewer

"*Christmas Lights and Cat Fights* by Heather Weidner is a delightful and cozy mystery that combines the joy of the holiday season with an entertaining feline twist. With engaging characters, a charming small-town setting, and a purr-fectly mysterious plot, this book is sure to keep fans of cozy mysteries entertained."—A Moment with Mystee, NetGalley Reviewer

"*Christmas Lights and Cat Fights* is a fun cozy with a nice winter-holiday theme."—Rebecca M. Douglass, Author and Book Blogger

"This is a charming cozy mystery for the Christmas holiday. Heather adds many festive details to the descriptions of Fern Valley, making me wish I could visit Jules' resort and stay in a tiny house. I particularly loved the descriptions of snow in the valley."—Sarah Erwin, *Kings River Life*

"This was a suspenseful holiday mystery that kept me hooked from the first page to the end of the story. It's the 3rd book in the series and is full of surprises. The characters are engaging and entertaining. Many are suspects with secrets that kept me guessing. I also enjoyed reading all the recipes following the end of the story. I look forward to reading another book by Heather Weidner. If you like cozy mysteries, then I am sure you will love this one."—Eadie Burke, NetGalley Reviewer

"A fun cozy. Throw together a wife, ex-wife and Christmas time along with a huge blow up between them and you get mayhem. And some cats are missing! Not your everyday house cats either! Yikes! Jules is trying to keep everyone happy while finding out who did the ex in. Great setting. Good characters."—Renee Winter, NetGalley Reviewer

"Christmas mystery meets the Tiger King! I was excited to read this book. Weidner's book had me guessing until the end. It's a perfect read for a cozy night!"—A Book to Mark, Book Blogger

"I was looking for a fun mystery set during the Christmas season to get me in the holiday spirit. *Christmas Lights and Cat Fights* by Heather Baker Weidner was just the book! I was delighted to find that it was set in Virginia, and I recognized many of the towns. I want to continue to follow the adventures of Jules Keene."—Theresa Werner, Journalist

"This is a fast-paced mystery with an interesting setting and an engaging amateur sleuth. A fun read around the holiday, or anytime."—Anna St. John, mystery author

"This was such an amazing holiday cozy mystery. I couldn't stop reading this book!! I hope more comes out with Jules as the main sleuth. I think that they would be awesome. I loved the writing style of Heather Weidner, and I will definitely be reading more from her."—Lori Clenderin, NetGalley Reviewer

"Christmas, Oh I do love Christmas at any time of year. This is a book that is a bit of fun, a bit of murder and of course an amateur sleuth. A cosy mystery and an entertaining read. A good story and it is very easy to read, I enjoyed the characters and the setting. And to top it off. Recipes! I wasn't expecting that."—Donna Robinson, NetGalley, Reviewer

Praise for Film Crews and Rendezvous

"Lights! Camera! Action! Heather Weidner has penned a delightfully entertaining cozy mystery with a strong female lead, a handsome love interest, realistic connection to law enforcement, a snuggle-worthy dog, clever nod to Baum's *Wizard of Oz*, and just the right amount of trials and tribulations to keep readers on their toes. Starting with the perfect karmic choice of victim, the additional murder, questionable accidents, evasive suspects, overheard arguments, revealed secrets, and incriminating photos made this a 'couldn't put down' tale of illicit affairs, professional conflicts, and a social media smack down. And the final arrest? I didn't see that coming ... loved it!

"Heather's writing style is very entertaining worthy of reading more of her work. She has created a delightful environment and characters that work, play, and love in endearing ways to make this a book you'd like to enter. Jules is a determined woman with tight family and friend relationships including the Sheriff, a connection which offers a more natural involvement in the murder investigation ... sure she goes off on her own snooping and finds herself in jeopardy, but it meets the realism I expect."—Kathleen Costa, *Kings River Life Magazine*

"With the inviting setting of a luxury camping resort in the Blue Ridge Mountains, a plucky protagonist, and a twisty murder to solve, *Film Crews and Rendezvous* has all the ingredients that appeal to cozy mystery readers."—Kim Davis, Reviewer

"Weidner hits it out of the park with this Jules Keene Glamping Mystery. I loved FILM CREWS AND RENDEZVOUS. Jules is a fun character in this great mystery. Weidner keeps you guessing throughout this delightful story. Of all her books I've read, this is definitely one of my favorites."—Cat Brennan

"This series is something truly original."—hsim3691, BookBub Reviewer

"This is a fun addition to the Jules Keene glamping mystery series. As always, it presents a cast of quirky characters and a surprise twist at the end. Highly recommended."—Mary Miley, mystery author

"I had never heard of glamping until I started reading the Jules Keene mysteries. Jules is a savvy business owner who always seems to be in the middle of a new adventure which includes murder. Fun to read to figure out who done it. Keep these mysteries coming!"—Vince A., Reviewer

"This is a great book!! I really enjoyed it! When I started reading and discovered that it is set pretty close to where I live, I wasn't sure if I would be able to enjoy it or if I was going to constantly be noticing things about the area that are wrong, but the location didn't end up bothering me at all. It held my interest the whole time, too. I'll be keeping an eye out for the next book in this series."—Sarah Manspile, NetGalley Reviewer

"I thoroughly enjoyed this mystery story set in a Hollywood setting. This had me guessing and guessing who the murderer was and in the end I was wrong. Heather has created characters who are colorful, and she develops them in a way that you will learn about them as you read."—Katie Edgard, Net Galley Reviewer

"This latest book by Heather Weidner is great fun. The descriptions of the resort setting are visual, the film crew characters come alive, and there are enough plot twists to keep you guessing. In addition, all the references to food make you want a snack. (Spoiler alert: there are recipes at the end.) A good holiday read and stocking stuffer!"—Charlotte Stuart, mystery author

"The second of the Jules Keene Glamping mysteries and the apparent arrival of Hollywood in Fern Valley is raising more than a few eyebrows. The glamping resort has, in fact, never seen anything like it - as the divas and the drama arrive in droves. Amidst the menagerie, however, a killer lurks and it's not too long before chaos ensues and bodies pile. Jules needs to act fast before her previously booming business goes bust. With a cast of eccentric characters, a pacy plot and a frothy narrative this is an entertaining entry in the series."—Ruth Giles, NetGalley Reviewer

"Although I haven't yet read *Vintage Trailers and Blackmailers*, the first book in the Jules Keene Glamping Mystery series, I was soon hooked after beginning *Film Crews and Rendezvous*! It didn't take long for me to become acquainted with Jules and her dog, Bijou, from Fern Valley in the Blue Ridge Mountains. With an obligatory murder, the characters are beguiling, and the mystery held my attention and kept me guessing. A great tale."—Bridget East, NetGalley Reviewer

"An entertaining story and I like the idea of the tiny houses. They intrigued me and off I went researching them. I do like stories that pique my interest in something new."—Kate Merson, NetGalley Reviewer

"A very fun read!!" —Liz Boeger, mystery author

"*Film Crews and Rendezvous* gets five stars from me! The entertaining characters, cozy small town setting, humor, and twisty mystery make Film Crews and Rendezvous a cozy I highly recommend."—Kristy's Cozy Corners

"Hollywood, glamping, and murder… oh my! *Film Crews and Rendezvous* by Heather Weidner had me at the Blue Ridge Mountains setting (aka, one of my happy places) and then kept me engaged by the various layers to this murder mystery. As the title suggests, Jules' glamping resort is overrun by a film crew—and the crowds it attracts—and trying to keep up with who is rendezvousing with who (all off-scene) becomes an almost full-time job for poor Jules. All in the name of investigating the double murder, of course. The author does a great job of setting the scene and moving the mystery along at a steady pace. Sorting the clues from the misdirections will take some skill for readers-slash-armchair-detectives and keeps us invested in the outcome – a cleverly-crafted outcome, at that. Also, I want the tiny homes at Jules' resort to be real because I want to stay in the Rowling one. Such a fun idea!"—Carrie Schmidt, Reading is my Super Power Blogger

"What a fantastic addition to the series! This has to be my new favorite in the series! I love the setting—Blue Ridge Mountains, the characters (Jules, Aunt Roxanne, Jack, Pixel and of course, Jules' dog Bijou), and this time we have a film crew on set. So, more drama, more saucy gossip and rumors, and more action… with a dash or two of murder."—The Book Decoder, Book Blogger and Reviewer

"What do you get when you mix Hollywood people and a small town in the Blue Ridge Mountains: you get this amazing book. I need to read the first book in the series."—Riley Wiederhold, Book Reviewer

"With lots of twists and turns, a little romance, a murder and a strong, take charge protagonist in Jules Keene and you have a winning cozy murder mystery!"—NorthStarVance, BookBub Reviewer

"All the characters are well written and interesting. The dialogue is smart with a bit of sass. Heather Weidner has done a great job writing Film Crews and Rendezvous. I'm looking forward to reading more books in this series."—rmkrejsa42, BookBub Reviewer

"A new to me author and series. It was the first I read and won't surely be the last as the author did a good job in developing a solid plot that kept hooked and guessing. The fleshed-out characters are likeable and I had a lot of fun. Recommended."—Anna Maria Giacomasso, NetGalley Reviewer

"Such a cute, fun read! I really enjoyed the mystery in the book, and I thought the story flowed really nice. Such a good book!"—Noelle S., NetGalley Reviewer

"I really liked this book! The setting was great and very well written. I am now very interested in glamping myself. The author really involved every part of the setting in a well thought out way and it really made the book better. I liked the steady pace which never made the book boring or to intense. It was a good mix between the author telling us what we needed to know and stuff the reader had to figure out by themselves. I was very invested in the book and liked all aspects of it!"—Molly Bossel, NetGalley Reviewer

"I absolutely loved this book! The story is so well developed, and the characters are so relatable. I love the tiny homes that are in the book. If you are looking for a fun fast paced reed, I highly recommend!!"—Katie Burleson, NetGalley Reviewer

Praise for Vintage Trailers and Blackmailers

"I love the premise of this well-written and light-hearted whodunit where we meet Jules Keene, who owns a camping resort where murder does not mix with vintage trailers, but alas a guest fell victim and it was up to Jules to figure out the who, the what, and the why this person was murdered and to protect her business.

"From the introduction of the characters to the small-town atmosphere to the vintage trailer camp to the victim to the events leading up to his death and the killer's identity and apprehension, the author did a great job in presenting this well-crafted mystery that kept me immersed in all aspects.

"The suspect pool was short, but it was the follow-ups that kept me in the guessing game. The author knows how to tell a story that was both intriguing and suspenseful with visually descriptive narrative and engaging dialogue.

"The pacing was on par with how well this story was being told. Overall, this was fun book and I look forward to more adventures with Jules and her friend in this delightfully entertaining series."—Dru Ann Love, Dru's Book Musings

"In *Vintage Trailers and Blackmailers*, the calm of Jules Keene's Blue Ridge Mountain camper resort is disturbed when a man's lifeless body is found in the woods. What follows is a cozy mystery full of blackmail, secrets, mysterious strangers—and handsome security guy, Jake Evans. Jules and her loyal pup Bijou are in for a suspense-filled adventure. I love the warm and friendly characters and the twists and turns in this new down-home, mutt-loving series."—Susan Van Kirk, author of The Endurance Mysteries and *A Death at Tippitt Pond*

"Jules Keene is focused on her vintage trailer camping resort, but when a dead guest is discovered in the woods and her aunt is questioned, Jules decides to help catch the killer. She must stop the culprit, keep her guests satisfied, grow her business, run for president of the town's business council, and stay alive when the bad guys come after her. This book is a joy to read."—Jackie Layton, author of the Low Country Dog Walker Mysteries

"Packed with action and filled with "Oh, man, I didn't see THAT coming" moments, this first installment in the Jules Keene Glamping Mysteries series will not disappoint. And Weidner made glamping sound so glamorous that I think I'll take my husband up on his suggestion to go camping…but only if it's Fern Valley Camping Resort style!"—Jayne Ormerod, author of *Goin' Coastal*

"Smart and persistent businesswoman Jules Keene puts on her amateur sleuth hat to track down murderers at the upscale Fern Valley Camping Resort, set in the beautiful Blue Ridge mountains. The bad guys have met their match in this fast-paced mystery."—Frances Aylor, author of *Money Grab*

"Heather Weidner's *Vintage Trailers and Blackmailers* is an exciting addition to this year's cozy mystery line-up. Fern Valley Camping Resort, with its refurbished vintage trailers and tiny houses, is as enjoyable as can be, but don't be fooled, this book is all excitement. I don't know how she combines charm with a fast-paced story but I'm so glad she did."—Lane Stone, author of the Pet Palace Mysteries and the Tiara Investigations Mysteries

"Heather Weidner writes a fun and intriguing mystery that's full of twists and turns. Jules Keene, the owner of the posh Fern Valley Camping Resort in the Blue Ridge Mountains, brings sass and adventure as she works to figure out what's happening in her glamping get-away. The other characters are also well defined and add romance, humor, and hair-raising antics! Hard to put down once you start!!"—R. Lambertson, Amazon Reviewer

"I really enjoyed this fun read and would highly recommend it for anyone. I especially liked the idea of the vintage trailers. What a great idea for a campground!"—Sandra Fehr, Amazon Reviewer

"With an appealing cast of characters and a smart amateur sleuth, this series kicks off with a bang. I recommend this to readers who like their mysteries with plenty of red herrings before the satisfying end. Five stars!"—K. M. Rich, Amazon Reviewer

"A mystery with humor, full of secrets, one very handsome security guy, Bijou the dog, blackmail, and some interesting strangers. A fun mystery and look forward to what happens next."—Amy, Goodreads Reviewer

"Heather Weidner wrote a really great storyline with great characters. I think Jules's dog, Bijou, will be everyone's favorite character. The town of Fern Valley seems like the ideal spot for tourists, but it has that warm familiarity to it that could easily make it home for anyone. I'm so excited to see what Heather will come up with next for Jules and Bijou."—Valerie Blankenship Book Reviews

"*Vintage Trailers and Blackmailers* by Heather Weidner is a fantastic start to a new series for Ms. Weidner. I can't wait to read the next book in this series to find out what else Jules can get into when it comes to solving a mystery. Jules, Roxanne, Jake, and Emily are all great characters, and I can't wait to see what else can happen with them. I am giving *Vintage Trailers and Blackmailers* by Heather Weidner five stars and recommending it to everyone that likes to read cozy mysteries."—Karen Baron, The Baroness Book Reviews

"This is my first book by this author, but it definitely won't be my last! I was hooked from the very first page!"—Tonya S., BookBub Reviewer

"The unique setting at a campground pulled me in and gave me a vicarious "glamping" escape. Memorable characters, unique setting and twisty-turny plotting made this a great weekend read. Waiting (not so patiently) for the second installment in the Jules Keene Glamping mysteries."—Mystery Loving Mom, Amazon Reviewer

"Take a break from routine with a visit to a charming mountain resort that features vintage trailers and other whimsical lodging options. While there, get caught up in a puzzling death of a guest. Resort owner Jules investigates murder with the help of an interesting cast of characters. A satisfying and enjoyable read."—S. E Warwick

"Now, this is my idea of camping! Cute, upcycled vintage trailers are so much better than tents! (Not that I have camped in a tent in the last 30 years…..) If Fern Valley Camping Resort was real, you can bet I'd be vacationing there. As owner of this resort, Jules Keene has got a great thing going. The campers are full, and people are happy. One reason they might be happy too is the delicious breakfasts that they can get in the lodge. I'd fill up on cinnamon rolls.

"*Vintage Trailers and Blackmailers* is a fantastic start to what I'm sure will be a wonderful series! Heather Weidner paints us a vivid picture, and it's easy to feel as if you're in Fern Valley. She describes not only the camping resort but also the town. You're going to get hungry since Jules visits several trendy restaurants in Fern Valley. So, get some cookies or carrots (or better yet, cinnamon rolls) for your book reading snack. I also love the fact that she doesn't tell us about many of the trailers because that leaves more surprises for the next book. And, speaking of more surprises, I can't wait to see how the tiny house village that they're planning comes along.

"The book was a light, fun, quirky read with interesting characters. It sets up for a unique series. I found it very entertaining and enjoyable to read this clean, fun cozy mystery! I highly recommend this book and series!"—Nellie Steele, Nellie's Book Nook

"Heather Weidner has done an outstanding job with this engaging and enjoyable debut novel that features Jules Keene. The story introduces a group of realistic characters. Jules is likable and believable in the central role, and the supporting characters are an interesting mix of personalities. The story is not just about a mystery to be solved. It also encompasses secretive behavior, interpersonal relationships, perseverance, political aspirations, business undertakings, the close connection between a pet and its owner, and a juggling act between amateur sleuthing and fulfilling job-related duties."—Diane Woodman, Amazon Review

"*Vintage Trailers and Blackmailers* is the first book in a new series but doesn't read like one. I mean that in the best possible way. Often, first books tend to spend a lot of time setting the scene and introducing the characters, with the murder almost taking a backseat to the series background. This book launches right in with the mystery element, and does an excellent job of introducing characters, relationships, and the location as part of the narrative.

"I very much enjoyed the setting at a glamping-style campground near real-life Charlottesville, Virginia. I liked reading about the different themes of some of the refurbished campers, and the tiny houses. I look forward to seeing more featured in the next book in this series. Five out of five slices of perfect Provolone!"—Chewie the Mouse Amazon Review

Chapter One

Sunday

"Good morning. Brrrr. It's freezing out there." Roxanne Mallory stepped toward the dividing door between the Fern Valley Luxury Camping Resort's store and office. She paused and bent over to give Bijou, the wiggly Jack Russell Terrier, a squeeze. "You all ready for the Valentine's festivities? I can jump in and help you after I make myself a café mocha and get some feeling back in my fingers. I'm hoping this one is fun and not like the last time we had that so-called author here. That didn't work out well for anyone." She sashayed over to the counter in her cream-colored slacks, a red cashmere sweater, and her signature pearls.

Jules Keene, owner of the facility and Roxanne's niece, looked up from her laptop and pursed her lips, trying not to dredge up old memories of a cranky guest who was killed on her property a year ago. Changing the subject, she said, "It was a bit frosty when Bijou and I walked over this morning. She wasn't in any mood to dawdle, which is unlike her. Curiosity is usually her middle name. Chilly as it was, the frozen trees look pretty in the morning sun."

"And the three-sixty-degree view of the mountains makes it a perfect location for photos. I should have snapped some, but I was in a hurry to get inside and warm up. Winter looks magical, but I'm counting the days until spring. It's thirty-seven, in case you're wondering." Her aunt tapped the coffee maker with her ruby-red nail like she was directing it to stop sputtering.

"I'm excited that we're booked solid for the next two weeks." Jules worked hard to keep guests coming to her resort all year instead of only during the summer season. This year, she and the business council cooked up the idea for a two-week, jam-packed festival of all things romance. Authors, editors, publicists, and readers were about to descend on the sleepy little one-stoplight town of Fern Valley, nestled in the heart of the Blue Ridge Mountains, and turn it into love central.

"I think we're good to go," Jules said. "All of today's check-ins are highlighted in the reservation app. I spread the authors and book people out among the vintage trailers and the tiny houses." Jules's resort catered to visitors looking for luxury, along with the traditional outdoor adventures. Her themed, refurbished trailers, stocked with posh amenities, were perfect for today's visitors seeking a glamping experience. Jules and her boyfriend, Jake Evans, had added tiny houses to the resort's offerings recently to give visitors another type of glamping experience.

"Love is in the Air," Roxanne sang in a dramatic operetta voice. "That title always makes me want to break out into a musical number. It's perfect for all those romance writers. I'm looking forward to your Death by Chocolate thing and the romance cover model fashion show. Oh, and meeting my favorite authors. I saw on the library poster that Allegra Rhodes is coming. I've read all her books, and I used to watch *Enduring Love* on TV when Max was little. I've never met a soap opera writer before. That'll be a blast from the past." Roxanne waited for the coffee maker to spew out the final dribbles.

Before Roxanne could settle on the stool behind the front desk, the bells on the door tinkled. A smallish woman with silver hair coiffed in a stylish bob stepped inside and glanced around at the shelves of supplies and racks of brochures. A tiny yip emanated from behind the Dutch door as a younger blond with a messy bun and puffy coat pulled in two rolling suitcases and shut the door hard enough to rattle it, setting off the bells again.

"Sorry, Ms. Abernathy. I guess I don't know my own strength," the younger woman said, untangling her hand from the suitcase handles.

Ms. Abernathy gazed around the room and frowned at her companion.

Then, turning toward Roxanne and Jules, she said in a soft voice, "Hello. I'm Windsor Abernathy. The reservation for two is probably made under Joyce Jones, my real name," she whispered. She glanced around the store again like she was looking for spies and then continued, "This is my personal assistant, Tiffany Blake." Turning toward the blond, she asked, "Do you have our reservations?" The woman made sure to overpronounce each word with her British accent.

Roxanne's eyes widened. She smiled and tapped on the keyboard as the younger woman fished through the side pouch in one of the bags. Then she rummaged through her oversized purse. A panicked look crossed her face as she continued her frantic search.

"That's okay. I have it right here, Ms. Abernathy. We have both of you in the tiny house that's themed for Beatrix Potter and all her stories. Here are two keys, and I'll call someone to take you over in the golf cart. This is a welcome gift that contains the schedule of the festival's events and the breakfast times. We can also help you if you need lunch, dinner, or sightseeing options," Roxanne said.

"Thank you." Windsor reached for the red and purple gift bag and handed it to Tiffany. "I'm correct in assuming that our accommodations have two bedrooms."

"Yes. Two bedrooms and a fold-out couch, if it's needed. I can take you when you're ready," Jules said.

"That won't be necessary if it's not too far. It'll give us a chance to see some of the surroundings. This is my first trip to the Blue Ridge Mountains. The area is lovely. We've been on a plane and in a car too long. The walk will do us good, and it's not that cold. I'm a native of Rhode Island, so it will be nice to see this part of the country." Her British accent faded the longer she talked.

"Would you like me to bring your bags over? The tiny houses are on the other side of the parking lot. It's no trouble to get the golf cart for you ladies," Jules said.

"No, thank you. We can manage. I'd prefer to walk." Windsor reached for the keys and the papers that Roxanne slid across the counter. "Tiffany, the bags. Let's go."

"This is the information packet with the WiFi and amenities list. Please don't hesitate to call if you need anything. I am such a fan, and I look forward to your talks this week," the normally calm and collected Roxanne gushed.

Windsor smiled and shooed her assistant toward the front door that flew open as a tall woman in a ski parka barged in and glanced around the room. She flipped her long dark hair over her shoulder and stomped her boots on the pine floor.

"It is freezing out there," the woman exclaimed, rubbing her bare hands together. "This is not like February in Miami. Who knew this week would be frigid?" She waved her arms around and scooted closer to Roxanne and Jules.

"It is winter," Windsor said softly, pulling the door behind her.

The brunette glared over her shoulder at the closed door. She made a face and waved dismissively with one hand. "Hi, I'm Tracey Abbott, but you know me as my pen name, Phoenix. I have a reservation for one."

"Here it is, Ms. Abbott," Roxanne said. "You're in our 1959 Sunliner Caravan. Jules here decorated that one with a pink, high fashion theme in honor of the year that the camper and Barbie debuted."

"Cute," Phoenix said. "It should be fun. I'm looking forward to the book festival. I can't wait to meet all the people and sell some books. The camper thingy has WiFi, right? I've got to keep up with my socials, and I have some writing to do while I'm here. I can never truly unplug."

Before Roxanne could repeat her spiel about the welcome packet and the amenities, the door burst open again, and a blond blew in like a tornado. "Hello, all. I'm Gigi Johnson. Virginia Johnson, I'm here to check-in. I'm one of the headlining authors for this weekend's festivities. My name should be on your VIP list."

"Welcome, Ms. Johnson. We'll get you checked in a moment," Jules said. Gigi gave Phoenix, Roxanne, and Jules a once-over that looked like she was auditing their assets. She let out a puff of air as she crossed her arms across her ample chest.

"Ms. Abbott, here are your keys and your welcome packet with the breakfast schedules. Your trailer is right across the field as you step off the porch. It's the second one in the first row. The WiFi info is here, too."

"Thank you," Phoenix said, turning on her heels and giving Gigi an almost-sneer on her way out.

"Now, Ms. Johnson, we have the red and white 1947 Westwood Coronado for you. Its theme is *Miracle on 34th Street,* since the movie with Maureen O'Hara and Natalie Wood premiered that same year."

"Thank you," Gigi snatched the gift bag from Roxanne. "I heard all the details earlier. And I really don't care about cute old movies."

Roxanne pursed her lips and paused. "Very good. Here are your keys and your receipt. Your trailer is the first one in the second row."

"Who will carry my bags? I have others in the car," Gigi said.

"I can get the golf cart and meet you on the front porch in a bit," Jules said.

Gigi paused and glared at Jules and her aunt. "No, that will take too long. Never mind. I can manage. I need to get settled and make some phone calls to let my people know I made it to this backwater town." The author's three-inch heels clicked on the floor on her way out.

When the door shut behind her, Roxanne said, "Well, can't you feel all the love? I can't wait to meet the rest of the authors. Hope they're not all like her."

Jules stifled a laugh. "Well, at least Valentine's Day won't be boring."

"It may be more like the Fourth of July if the authors keep setting off fireworks." Roxanne pulled out an emery board and touched up her red nails.

Chapter Two

Monday

The bells on the front door jingled behind the last of this morning's check-ins.

"Whew. That was a sudden rush." Roxanne plopped on the stool behind the counter and fanned herself with her hand.

Jules tapped on her computer. "By my count, all of the authors and most of the fans have arrived."

The door popped open, and Tom Jenkins juggled a pouch and a stack of boxes. "Morning, ladies. I have a couple of packages for you." Stacking the boxes on the counter, the postal carrier rummaged through his bag and handed a rubber-banded stack of envelopes to Jules. "Here ya go. How's life in your corner of Fern Valley?"

"All's well. How about you?" Jules asked, setting the stack of envelopes next to the boxes.

"Can't complain. And nobody would listen if I did," Tom winked. "Take care, and say hey to Jake and Lester for me," he said over his shoulder.

By the time Jules returned from putting the envelopes on her desk, Roxanne had moved the three boxes behind the counter. "That's better," her aunt said. "They were blocking my view." She picked up the phone and tapped in a number. "Good morning. Ms. Abernathy. This is Roxanne Mallory in the front office. Your packages arrived this morning. Oh, okay. We'll be here," she said, disconnecting." Turning toward Jules, "She's on her way. I was about to offer to bring them over, but she saved me a trip."

Minutes later, Windsor Abernathy, in a long aqua tunic and no winter coat, breezed into the office. Her oversized shirt seemed to float behind her like a cape. "Hello. I'm here to pick up my packages." She stomped her feet and rubbed her hands together. "Brrr. I was so excited that my packages had arrived, I rushed out without my coat. I live in Florida for most of the cold parts of the year, and I'm not in the habit of bundling up. It's a tad nippy here. It reminds me of winters from my childhood in New England."

Roxanne pulled the first box out and set it on the counter. Before she could get the other two, Windsor chirped, "Ooooh. My pretties. I have to show you these. I'm doing a presentation for the library one day on antiques and women's treasured trinkets of bygone eras." She pulled out her keys and used one to slit the tape.

Tossing out tissue paper and bubble wrap, she undid the packaging and held a ring with an amethyst stone the size of a quarter, surrounded by a silver filigree setting with an ivy design. "This is one of my favorites. It's an antique that dates back to the Victorian era. It's a poison ring. See the top flips open to provide access to a secret compartment. Women could literally take out their tea or dinner companion with a flick of a wrist," she said with a wink.

Jules opened her eyes wide. Before she could comment, Windsor continued, "And look at this. This is my ladies' dagger, which dates back to the early 1800s. It's small enough to hide in a sleeve or a blouse, and it's the perfect size to be pretty and lethal. I have a ton of these types of items and some great stories to share with folks. You will have to come to the presentation and see all of my treasures. I do a whole presentation on Victorian poisons and another on dainty but deadly weaponry. I think that one's still on my YouTube channel if you're interested. I find it fascinating that so much deadly stuff was lying around people's houses. But that's a whole 'nother story."

"They are lovely," Roxanne said, fingering the metal detail on the dagger's handle. "It looks like a piece of jewelry with roses and ivy. Not what I would expect on a weapon."

"I use them in my stories. They are perfect weapons for my spunky heroines…." Before Windsor could finish her thought, the door banged open, and Gigi stomped across the floor. I'm here to check on my packages. I saw the mail guy drive off. My publisher shipped some books, and I sent some things I didn't want to take on the airplane. I'm here to collect my items." She stepped closer to the counter and pushed Windsor's packing materials out of the way, and several pieces fluttered to the floor.

"Ms. Johnson, we don't have any packages for you. I'll make sure that we alert you when they arrive." Roxanne stared at the discarded packing materials on the floor.

Gigi made a harumphing sound and tapped the toe of her boot. "I shipped it four days ago. Are you sure it hasn't arrived? It should have by now. I sent it in plenty of time. Can you check in the back or wherever you store things? And if it's not there, can you call someone?"

"Nothing has arrived for you," Roxanne repeated. "But I'll check to be sure." Roxanne pasted a plastic smile on her face and disappeared through the dividing door.

"Thanks, ladies, for my packages. I've got to get a move on," Windsor said, rewrapping her items and stacking the boxes. "I'm having tea in town with my sweet friend Allegra Rhodes and a podcaster. We're doing a fun interview about our characters."

Gigi's eyebrows shot up about two inches. "That sounds divine. I would love to go to tea and chat. I find podcasters so interesting."

"I'll let you know how it goes, and I'll send you the link so you can hear it in its entirety. And I'll pass on the name of the interviewer if all goes well. It sounds like a fun afternoon. I am looking forward to catching up with Allegra." Windsor waved her hand and picked up her boxes.

"Let me help you with those," Jules said, taking the two boxes that teetered off the top in front of the author's face. "I've got a golf cart out back. I can give you a lift."

"Me, too. Me, too. I need a lift," Gigi said, waving an arm in the air. "Don't forget me. It is such a long walk to our accommodations. And it's hilly around here."

"Certainly, I'll get the cart and meet you both on the front steps in a jiff. I hope to see you all at the Death by Chocolate event this evening. Our caterers have prepared some decadent desserts," Jules said.

"Delightful. And I can't wait," Windsor said.

Gigi shrugged. "I'm sure it will be, uh, nice. I don't really eat sweets."

Roxanne returned empty-handed. "Sorry, ma'am. There aren't any packages for you. I'll be sure to let you know when they arrive." Roxanne's voice dripped with honey.

Gigi's face darkened. "I guess that's to be expected in a podunky town, far from civilization." She turned when she noticed Windsor near the door. "Windsor, wait for me. We can use the ride over to talk about some joint marketing opportunities. We should do some book signings together. You know, like a mini book tour this spring."

"My calendar is pretty full this year. I have three books coming out, but I guess we could talk. Come on then," the older author said. "We can wait on the porch. I want to get some fresh air."

When the door closed, Jules tried not to roll her eyes. "I'll be back in a bit. I don't want to keep the ladies waiting."

"Buckle up. It sounds like we're in for a roller coaster of a ride with this bunch. Hope you don't have to break up any altercations." Roxanne reached for her phone. "I'm curious about these authors. While you're gone, I'll see if I can find out anything juicy on the wild web."

Chapter Three

Monday Evening

Jules took a break from the event setup to wander through the lodge's dining room with the wall-to-wall windows flanking the oversized stone fireplace. This was her favorite spot at the resort. She paused a moment to soak up the fabulous view of the mountains that looked several shades of blue in the fading sun. Gorgeous. No matter what the season.

Jules hip-checked the dining room door that opened into the large, industrial kitchen. "All the tables are set and ready to go. I added all the place cards," she said to Mel Carson, the mother-half of the mother-daughter duo who catered all the meals and cleaned for the resort.

"It looks lovely out there. The centerpieces and decorations on the mantel are perfect for a Valentine's Day soiree." Mel closed the door to the oversized dishwasher and pushed a stray strand of hair that escaped from her ponytail.

"This will be fun. Death by Chocolate sold out in a day. I'm excited that there'll be so many authors and fans here. You and Crystal have outdone yourselves with the menu. I had no idea that there were so many ways to showcase chocolate. The guests will love it."

Mel beamed as Crystal pushed a cart full of chocolate fountains from the stock room. "Oh, hi, Jules. Love all the decorations. It's so festive. I'll put these on the buffet table, and we should be ready for the party. The business council volunteers should be here soon, and we'll get them situated." Crystal's long blond braid bobbed as she guided the cart to the dining room.

Before Jules could comment, she and Mel heard, "May I help you? Excuse me, may I help you?" from the dining room.

Jules and Mel popped their heads out as Crystal strode toward a tall woman in a red velvet evening gown and arm-length, vintage white gloves. Her chestnut-colored hair, styled in a swanky updo, reminded Jules of classic Hollywood.

By the time Mel and Jules wended their way through the round tables to where the woman stood, she jerked both gloved hands behind her back like a five-year-old who got caught being naughty.

"Hi, I'm Jules Keene. How can we help you?"

"Hello. I'm Echo Aames," the tall woman said in a breathy voice. "I'm, uh, trying to find my seat for tonight. I saw this amazing building and popped in for a preview. This view is gorgeous," she said, turning at the waist without revealing what was behind her back in her hands.

Glancing at the table with the crooked tent card, Jules turned toward the window. "Thank you. My dad worked with the architect to incorporate the mountain view into this building. I like to think of it as the focal point of the resort. We're excited to host the event tonight for all the authors and readers. The planning team spent a great deal of time organizing all the details. I hope you enjoy your evening."

"I am sure I will. This is lovely. I wanted to get the lay of the land. I think I'll get some air before we get started. Ta ta." The woman gave a dramatic wave, along with a toss of her head, as she traipsed toward the door.

Crystal smiled and moved on to put the finishing touches on the buffet table. Jules meandered through the tables to where author Cinnamon Moon's tag sat askew next to the place setting. Picking up the tent card, she returned it to its original table and put Echo's back on her assigned table. A wry smile made its way across Jules's face. *Some of these authors are high maintenance. I have to keep an eye on this bunch. Everyone seems to have an agenda.*

The next hour was filled with a whirlwind of last-minute tasks. Jules got her quota of steps in on her fitness tracker while Mel organized the small army of volunteers, and Crystal put out a spread of what looked like hundreds of ways to enjoy chocolate delights. Jules gave the dining room one final glance and wandered out to the foyer to the reception table.

"Everything looks great," Elaine James, owner of the Birds and Bees shop, said, ensuring that all the flyers were aligned horizontally and vertically. "I'm all set up here, and we should be ready to open the doors at seven on the dot."

"One of your authors, Echo Aames, popped in earlier and switched her seating arrangement. I put it back where it was supposed to be. Not sure if you'll hear any feedback from her when she notices," Jules said.

Elizabeth Rhoney put her arm on Jules's shoulder. "Authors are a special bunch. I prefer the easy-to-get-along-with ones, but they're often few and far between," the owner of the bookstore said quietly, moving some of the stacks of handouts on the table that Elaine had just arranged. "I smile and nod a lot. That usually seems to work. Lots of princesses."

Jules laughed. "They definitely brought the drama with them."

Elaine rolled her eyes. "It's always something. I'm thrilled that all of our events have sold out. We'll have to check the final numbers, but regardless, tonight is a boon to the youth reading fund. Kudos, ladies."

"Everybody ready?" Elizabeth and Elaine nodded. "Then, it's time to get this party started." Jules opened the door to a flood of guests.

The evening zipped by. Greeting guests, answering questions, and helping to clear plates and utensils kept Jules hopping. She barely had time to talk to her valentine, who stopped to check on things. Jules had known Jake Evans since they were teens, but they hadn't started dating until recently. The handsome maintenance and security guy had worked on and off at the resort for her parents and returned to Fern Valley after a couple of Army tours in the Middle East. Jules smiled as he made his way through the throngs of romance novel fans. He stood head and shoulders above most of the all-female crowd.

"Hey, great crowd tonight," he said, resting his hand on her shoulder. His face lit up with a grin that showed his boyish dimples.

"I'm glad. You never know who will turn out after all the planning and hard work. What are you up to this evening?"

"Making my rounds and checking on the wild party you're throwing." Jake winked at her. "Plus, I heard there were snacks."

Before Jules could reply, two women approached, waving at the pair. "Excuse me, can you tell me where I can get the books for tonight?"

"I'll show you," Jake said, turning on his mega-watt smile. "It's right this way." He saluted Jules with two fingers and escorted the women to the lobby.

When Elizabeth Rhoney approached the lectern to introduce Allegra Rhodes's author talk, Jules had a minute to sample some of the decadent delights like the chocolate volcano lava cake. After the final, delectable bite, Jules wiped her hands on a napkin and found a quiet spot near the kitchen to listen to the presentation.

Allegra knew how to command an audience and hold them in rapt attention. Her talk on writing for publication and TV was full of pop culture anecdotes that held everyone's attention and kept the applause coming.

The crowd rose to their feet to show Allegra their appreciation. When the applause subsided, Elizabeth gave the crowd a fifteen-minute break to refresh their snack plates before Cinnamon Moon took the stage.

Cinnamon floated across the stage in a flowing dress and matching cape to her own round of applause. The petite woman with platinum hair did a royal wave to the crowd. She cleared her throat several times and said in a breathy voice that reminded Jules of Marilyn Monroe, "Thank you all so much. Thank you for the wonderful welcome." Then she launched into her presentation about romance through the ages and the history of Valentine's Day, complete with slides set to popular romantic songs.

When she finished, Cinnamon nodded her thanks to the crowd as Elizabeth adjusted the microphone. "What do you think of our speakers tonight? And the fabulous chocolate goodies?" When the crowd's roar died down, she continued, "What a fun night. And it's not over yet. The booksellers are out front in the foyer. Allegra, Cinnamon, and Echo will be here autographing books. Go back for seconds or thirds of those amazing chocolate treats created by the ladies here at the Fern Valley Luxury Camping Resort. Then go get some books signed. Please make sure to check out all the events happening over the next weeks." Elizabeth waved her copy of the program.

Jules smiled at the applause. Her team had put in some long hours to make this event special.

After another standing ovation for the authors, guests chatted and moved toward the booksellers. Jules double-timed it for the welcome table where Echo Aames had Elizabeth and Elaine cornered.

"Well, I want it on record," Echo said. "I was not happy with my table assignment. I was stuck over in the corner in the back with three empty seats while the other authors, some of whom are self-published, were front and center with full tables. Someone of my caliber and draw should have had a prominent place. I am expecting better treatment at tomorrow's event. I didn't come all this way to be ignored. And I didn't even get a spot on tonight's program. It's like I was added at the last minute. I am not accustomed to this kind of neglect." Her voice rose an octave as she swung her gloved hands around, almost bumping an older woman on her way out.

"Ms. Aames, your table was sold out, too. I'm terribly sorry if some of the guests did not attend. The team has worked hard planning these events to showcase the authors and their works," Elizabeth said.

"I think some of them moved seats to other author tables. Very tacky." Echo's brows formed a "V" right above her nose. "For everyone's sake, I hope tomorrow's event is better." She turned on her heels and strode toward her spot at the signing table. Her exit looked like it belonged to a starlet on a red carpet.

Elizabeth stifled a laugh. "I guess she would know about moving seats. Jules, everything was lovely. I hope the author speed-dating tomorrow meets her expectations."

"You'd think these romance writers would be all sparkles and hugs. So far, all I've gotten are a bunch of complaints and demands. Maybe the arrival of Valentine's Day will bring out the joie de vivre," Elaine muttered with a half-hearted smile. "The romance writers should be in their element. It's their holiday."

Chapter Four

Tuesday Morning

"Happy Valentine's Day" echoed through the store. Jules and Bijou poked their heads through the doorway.

Before Jules could speak, Roxanne squeezed in between them and set a platter of fudge on the counter. "I was productive and a little creative. I made some different kinds of fudge for Matt, and I brought some for you all, too. This one is my favorite. It has cayenne pepper in it to spice things up." Roxanne winked and stowed her purse in the desk across from Jules. Her eyes sparkled at the mention of her beau, Sheriff Matt Hobbs.

"Yum," her niece said. "Perfect for my after-breakfast snack." Jules pulled a yogurt from the refrigerator and settled in at her desk. "Want one?" she asked, holding up the plastic container.

"No thanks. I had oatmeal after my workout. What exciting things do you and Elaine have planned for us today?" Roxanne asked.

"It's author speed-dating at the high school tonight. I've never seen one, so I'm curious about how it will work. Elizabeth said it gives readers a chance to talk to all the authors as they visit each table. I'm not sure if the guests move every five minutes or the authors. We'll find out. It sounds like fun and a little chaotic. You going?"

Roxanne shook her head. "It's date night for us. Sheriff Matt's coming by this evening for dinner and a movie."

"You're making dinner?" Jules raised one eyebrow.

Roxanne returned her niece's stare. "Just 'cause I made fudge doesn't make me fully domesticated. Don't get any crazy ideas. I ordered dinner from the Good Thyme Bistro. They had a nice holiday take-out menu. What are you two doing on Cupid's big day?"

"Jake said he had a new project that he wanted to show me, so we're going out for lunch since I told Elaine and Elizabeth that I'd help with the thing tonight."

Roxanne nodded. "You and Jake are always working." She pushed a mug under the coffee maker's spout and mashed the button. "As soon as I get properly caffeinated, I need to get busy on the books and balance the accounts. Anything else you want me to concentrate on?"

Jules shook her head. "Everyone is checked in this weekend. So far, everything's been fairly quiet with the new batch of guests. Slightly different from the author check-in. And we weren't the only ones to remark about some of the authors. Elaine said she was bombarded with demands from some divas."

Roxanne chuckled. "We've had enough drama and excitement around here for a while. I know Matt and his team are enjoying the calm. After the spate of murders and all those Hollywood people last fall, everyone in Fern Valley can use a breather to start the new year off right."

Jules busied herself with drafting content for the resort's newsletter, and then she scheduled social media posts to stir up interest in some of her warm weather getaway packages. The mountains were beautiful in the spring with all the blooms and bright colors. Jules worked hard to keep the resort fully booked ahead of the vacation season.

Around ten-thirty, Jules heard the front door close and a series of whispers, followed by more whispers. Curious to see who was in the store, she slipped through the doorway and spotted Jake and Roxanne huddled near the counter by a vase full of red roses.

"Oh, hi," Jake said, straightening up. "Happy Valentine's Day."

"They are gorgeous. Thank you so much." A tingle of excitement arced through Jules. It had been a while since she'd had someone to celebrate Valentine's with. She pushed memories of the Idiot and her divorce out of her head. Most of those holiday memories weren't worth stirring up. "Let me get your present." Jules hurried to her desk and returned with an oversized red envelope.

She bounced on her toes as he slid the flap up. His eyes widened when he spotted the two Nationals tickets. "I thought maybe we could go on opening day," she said.

"These are great. Wonder who I'll take? Roxanne, are you free?" Jules punched him lightly on the shoulder as her aunt gave him a side-eye.

"Hmm. Would you like to go? Just kidding. Thanks." Jake enveloped Jules in a bear hug. "Still have time for lunch today?"

Jules nodded and moved the vase to her desk.

"Y'all have fun," Roxanne said as Jules grabbed her coat and Jake's hand.

"Before we head to town, I want to show you something," he said.

Jules walked with him across the field toward the neighborhood of tiny houses, each themed in honor of a writer. She loved all the touches Jake had added for their guests, like the revolving bookcase and the cozy reading nooks.

The February breeze sent a chill through Jules, and she zipped up her puffy jacket. The pair walked past the Potter, Baum, Rowling, and Stoker houses, and Jake stopped suddenly at the base of a copse of oak trees.

"I had an idea for a new project," he said, looking up at the bare limbs. "Instead of another tiny house, what do you think of a tree house? It doesn't have to be completely in the branches. I saw a design that had parts on stilts. I'd build it to blend with the environment. It'll fit in with our tiny houses."

"I always wanted a tree house. I think it would be awesome. And the view…"

"That's why this bunch of trees is the spot. If I do the design right, you can have almost a three-hundred-sixty view." Jake pointed to the surrounding mountains.

"I love it," she said, staring up at the trees that seemed to poke through the vast expanse of blue sky. Hundreds of marketing ideas for the new offering bounced around in her head.

Jake put his hand on her shoulder and brought her back to reality. "I'm starving. What do you feel like for lunch?"

"Pop's Diner has always been my go-to place," Jules smiled at him. "You can't go wrong with killer burgers and shakes."

"Always a fan favorite, especially after football and basketball games. It's an institution," Jake said, heading toward his Mustang in front of his cabin.

Jules barely had time to fasten her seatbelt before Jake sped out of the driveway and down the resort's maintenance road toward Fern Valley's downtown. They made it to the diner in record time. Finding a parking spot away from the other cars, the couple hiked around the sprawling building. Three different Pops had expanded the original little silver diner several times over the years.

A gal in a poodle skirt seated Jake and Jules in a cozy booth in a corner of the room decorated in honor of Buddy Holly, the Big Bopper, and Richie Valens. Jules set her menu down and looked at the memorabilia covering most of the wall space.

Marsha Stokes, the fifty-something waitress with the pink bouffant do, sidled up to the table. "Hey, guys. Long time no see. What can I get for you on this fabulous Valentine's Day?"

"Hi, Marsha. Happy Valentine's Day! I hope all's well. I'll have the all-American cheeseburger with cheddar, ketchup, and mustard, and Pop's famous steak fries. May I have a cherry Coke, too?"

"Gotcha, and what about you, handsome?"

Jake grinned. "I'll have the bacon and Swiss burger with fries and a chocolate malt."

"Be right back, and I'll bring you some water, too. It's been hopping around here for February. I'm glad to see all the folks in town for the romance festival. Pop loves it when we fill all the tables in the winter."

When Marsha retreated to the kitchen, Jake pulled out his phone and swiped through a series of pictures. "These are some tree house designs I found. Most surround the tree. The bedrooms are usually elevated, and there's always some kind of deck. Most of the living area is on a different level. I want to do a wrap-around deck with lots of windows in the bedroom."

"This will be the perfect addition. And I may have to make it my secret office when it's not booked. Though when word gets out, everyone will want it. I really did want a tree house as a kid. My dad and I talked about it a couple of times, but we never got around to actually making it happen. Stuff always got in the way." Jules's voice trailed off.

"This shouldn't take too long. It's modularized. It'll take time to put in the footings and build the decking. I was thinking about adding some sort of elevator or lift thing for moving stuff in and out. I know the steps will get old fast when you're lugging suitcases or supplies. Something like a dumb waiter."

Jules scanned through the photos. "I like the deck on this one and the house design of this one. It blends in with the trees. Now we need to think of a theme for it."

Before Jules could continue, Marsha popped over with their lunches. "Here you go, folks. Condiments are on the table. Holler if you need anything else."

"Will do," Jake said, reaching for the ketchup.

Pausing their conversation, the pair concentrated on their lunches.

The hostess breezed into the dining area and seated Allegra and Windsor in a booth across the aisle. Both women nodded and waved when they recognized Jules.

"Who're they?" Jake whispered as Jules waved back.

"It's two of the authors from the festival. That's Allegra Rhodes, and she's Windsor Abernathy…" Before Jules could finish, a high-pitched squeal echoed through the restaurant. Three fifty-something women huddled around the authors' table for photos and autographs. The taller of the three whipped out a book from an oversized bag for Allegra to autograph.

"More like rock stars," Jake added.

Gigi and Phoenix sidled up to the crowd and wormed their way to a spot with a clear view as Allegra autographed the woman's book.

"Phoenix Abbott and I are also featured authors at this week's festival. We'd love to chat with you all about our books, too," Gigi said, patting one of the fans on the shoulder.

Allegra handed the woman her book. "Thanks so much, Charlotte. It was so nice to meet you all today."

Charlotte gushed and reached for the book. "We'll let you all get back to your lunch, but could you take a picture of my friends with these two authors?" she asked Gigi.

A flush covered Gigi's face in a matter of seconds. She glared at the woman. "What?"

"Could you take our picture with Windsor and Allegra?" Charlotte repeated.

Gigi threw her hands in the air and stormed off.

After a long, uncomfortable pause, Phoenix reached for the woman's phone. "I'll take it for you."

Jake said, "Wow! Roxanne said some of them were prima donnas. That was awkward."

Jules's eyes widened. "Not the best way to win new fans. Definitely an interesting bunch. The one who stormed out wasn't too happy when Roxanne told her that her package hadn't arrived yet. She lets everyone know what she likes and doesn't."

Marsha approached, looking over her shoulder. "Is that Allegra Rhodes? She used to write and have a bit part on that soap years ago."

"That's her," Jules said.

"I need to get a picture before they leave. I used to love my daytime stories. Can I get you all some dessert? Pop's got some awesome cheesecake, sundaes, and a red velvet cake to die for in the case today. You know you want something."

"How about if we split something? Jules asked.

Jake nodded.

"You pick. It all sounded good," Jules added.

"How about New York cheesecake with raspberries?"

"Perfect choice. Be back in a flash." Marsha turned on her rubber-souled shoes that squeaked on the black and white tiles and disappeared in the back.

A few beats later, Marsha returned with their dessert and two forks. But before Jules could dig in, her phone alerted staccato style with a series of texts.

More complaints from the authors.

The festival has barely started.

Can you be at the event tonight by 6 for a powwow?

Jules tapped a quick affirmative to Elaine's group text and shrugged a shoulder.

"Emergency? Do we need to head back?" Jake asked.

"No. Elaine's getting some not-so-constructive feedback from some of the authors. She wants to have a quick meeting before tonight's thing."

"Sounds like a fun way to spend Valentine's Day," Jake said, snagging a big bite of cheesecake. "I'll be hanging out in the barn where it's quiet. I want to get a jump on the tree house plans."

"But this is a great way to spend Cupid's holiday," she replied, spearing a raspberry. "I've had the nicest Valentine's Day in as long as I can remember." She blew him a kiss across the table.

Chapter Five

Tuesday Evening

Jules checked her hair and makeup in her Jeep's rearview mirror and shimmied out of her coat. Stuffing her phone and keys in the pocket of her black jeans, she jogged to the high school's front doors. The blast of heat and the antiseptic smell gave her a flashback to her teen years in the public school system.

Rubbing her hands to shake off the cold, she hurried to the information area in front of the cafeteria. At a long row of tables, Elizabeth arranged gift bags, name tags, and instruction packets for the authors.

"Hi, Jules. Here's your lanyard. Kim and Darlene are making sure all the tables are ready. The Good Thyme Bistro folks are in the kitchen. Elizabeth will take care of the authors. These gift bags are for them. Then, she and her team will take care of the book sales. Jules, you, Kim, and Darlene will handle the guest registration. The nametags are in alphabetical order. Give them that, and they can slide it into the plastic thing on the lanyard. Then everyone gets a program." Elaine took a pause for a breath and looked at her clipboard.

"The guests can sit wherever they want. The authors find a table. All the tables have numbers on them. Every ten minutes, we'll have the authors switch tables. By the end of the evening, they'll have visited all the tables. I think that about covers everything in a nutshell. Elizabeth, did I forget anything?" Elaine asked.

Before the bookstore owner could answer, Elaine added, "Oh, when it's time to start, I need Kim and Darlene to staff the table in case there are any late arrivals. Jules, you can help me make rounds inside and keep order. I've got my airhorn and stopwatch." Elaine patted her hot pink fanny pack.

Jules tried to suppress a laugh when she caught Elizabeth rolling her eyes. "Sounds like a plan. I'm willing to help wherever you need me." *I hope the air horn doesn't deafen the guests or us.*

Elaine stuck her head in the cafeteria and let out an ear-piercing wolf whistle. "Whoo hooo," she waved at the pair of volunteers inside. "Let's do a quick pull-up and get this party started."

When Kim and Darlene joined the crew at the welcome table, Elaine took a swig of her iced coffee. "Thank you all for volunteering to help us this week. Tonight is author speed-dating, and the event is sold out. I'm so glad that the Good Thyme Bistro is our caterer. We've heard from a bunch of guests today, and they are so excited about this event. It should be unique and fun and noisy." She paused and lowered her voice. "Then there are some of the authors, the drama llamas. Echo, Phoenix, and Gigi seem to be the most vocal. They're not happy with panel placements, publicity, and life in general in our small town. I'm trying to tamp down any scenes and make our events enjoyable for all. If you come across fussing or complaints, let me know. I want to nip it in the bud."

Jules nodded and faked a cough to cover up a snicker. She had images of Mayberry's Barney Fife and his favorite "nip it" line.

The group disbursed as Elaine checked her watch every five minutes. Jules wandered over to the long row of tables where Elizabeth and her team arranged stacks of books. Jules picked up some by Windsor, Allegra, and Cinnamon. Autographed copies would make nice additions to her book collections in the tiny houses. She handed Elizabeth her credit card, flipped Cinnamon's latest over in her hands, and stared at the back cover.

"What's wrong?" Elizabeth asked, scanning the book Jules held.

"I find it interesting that some of these author photos don't quite look like the in-person version," Jules said in just above a whisper.

"That happens a lot. I've been surprised when an author shows up at the shop and looks like the book photo's grandmother. I guess we all want to hang onto our youth in some way or another. The photos are either twenty years too old, or they've been touched up to the point that the author looks like a Disney princess with soft, doe eyes. Me, I plan to embrace all the platinum hair and the laugh lines. I earned them."

Jules smiled and retrieved her card and shopping bag from Elizabeth. "You always look lovely. And thanks so much. These'll be the perfect addition to the resort's libraries."

Midway down the book table, a loud voice caught everyone's attention. "Hello. Are you the one in charge here?" Echo demanded, pointing her bony finger close to Elizabeth's assistant's nose. "Who's in charge here?" Her shrill screech was as bad as Elaine's sharp whistle.

The startled assistant opened her mouth to answer, but Elizabeth stepped in. "I'm Elizabeth Rhoney, owner of Between the Covers. What can I do for you?"

"I'm Echo Aames, and I want to talk to you about my placement on your table. My series is jammed all the way down there at the end. My books are almost at the end of the hallway. People are not going to walk all that way. We know people are lazy. I would like you to move me closer to the door area where I can be seen." She stomped down to the end of the table and retrieved a stack of her books. "My surname is Aames. A-A-M-E-S. I should be at the front. It's better that way. People expect the A's to be first."

Jules and the booksellers stood and stared as Echo balanced a wobbly stack of paperbacks and plopped them down by the cash register. "See. It looks better already."

"Thank you for your feedback, Ms..."

"Aames. I told you. It's Echo Aames," she interjected before Elizabeth could finish her sentence. "And I'm a New York Times best-selling author and one of the headliners here," she huffed. The vein in her sinewy neck bulged as she enunciated each word and waved her nametag in front of the booksellers. Her eyes flashed, and her stare was laser-focused on Elizabeth.

"Thank you, Ms. Aames. My team will take your display suggestions under consideration."

"You should know that your A-listers must be in spots of prominence. Placement is everything, especially when there's so many to choose from." She turned on her heels and strode into the cafeteria as the guests started streaming into the school's main entrance.

The assistant's mouth formed a small "o" as she stared at her boss, Jules, and the line forming at the book table.

A lightbulb popped in Jules's head. She had wondered why so many of the authors' pseudonyms started with the letter "A." *That makes sense. They all want to be at the head of the line or first on the shelf.*

"Debbie, please put those back where I had them," Elizabeth said to her assistant. "They're fine where they were at that end of the table. And I guess I should let Elaine know that the drama has arrived." The owner of Between the Covers pressed her lips together and watched Debbie restack the books.

Chapter Six

Tuesday Evening

After an hour or so of cleanup at the end of the author speed-dating event, Jules surveyed the high school cafeteria. Everything looked ready for the return of students tomorrow morning.

"Well, ladies. We did it. Thanks so much for all of your hard work," Elaine said, leaning on a push-broom. "I think this was a tremendous success. What a day."

"Everyone seemed to have a fun time," Kim Lacy said. "I heard lots of scuttlebutt from guests. They were thrilled for the chance to get up close and personal with their favorite authors. We had a big hit, ladies."

"And once some of the authors climbed down off their high horses, I think they enjoyed themselves, too. Book sales were excellent. If this keeps up, I may have to put in a restocking order for the rest of the events." Elizabeth did a fist pump and a little shimmy.

"Good to hear," Elaine said. "Go home and rest up. We have workshops and meet and greets tomorrow. And, hopefully, all the guests are spending money around town. Excellent work, team."

"Yes. Great work, everyone. See you all tomorrow." Jules picked up her bag and headed for her silver and black Wrangler, one of the few remaining vehicles in the parking lot. Jules hustled across the chilly lot. Once inside, she cranked up a classic rock station on the radio and blasted the heat in the Jeep.

By the time she pulled into the resort's gate, the interior felt toasty, and she almost didn't want to open the door. The white twinkle lights on the trees lining the entrance provided a magical greeting, perfect for Valentine's Day celebrations. *I'm glad I left those up after the Christmas holidays.*

Jules opened the front door of her cabin, and a white and brown fur bomb pounced on her, almost knocking her off balance. "Well, hey to you, too, Bijou. Let's get your leash and head out for an adventure. I have to tell you all about author speed dating."

The tiny dog bounced around the living room and in and out of the open door. She had the zoomies tonight. Jules finally got her to stand still long enough to click her leash in place. "Come on. Let's go sniff something."

Bijou bounded out the door and stopped to examine everything in the flowerbeds. The little dog froze and sniffed the air. Then she darted toward the tree line. Wishing she had turned on the cabin's floodlights, Jules picked up her pace to keep up with the little dog. She used the flashlight app on her phone to try to light the way.

As the pair edged closer to the barn, Bijou froze again and stared off into the inky darkness. Jules strained to listen to what got the dog's attention. Not hearing anything, she nudged the Jack Russell Terrier toward the cabin.

A crunch and twigs snapping caused Jules to freeze. Bijou let out a guttural growl. After a couple of barks from the spunky guard dog, all Jules could hear was wind and an occasional frog. She strained to hear anything that sounded like footsteps.

The pair waited for what seemed like an eternity, and as Jules shrugged the noise off as a guest out for an evening stroll, she heard someone running in the heavy underbrush.

As they turned to head home, a pale flash of something disappeared into the woods. Then in the shadows, it looked like another figure followed. But it was hard to tell. The sounds disappeared into the woods, and Bijou ramped up to Def Con four.

What is going on out here? Who is running around in the woods this late in the evening. I haven't had trespassers on the property in a long time.

She stroked the soft fur on Bijou's back while she waited to see if the strangers would return. The minutes ticked by and felt like an eternity. Jules's heartbeats pounded in her ears.

Her curiosity and the anxiety of trespassers battled it out while she waited. Not able to stand out in the cold any longer, she scooped up Bijou and jogged toward home.

After fumbling with her keys, she rushed inside and threw the deadbolt in place. Jules let out a long sigh and texted Jake to be on the lookout for any weirdness when he made his evening rounds.

Got it, he replied. **Probably kids.**

The flashbacks of recent murders crept into her thoughts. A guest, a reporter, two people from a film crew, and then two vendors from the Christmas festival all died in Fern Valley over the past year or so. Maybe J. P. Gross and his followers on the business council were right that her efforts to bring visitors to the area also brought big city problems. She shook off the creepy memories and chided herself for mentally jumping from someone running in the woods to murder. *You are antsy tonight. It might be nothing.*

She grabbed her phone and scrolled through the security camera feeds. Scanning through the past hour of footage wasn't productive. Nothing looked out of place. Just guests returning to their campers after the speed-dating event or an evening out. All quiet in the valley. The cameras didn't capture the mysterious figure or the person who followed her.

Shaking off the foreboding feeling that made her skin prickle, Jules picked up her copy of Windsor's book and settled on the couch next to Bijou, who was already snoring. Maybe this was something random. Every little outside noise made her twitch or jump up to peek outside. *Girl, what is wrong tonight?* She took a couple of deep breaths and willed her pulse rate back to normal.

When the book didn't hold her attention, and she couldn't find anything on TV, she emptied the dishwasher, cleaned out the almost empty fridge, and scrubbed down the counters. *Might as well use all this energy to accomplish something.*

Chapter Seven

Wednesday

After a fitful night's rest, Jules decided to shower and dress and start work early. There was no sense tossing and turning until the alarm blared. Stuffing a banana and a yogurt in her messenger bag, Jules said, "Bijou, 'bout ready to head to the office?"

The little dog trotted to the front door and waited for her leash. "There you go. Let's see if there are any hints as to who was running around in the woods at night."

The pair walked around the cabin and the perimeter of the property. At the barn, they turned and headed for the office as a purply gray dawn crept over the mountain ridge. No noticeable footprints, red flags, or signs of anything nefarious.

Jules settled in at her desk as the coffee machine chugged into action on the nearby counter. Not interested in caffeine or catching up on emails, Bijou circled her puffy bed twice and plopped down for her first nap of the morning.

Jake had texted after his rounds. **Nothing looks out of place. No one out and about.**

Chalking up the creepy footsteps to someone goofing around in the woods, Jules pushed thoughts of pranksters and trespassers to the back of her mind as she plowed through resort and business council emails. Lots of positive feedback on Love is in the Air. There were even a couple of suggestions for spring and summer council events.

Feeling pleased that she had caught up on her administrative tasks, Jules focused on a coffee refill. The sun peeked over the top of the mountains, casting a golden glow on the resort. It looked warmer than the thermometer showed.

Before she could work on her own event planning for the spring, her phone vibrated, announcing a string of rapid-fire texts.

Not all the authors are here. Missing Cinnamon and Gigi.

Cinnamon's the second speaker. Why today?

Can you check to see if they're still at the resort?

We'll have to come up with plan B if they don't show. Hate it when people don't do what they say they are doing to do. Actions have consequences.

Jules let out a sigh. She could picture Elaine's fretting and pacing. The owner of the Birds and Bees wanted everything to run smoothly. It was nine-o-four. The workshops didn't start until ten.

I'll walk over and check on it, she tapped into her phone.

"Do you want to go, too?" Jules asked the dog.

Bijou opened one eye and snuggled into her bed.

"I'll take that as a no. Be back in a bit." Jules slid into her parka and grabbed her phone. Circling back to her laptop, she pulled up the numbers of the authors' vintage trailers before she headed out.

The February chill cut through to the bone. Jules shivered and picked up her pace. Stopping first at Gigi's Barbie-themed pink and white trailer, she knocked on the aluminum door. No human noises. The scalloped edges of the patio awning fluttered in the morning breeze.

Jules repeated the exercise at Cinnamon's trailer, the 1954 Airstream, decorated in honor of Elvis's first recordings at Sun Studio. No answer or sign of life there either.

Deciding to swing by the lodge to see if either of the authors were enjoying breakfast, Jules jogged across the field. Inside, guests milled around the buffet table. Mel and Crystal's menu today featured bananas foster French toast, yogurt parfaits, and a variety of quiches and muffins.

Jules made a circuit through the tables, greeting her guests. No Cinnamon. No Gigi. She headed to the industrial kitchen, where Mel refilled the tea and coffee carafes. "Hello. Everything looks great. Everyone's enjoying breakfast. Have you seen Gigi Johnson or Cinnamon Moon this morning? Elaine said neither of them are at the library for the workshops."

A puzzled look crossed the woman's face. "Not sure I could identify them by sight. We've had a steady string of guests come through here today."

Jules pulled up the "Love is the Air" website and pointed to the two authors.

"Nope. Can't say that I remember seeing either one. Maybe Crystal did," Mel said.

On cue, Mel's daughter hustled through the swinging door with empty food trays. "We've got a hungry bunch out there. I need to get a refill on the quiche and some more bacon."

"Got it," her mother said. "Take a look at Jules's phone. Have you seen either of these ladies today?"

Stepping closer and leaning toward the phone, Crystal slowly shook her head. "Nope. Maybe they ate in their trailers?"

"Could be." Jules pocketed her phone. If you see them, let them know that Elaine is looking for them. They're supposed to be getting ready for today's workshops. Elaine is a little frustrated that she's missing two of her speakers."

A slight smile crossed Crystal's face. She nodded as Jules reached for a to-go box for a sampling of breakfast before she headed back to continue her search for the wayward authors.

Jules made a loop and checked the trailers one more time before she hurried back to the office. Popping a quiche in her mouth, she fired off a text to Elaine. **No Gigi or Cinnamon here. Not at breakfast either.**

Gigi waltzed in the front door like the queen, Elaine replied.

Still no sign of Cinnamon. I guess we'll figure out something if she doesn't show. It'll ruin the order of today's program. She was supposed to talk about the adaptation of her books for TV. Hmm.

How unprofessional. Elaine ended her text with a string of unhappy emojis.

I'll let you know if she turns up here, Jules replied.

"Wow. Elaine's on a tear this morning. I hope they can find a sub for Cinnamon's slot."

"What's up?" Roxanne asked as she breezed in with a to-go carton. "Had to stop in and see Mel and Crystal. Things were hopping over there."

"You must have popped in right after I left. The baby quiches are yummy." Jules wiped her mouth on a paper napkin. "I received a frantic series of texts from Elaine this morning. Two of the authors are AWOL. She found one, but the one who's the headliner hasn't shown up yet. You didn't see any of the authors on your travels, did you?"

Her aunt shook her head and rummaged through the cabinet for a coffee mug. "Nope. Just a bunch of happy guests. The guests in the food line chattered on and on about all the fun."

Jules gave her a quick thumbs up. "When you get settled in, I'm going to drive over to the library to check on things. Can you cover here?"

"No problem. Bijou and I will have a staff meeting while you're gone." Her aunt popped a tea pod in the coffee maker and waited for it to heat up.

Jules picked up her coat and purse. "Be back soon."

Inside her silver Wrangler, she fished through the glove compartment for her sunglasses. She cranked up the classic rock station and enjoyed the quick ride to the government center, a name that was bigger than the actual complex that housed the sheriff's office, library, and administrative buildings.

Not finding an available spot in the library's parking lot, she put the Jeep in a lower gear and made her own place in the nearby grass. "That'll do," she said to herself.

After a quick jaunt to the library, Jules slipped inside and found Kim Lacy and Darlene Denunzio chatting at a nearby table. She stared at the line that inched toward the registration desk.

When a pair of women in front of Jules collected their name tags and programs, Kim let out a long sigh that sounded like air escaping from a leaky balloon. "I think almost everyone is checked in. We had a mad rush when Elaine opened the doors."

"Good turnout. The parking lots are full. Did Cinnamon Moon ever show up?" Jules asked.

"Nope," Darlene muttered. "And Elaine was ready to declare war. Thankfully, Elizabeth has a calming effect, and they came up with a substitute panel, but I know people will be disappointed. They wanted to hear how her stories were optioned for TV."

"Who did they get to sub?" Jules asked, flipping through a stack of programs on the table.

"A gal named Carrie Shultz," Kim said. "She's Cinnamon's agent who pitched the TV deal, so maybe people won't be too disappointed. Elaine was ready to hunt the author down. If the sheriff had been around, I'm sure she would have asked him to send out a search party and drag her over here."

Jules smiled. "That's why she's a perfect event planner. She can keep the trains running on time. I'm going to take a walk and check things out before I go back to work. Is there anything I can get for you all or spell you for a break?"

"We're good. The food trucks will be here before lunch. That'll be fun. And I don't think we have to do much. If it gets too quiet, we'll take turns popping into the panels and workshops," Darlene said.

"Have fun," Jules waved and made her way to the conference room near the children's section.

Jules listened to part of Windsor Abernathy's presentation on Victorian trinkets with interesting uses. She waved to Elaine, who lapped the perimeter of the room and scanned the crowd for any untoward behavior.

Jules slipped out between presentations. Distracted by her vibrating phone, she paused behind some tall bookshelves. "Hey, Roxanne. What's up?"

"You may want to head back over here as soon as you can."

"What's up?" Jules pursed her lips.

"Uh, the sheriff and his team are here. Jake and Lester found something in the barn." Her voice trailed off.

"What?" Jules said, concern creeping into her voice.

"Sheriff Matt's not saying much. He's busy, but Jake said that Lester found a woman under his big lawn mower this morning."

Bats bounced around in Jules's stomach, and she felt her heartbeat pound in her temples like a bass drum. "I'll be right there."

Chapter Eight

Wednesday

Jules broke the sound barrier on her drive back to the resort. She flew down the maintenance road and skidded to a stop near her cabin. Without missing a beat, she slammed the door and ran across the grass to the barn.

Yellow crime scene tape surrounded the perimeter and wiggled in the breeze. A shiver zinged through her, and memories of recent crime scenes flashed across her thoughts. Taking a deep breath, she tried not to panic before she knew the details.

Spotting Jake and Lester under a tree, she made a beeline for her team. "Hey, guys. What's up? Roxanne called me." Jules paused to catch her breath.

"What a morning. I think it took a couple or three years off my life," said Lester Branch, the groundskeeper who had been a fixture at the resort all of Jules's life. He let out a long stream of air through his nose. "I woke up this morning like any other. After oatmeal, coffee, and my vitamins, I put on my steel-toed boots and a big coat. When you get to be my age, you have to bundle up. Anyway, the grass needed a little trimming. Perfect day for outside work with all this sunshine, if I do say so myself. It's been a little chilly, but the grass needed tending to. Anyway, when I went in the barn, I tripped on something near Old Bessie."

"The lawn mower," Jake added.

Jules nodded, and Lester continued with his tale. "Yes, the lawn mower. The light's not that bright in the back part of the barn, and I forgot to put on the overhead lights since I was only there for a quick minute to get Old

Bessie chuggin'. Who would think I'd ever trip over a woman's shoe in the barn? That is the last place I'd expect to find something like that. I thought someone was messing around where she shouldn't be, so I did some poking around. It was too early for any hanky panky. Almost gave myself a heart attack. There was a woman curled up under the mower's blades." Lester took a deep breath, pulled out a handkerchief from his pocket, and wiped his forehead, despite the chilly temperatures.

"Lester, are you okay?" she asked the older man. "Can I get you anything?"

"Nah. I'm fine. It was a shock to the old system. Glad I didn't lose my breakfast. For the life of me, I couldn't figure out why some lady would be hiding out in the barn. She was dressed too fancy. None of it made any sense. Jake and I are stickin' around out here to see if Sheriff Hobbs needs anything. And to see what else they find. There's been a lot of comings and goings. So much police activity." Lester folded his hands and leaned against the barn wall.

"They brought the forensic team in about twenty minutes ago. And two or three state troopers arrived after that," Jake added.

"Any idea who it is and what she was doing in the barn?" Jules wanted details about the body and where he found her, but she decided to let Lester tell his story his way. She stood on her tiptoes for a better view.

Lester shook his head. "Nope. Don't think I'd ever seen her before. She was dressed too nice to be a vagrant. Sad to say, but it's probably one of your guests. Not somebody hiking the Blue Ridge parkway or hoboing around these parts."

Jules pulled out her phone and located the "Love is in the Air" website. "Was she one of these folks?" She swiped slowly through the author pictures.

Lester pulled his glasses out of his shirt pocket and leaned closer to her phone. "Hmm. Go back to that one. That poor woman looked a little like this gal. What do you think, Jake? Could be our mystery woman?"

"I think that's her. She was wearing that pin." Jake pointed to the image on Jules's phone.

Jules sucked in a mouthful of cold air. "Cinnamon Moon. What was she doing in the barn? Any sign that anyone was there with her? And any idea how she died?" Jules's voice faded to almost a whisper. Thoughts of all kinds of gruesome deaths swirled around in her head.

"Nope. Just her curled up under the mower like she was sleeping. Even though that is the darndest place to take a nap. And how in the dickens did she get under there? Well, uh, there was one thing. It's kinda weird…" Lester paused.

Jake and Jules stared at the older man, and he continued, "She had some big fancy needle in her neck."

"A syringe?" Jules gasped.

"No, not like that. Like one of those knitting needle things. It had a silver cap on the end, and it was as big around as a dime. The kind that Kim has in her shop in town."

Jules furrowed her brows. *Why a knitting needle?*

"Sheriff Hobbs and Bubba, I mean Deputy Dempsey, arrived first and cordoned off the barn. Then, the others arrived. Your field looks like a parking lot for police cars. They've been in there for about forty-five minutes or so," Jake said. "We haven't heard much chatter from any of them."

Jules leaned against Jake as he slipped his arm around her. *Another dead body could affect my bookings. People don't want to vacation where they don't feel safe. J. T. Gross and his allies will have a field day with another murder in Fern Valley. He already beats the drum that I'm bringing crime and unsavory people to our town.* Jules let out a long puff of air. Closing her eyes for a couple of beats, she tried to figure out what to do next.

Like he could read her mind, Jake hugged her with one arm and said, "Don't start worrying until we know the extent of it. We didn't have anything to do with her death. It could have been a freak accident. Let's see what the sheriff has to say."

Jules draped her arm around his waist and gave him a squeeze. "You're right. It's hard not to rev right into panic mode. You know how some of the locals feel about all the tourists in Fern Valley, and they point at me as the cause of all the town's ills every time something happens."

"Everybody knows what this town was like when I left for the army. Main Street was practically boarded up, and there was no money flowing in. They were cutting town services and jobs. The tourists that you and the business council are responsible for have saved this region. Without those dollars, we would have been plagued by the crime and drug problems that face other rural places."

"It's sad that Cinnamon passed away. She recently signed a big contract to have her books optioned for TV, and now she won't get to see the fruits of her labors." Jules wiped away a tear that slipped out of the corner of her eye and took a deep breath to ward off her quaking voice. "I'm heading back to the office to help Roxanne with damage control. I'm sure the town's grapevine is already buzzing. Let me know if Sheriff Hobbs needs anything."

Lester nodded, and Jake said, "Will do. I'll text you if anything big happens."

"I think I'll hang out here for a bit with Jake. This is more exciting than daytime TV or my police scanner." Lester shifted his weight from one foot to the other. His eyes twinkled with the possibility of front-row seats to a live police investigation.

Jules barely had time to get the back door of the office open before Roxanne and Bijou pounced on her. The dog wanted kisses, and Roxanne was after information.

"What is going on over there? Every time I look out the window, I see police cars."

"Any concerned guests or questions?" Jules asked.

"No. Not a one. I think everyone's in town. Who is it?"

"Lester said it was Cinnamon Moon. She's the one Elaine was looking for this morning."

"Now we know why she didn't show for the book thingy." Roxanne's lips formed a straight line across her face. "What happened?" her aunt asked in almost a whisper.

Jules looked over her shoulder, even though they were alone in the back office. "Lester said that he tripped over something and found her under his mower."

Roxanne's hand flew to her mouth as a horrified look darkened her face.

"I don't think it was a gruesome death," Jules said. "Lester said he found her curled up under the mower like she was sleeping."

"Oh, my stars. It's still so awful that she died, but I'm glad that she wasn't killed by the mower." Roxanne sank down in the nearby chair. "I had visions of a scene from a slasher movie when you said lawn mower." Her aunt let out a long sigh. "Oh, poor Lester. What a fright."

"That's not all. He said she had a knitting needle in her neck," Jules whispered.

"A what?" Roxanne asked.

"A knitting needle. I mean, I guess you could stab someone with one. But could that be the murder weapon? And how in the world did she get under the industrial mower in the back of the barn?"

"I have no idea. I was hoping the sheriff would stop by to talk to us." Roxanne fanned herself with a folder.

"Maybe you can work your feminine wiles to get some details out of your law enforcement beau." Jules cracked a half-smile.

"I'll try my best, but he usually keeps key details close to his bulletproof vest. We'll see what I can ferret out. I guess it's a matter of time before the story leaks. How famous was she? The press could get wind of this. We should have a plan in case it's a big story."

It was Jules's turn to sink down in her office chair. The energy seemed to seep out of her like she had a slow leak. "I plan to refer all inquiries to the sheriff's office. Let's see what her author website says about her." Jules woke up her laptop and started a search. "Hmm. She's been a best-seller for quite a while under the names of Cinnamon Moon and Amy Rivers. Her real name is Amy Bishop. Wow. She has over forty-five novels and a bunch of novellas to her credit. She, Echo, and Allegra have the same agent and publicist." Jules opened a blank Excel workbook and keyed in the random facts about the dead woman.

A little after one, a haggard sheriff stepped inside the office, knocking on the doorframe as he entered. "Hey, Jules. Can I get the key to Ms. Moon's accommodations?"

Jules found the key and handed it to Sheriff Hobbs. "It's in the third row, C4. You want a cup of coffee?"

"Thanks," he nodded and moved over to the small table near the counter. "I'll be back to drop this off later." He dangled the key. Anything I need to know about Ms. Moon?"

Roxanne popped her head in the doorway and fingered waved at the sheriff. A slight smile crept across his face.

"Uh, I don't know much about her except that her real name is Amy Bishop. She was mild-mannered, without any drama or complaints. A nice, well-dressed lady in her forties or fifties. Elaine texted me earlier that she hadn't shown up this morning for the event at the library. I went to check on her and another author who was late. I couldn't find either of them here at the resort."

Sheriff Hobbs jotted notes in his pocket-sized notebook as the coffee maker chugged on in the background. "What happened to the other gal?"

"Elaine said that she finally showed up at the library. Her name was Gigi Johnson. It's short for Virginia."

He nodded.

"Oh, one more thing," Jules added. "Ms. Moon was here to talk about her books, especially the series that was optioned for a film adaptation."

The sheriff continued to scratch notes as Roxanne placed a steaming mug in front of him and patted his shoulder.

"Thanks, Rox. Sounds like a big deal with big money. So, no altercations or disagreements with others?" he asked.

"No, none that we saw. She was overly polite and low maintenance. This was a sudden shock. And not what Lester was expecting to find in the barn this morning," Jules said.

"I'm sure." The sheriff took a long swing of his coffee.

"Was she killed there? I mean with the mower. How awful," Roxanne gasped.

"It looks like she was trying to hide, or maybe someone left her there. Though, it didn't seem all that practical when there were other spots in and around the barn that were easier to get to. My best guess is that she was placed there after she was killed. Lester said someone had jammed the blade release in the up position as far as it would go. The mower wasn't the cause of her death."

Roxanne let out a long stream of air as a look of relief crossed her face.

The sheriff took a gulp of his coffee. "Thanks for the coffee and the information. If you think of anything else, let me know. Rox, I'll try to call you later. I think I may need a raincheck on dinner."

She nodded as he rose and strode out the back.

Who would want to kill Cinnamon? All her books were happily-ever-afters that so many read for an escape from the mundane or the bad stories featured every day on the news. And what's the significance of the knitting needle?

Jules tried to concentrate on her email, but her thoughts kept returning to the knitting needle.

Chapter Nine

Late Wednesday Night

Jules's phone buzzed. She opened one eye and tried to figure out why she was on the couch. Two-thirty-three. Her living room lights were on, but the TV had long gone into sleeper mode after she started a binging session of the romance shows on the Love Channel. All in the name of research. Willing her brain to focus, she reached for the phone.

"Hey, Jake. What's up?" Jules hoped she didn't sound as groggy as she felt.

"Sorry to wake you, Boss. I wanted to let you know that I swung by Ms. Moon's trailer on my rounds. The forensics team finished their work, so I put the key that the sheriff had back in the lockbox."

"Thanks. Did you find out any details? I can't believe we've had another murder here." Jules rubbed her eyes.

"Not really. They've been all over the barn or at her trailer since this morning. They fingerprinted, photographed, and made videos of everything. Her trailer will need a thorough cleaning. That gray powder is everywhere."

"That reminds me. I need to call the sheriff to see what he wants me to do with her belongings." Jules tried not to sigh. *This isn't the first room that I've had to clean out before the checkout date.* Shaking off the eerie memories, Jules added, "Thanks for the update. Try to get some sleep. Love you."

"Night night. Love you, too," he said, disconnecting.

Too wide awake to head to bed, Jules turned on her laptop and perused her sparse notes about Cinnamon Moon. Not having much to add about the murder or the victim, she listed all the names of the authors who were staying at the resort. Then she spent hours on the internet looking at their websites. Most had polished headshots and carefully crafted biographies that highlighted their successes. Switching over to the fan and gossip sites, Jules uncovered some juicier details.

On one site, Jules found a discussion thread about traditionally published versus indie authors. The consensus in the comments seemed to be that the fans loved the bigger publishers' organized fan groups with meetups and lots of freebies over the handful of free books that the indies offered.

"Hmm. What's that?" Jules asked. Bijou rolled over, not interested in the romance genre.

On a "Love Bites" website, Phoenix Abbott had posted a whole diatribe and some snarky comments about other authors. It started out as a marketing post that turned sour. After some follow up comments devolved when someone called "Jessi Jewels" accused her of ripping off authors with some of her sell-a-ton-of-books schemes. Then, some readers piled on with comments that Phoenix didn't pay attention to the quality of her work. Several people suggested that she might benefit from an editor. *Might be worth looking into.* Jules jotted down the names of the commenters that Phoenix sparred with online.

From what Jules could find, Windsor, Allegra, and Cinnamon were adored favorites with thousands of followers, active street teams, and fan clubs. For Echo, she found an outdated website with old pictures, but oddly enough, her book information had been updated.

Jules shut down her laptop and stretched. The inky darkness outside faded as dawn approached. She padded off down the hall for a hot shower and some thinking time that she hoped would help her come up with ways to find information on these authors. Cinnamon could have been killed by someone here at the resort. It doesn't seem plausible that some random killer would go to all the trouble to pose her. And she didn't do it to herself. She was about to have a TV series based on one of her books go into production. None of this made sense. Why my barn? Maybe it could be someone who was in town for the festival. The haphazard thoughts banged around in her head. None of them seemed to fit together for a plausible explanation. She closed her eyes for a few beats, hoping that the headache would subside. When it didn't, she toweled off and threw on a sweater and jeans. She headed to the kitchen for an aspirin to dull the ache behind her eyes.

After settling in at her desk at the office, Jules answered all of the resort and business council emails. Glancing at her clock, it was still too early to call normal people. "Bijou, I'm going to see what Mel and Crystal have on the menu for our guests today. Be back in a sec."

She wriggled into her coat and trotted across the frosty field to the lodge. A handful of guests milled around the buffet table or warmed themselves in front of the roaring fireplace. Scanning the seating area, she smiled when she realized most of the guests were reading paperbacks. The perfect retreat for bookworms.

Literary agent, Carrie Shultz, sipped hot tea next to the fireplace and stared out the windows.

"Excuse me, Ms. Shultz," Jules said in a low tone as she approached the agent's table.

The woman, dressed all in black, looked up. Dark circles ringed her eyes and made her look ten years older. The woman nodded her head slightly.

"I'm sorry to interrupt. I wanted to check on you to see if there is anything my staff or I can do for you. I know this is such a hard time for those who knew Ms. Moon."

"Thanks." Carrie shook her head. "I've met with the police twice. We've got so much to do now that there's an estate." Her voice drifted off as she continued to stare out the windows.

"The sheriff said he would let me know when her accommodations could be packed," Jules said.

Carrie pulled out a business card from her messenger bag and handed it to Jules. "Yes, please let me know. I can arrange to get her belongings back to her family. I talked to her daughter yesterday. The family is devastated."

Lynette D'Angelo ambled up to the table, juggling two plates and a steaming mug. "Sorry to keep you waiting. I got stuck on another call after we talked." She set her food on the table and pulled out the chair across from Carrie. She let an oversized purse and a laptop bag slip from her shoulder, and she set them under the table. Without waiting for anyone to respond, she plopped down in the chair and dug into her food.

"Jules, this is Lynnette D'Angelo. She's Cinnamon's publicist." Carrie pointed across the table.

Lynnette paused with a forkful of eggs near her mouth and gave a little wave with her pinkie.

"This is Jules. She runs the resort," Carrie continued.

"It's nice to meet you all. I know you're busy. Let me know if my team can help in any way," Jules said.

"I wanted to go over some things we need to do for Cinnamon," Carrie said quietly, focusing on Lynette.

The publicist shoveled in another mouthful of eggs.

Nodding, Carrie glanced at her notes on her legal pad while Jules grabbed a to-go container and filled it with a sampling of breakfast casserole and a cinnamon muffin. On her way out, Jules snagged a fruity yogurt parfait for a snack later.

After breakfast and her second jolt of caffeine, Jules decided that it was a respectable enough time to make phone calls. She clicked on her contact for her college friend, Gwen "Pixel" Pierce. The gamer and computer geek was always Jules's best source of information, hidden away in the spooky corners of the Dark Web.

After two rings, she heard, "Hey, Jules. I've been meaning to call you. Life has been a bit nutty for me here. I've been in and out of town. Spending a bunch of time in training recently. But it's all worth it. How are you doing?"

"We're fine, but you never told me. What is your official status with the FBI?" Pixel had made her way onto law enforcement's radar when she helped Jules unencrypt a file that led to the arrest in the murder of one of the resort guests involved in a medical blackmailing scheme. "I can't wait to hear what you decided. Last time we talked, it sounded like you were suffering through a grueling interview process and weighing your options," Jules said.

"You can say that again. An alien abduction and probing would have been less invasive. The feds don't mess around with their background and security checks. I am still in training, but it will be official soon. I'll be a member of their support team. Most of my work will be from home, but I may have to head into Roanoke or Richmond or even D. C. from time to time. I'll be assigned to one of their fusion teams for cyber support. Most of my work will be done virtually. Can't wait, and I love that they'll let me work from home in my jammies most of the time."

"Pixel, that is so exciting. You still teaching at UVA?"

"Not this semester. I may go back in the summer and teach an accelerated class. We'll see. It depends on what I'm assigned to and how much of my life and free time the FBI assignments take."

Jules paused, wondering whether to mention the murder.

"What's up with you? I saw on your social sites that you've got a lot of events planned from now through the summer. That's exciting," Pixel said, tapping something in the background.

"I try to keep the guests interested and the trailers full."

"How's Jake?" Pixel asked.

"He's doing well. He's starting on a new tree house project for the resort."

"That sounds so cool. I want to come and see that when it's finished." Pixel paused, and her voice sobered. "I heard you had another murder. Do the police have any idea who did it?"

"Not yet. It was one of the romance authors who was here for the book festival. Lester found her under his mower in the barn."

"How awful. Was she, uh, killed by the mower?" Pixel asked.

"No, it looked like someone had tried to hide her there, or she crawled there to escape. But they did find her with a knitting needle in her neck."

"Eww. Creepy. Think someone was trying to send some kind of message?"

"I have no idea. I was kinda hoping you could do some of your amazing research if you had time. But I totally get it if you're swamped," Jules said.

"I can always make time for you. It's like we get to have our own little true-crime adventures. What's on your mind?"

"I've got a bunch of people staying here for a couple of weeks for the 'Love is in the Air' festival. I've poked around on the internet and found a ton of fan sites full of gossip and a little snark, but I don't have a clue to where to start looking for who would want to kill a romance writer."

"Send me what you've got, and I'll see what I can find on the wild web. You'd be surprised at what's out there. I'll see if knitting needles come up in any other murders. Maybe it's the killer's signature."

"You're the best."

"My pleasure. Plus, you helped me dodge a couple of jams in college. It's the least I can do. I'm always up for a twisty mystery, or I guess a romance in this case," Pixel said.

"I'll email you my sparse list of facts. Cinnamon Moon wrote popular love stories, and her stuff was optioned for a TV series. She's kind of a big deal. Cinnamon didn't seem like the type to be targeted for murder."

"No problem. You never know what secrets people are trying to keep buried. I could use an exciting quest to take my mind off all this work stuff and an overloaded brain from all my recent training. I'll let you know what I find."

"Perfect. And the next lunch or dinner is on me. We need to celebrate your new job."

"I haven't been to Pop's since in forever. Looking forward to it," Pixel said before she disconnected.

By the time Jules composed her email to Pixel, Roxanne blew in the front door with her breakfast and newest designer handbag.

"Hello," her aunt said, catching her breath. "What's shaking around here on this fine morning?" The resort's phone rang. "I'll get it," Roxanne said, taking her breakfast to the front counter before Jules could respond.

"Whew. Didn't think I'd ever get to my breakfast," Roxanne said, sinking into her desk chair across from Jules. That reporter kept going and going. I referred him to Sheriff Matt's office, but he kept pummeling me with questions. Oh, and Jake said he's got an errand to run. He'll be back after lunch. If we need anything, Lester's glued to his police scanner." He hadn't been this excited since the carjacking and big police chase last summer.

"Okay," Jules said, hoping this wasn't the first of many inquiries from the media. Before she could stress more about the murder, her cell phone interrupted her thoughts. "Hello, Elaine, What's..."

Before Jules could finish her sentence, the owner of the Birds and Bees wildlife store launched into a frantic plea, "Jules. I'm in a pickle. Two of the volunteers for today's fashion show called in sick. Is there any way you can come over here and help? The press from all over has shown up, and we're sold out. I could use an extra set of hands pronto. It is way too chaotic for my liking."

"Not a problem. I'll be there as soon as I can."

"You're a peach," Elaine said, disconnecting.

"Hey, Roxanne. Elaine needs help over at the high school. I'm headed over there. I'll be back as soon as I can. Call me if you need me."

"Will do. I heard today's steamy event was a fashion show with some real, live romance cover models. Call me if you need additional volunteers to escort the models around." Roxanne wiggled her eyebrows. "I want to see pictures of all the action when you return."

Chapter Ten

Thursday

Jules checked her look in the Wrangler's rearview mirror and dabbed on a touch of lipstick for some color. She hoped jeans and a baggy pullover weren't too casual for today's extravaganza. Nobody was there to see her. All eyes would be on the male models.

With parking at a premium, she ended up in the overflow lot across the street from the high school. On her hike to the auditorium, she spotted media trucks from nearby Charlottesville and Roanoke and let out a sigh that turned into a gasp when she realized the line at the front door snaked around the side of the school.

Picking up her pace, Jules maneuvered her way around the line until she was able to get near the door. Ignoring side-eyes and snarky comments about cutting in line, she texted Elaine. **I'm at the front door. Come and save me.**

One of the glass doors opened, and ripples of excitement ran through the crowd.

"Good morning, all. We'll open the doors soon. Thanks for your patience. Jules, it's nice to see you." Elaine grabbed her by the arm and pulled her inside.

Half-dragging her toward the registration table, Elaine chattered the entire length of the hall without taking a breath or giving Jules a chance to respond. "Thank you for coming so quickly. I'm short-handed, and I need another body to help with registration. The gals at the table will show you what to do. I have to make sure Windsor is ready to go for her opening presentation. Then, I have to check on the food trucks and get the fashion show models situated. Here we are. Kim, Jules is here to help you. Show her what's what, and I'll do a quick loop and then let folks in. Thanks to all of you. Holler if you need anything."

When Elaine flew off toward the backstage area, Kim, the owner of KnitWits, smiled. "Thanks for jumping in. All we need to do is give our guests a program and a lanyard for the event. There's a presentation first, the food trucks at twelve, and then the fashion show. Then, the models will be signing autographs in the cafeteria. That should be a hoot. Everything's in that box for last names A-H, and I have I-Z. Let me know if you can't find a tag. Oh, and we're not selling tickets today. I hope we won't get any disgruntled people at the door."

Jules nodded. "Got it. We should be okay as soon as we get through the rush. There was quite a crowd out there when I came in."

A roar of footsteps, laughter, and conversations filled the hallway, and a line of women rushed toward the table.

"Here we go," Jules said.

"We may need a coffee run after this," Kim said with a half-smile.

After about thirty minutes of answering questions, Kim and Jules sank back into their chairs.

"I think that's it," Kim said. "By my count, there are about eight people who haven't picked up their stuff. I need to make a pit stop and see if there's any fresh coffee in the green room. Want some?"

"Please. I definitely could use a caffeine recharge," Jules said.

While Jules skimmed through the resort's Instagram account, Kim returned and handed her a steaming cup of coffee.

"Here, I brought cream and sugar. I forgot to ask how you take it."

"You're a lifesaver." Jules stirred in enough creamer to change the color to a light tan. "Hey, by chance, did anyone from the sheriff's office talk to you about the murder?"

"Nope. Why would they?" a puzzled look crossed her face, and she pushed a stray curl out of her eyes.

Jules lowered her voice. "Cinnamon Moon was found with a knitting needle in her neck. I was wondering if someone was trying to send some kind of message. Any idea what that choice of weapon would mean?"

"They've been used as weapons before, but nothing comes to mind. My customers are interested in what their intended purpose is. I don't get too many questions about them as weapons." Kim pursed her lips and thought for a minute. "I mean, there are some valuable ones, especially some made of ivory or bejeweled, the collectible ones. I'd have to see it to make a better assessment." She paused and looked around the empty hall. "I guess it could be a murder weapon. Some are sharp enough."

"The investigation is ongoing. I'm sure the sheriff's team's looking into everything," Jules said. After a minute or two of silence, she continued, "If you'll be okay here for a while, I may go take a peek inside to see what's going on. Be back in a bit."

Kim nodded as Jules slipped inside the heavy auditorium doors. It took a minute for her eyes to adjust to the semidarkness.

Windsor Abernathy stood at the lectern, her image projected on the large screen. The author highlighted fashion trends and baubles from the Victorian era. She held up the ring closer to the camera. "This, ladies, is a poison ring. This handy dandy piece of jewelry could eliminate unwanted dinner guests with the flick of a wrist." She slid it on her ringer finger and popped open the ring's secret compartment, demonstrating how easy it was to poison someone.

"Next, I have a Victorian knitting needle like the one Lady Catherine Beckwith used to kill her paramour in my Duchess series." Jules caught her breath. *So, it has been used as a weapon in books.*

Windsor paused and fumbled with the row of items on a nearby table. She stared at the table and then bent down to look behind it.

Standing, Windsor let out a long puff of air in the microphone and rifled through her notes. After adjusting her reading glasses, she said, "Sorry about that. The next item I have to show you is an ornamental, fillagree hair comb to hold long hair in updos. And don't forget, like in my Heiress series, daggers and small knives could be secreted in fancy hairdos, piled high on one's head."

Jules slipped out to find Elaine hovering over the registration table. "What a morning. We've had a flurry of media requests, sadly none were to promote our festival. They were all looking for a scoop on Cinnamon's murder." Elaine fanned herself with a spare program. "Elizabeth has the green room in tiptop shape, and the sheriff is sending a deputy over later to help us if we have issues with crowd control. And I don't mean parking. After the rush came through the door earlier, I called the sheriff. We may need a law enforcement presence to keep order around the models. There's one more presentation, and the food trucks are getting ready outside. Let's hope the afternoon goes as smoothly. Any issues with registration?"

Both Kim and Jules shook their heads. "Just about everyone who registered showed up. Everybody seemed excited about today's program," Kim said, picking up the box of remaining lanyards. "Let's see, there are two no-shows."

"Good news, except, well, you know..." Elaine's voice trailed off. Applause drifted out from the auditorium, and Elizabeth Rhoney introduced a panel made up of Echo, Gigi, and Allegra for a talk about the importance of book covers and how they affect sales.

Before Elaine could continue, Windsor sped out the side entrance, dragging a wheeled suitcase behind her. The author zeroed in on the welcome table. Her usually coiffed hair stuck out at odd angles like she had run her hands through it repeatedly. She paused to catch her breath. "What a horrible fright. I need you to call the police," the author sputtered.

"What happened?" Elaine asked.

"I was doing my talk, and I realized that one of my daggers, a brooch with a secret compartment, an antique tatting shuttle, and a fancy Victorian hair comb are missing. Someone has stolen from me. It was so shocking that it made me lose my train of thought in the middle of my presentation. What a catastrophe. Who would do such a thing? I am beside myself. I need to find who took my precious antiques."

"Are you sure you packed them?" Kim asked.

"Of course, I packed them. They are props for my presentations. They rarely get unpacked." The author glared at Kim. "I bring them out for demos and interviews."

Elaine moved closer to Windsor and patted her arm. "Does anyone else have access to them?"

"Just my personal assistant, Tiffany. She's retracing our steps this morning. I can't imagine that they were lost. I insist that she take the ultimate care with my things."

Elaine pulled out her phone and made a call as Tiffany Blake scurried to the table.

"Mrs. Abernathy, I checked your coat and everywhere you've been this morning. And the rental car. There is no sign of the items."

The author's shoulders sagged. "I can't believe this. Besides being some of my favorite things. They are all antiques. I don't know where they could be." The older woman planted a fist on each hip.

Disconnecting her call, Elaine said, "The sheriff is sending someone over. Please have a seat until he gets here. Can I get you anything?"

"No, I'm fine. Just terribly disappointed. I can't believe someone would be this despicable. I plan to press charges." Windsor's fierce gaze settled on Tiffany, who fidgeted from one scuffed shoe to the other.

"Are you sure I can't get you something to drink while we're waiting? Water? Tea?" Elaine asked, hovering beside the author.

"I'm too worked up right now to concentrate. Tiffany, can you get me my pills and some water? This is all too jarring and disappointing. I may have to go back to my accommodations and lie down."

The assistant nodded and rummaged through her messenger bag.

"I'll get you some water. Anybody else want anything?" Kim asked. When no one responded, she headed for the green room.

By the time she returned with a bottle of water, Deputy Charles Dempsey, forever Bubba from the sixth grade, sauntered down the hallway. He hitched up his pants over his ample middle and approached the table. "Morning, ladies. What seems to be the issue this morning?"

Windsor stood and balled her right hand into a fist. "I have been burglarized. In the middle of my presentation, I realized that some of my precious objets d'art were missing. And I want you to find the criminal and return my things. Do you plan to check the nearby pawn shops?"

"Uh, we don't have any pawn shops nearby. We'll be sure to alert the antique dealers," Deputy Dempsey said.

"I should hope so. These items are quite popular with collectors." Windsor glared at the deputy, who tried not to make eye contact.

"When did you last see them?" Deputy Dempsey asked, pulling out a pen and notebook and flipping to find a blank page.

"When I packed my bag at home," Windsor replied, pursing her lips.

"Did you see them today?" he asked.

She paused and stared daggers at the officer. "Uh, no," she said quietly. "Tiffany did the setup. Hand me my phone," she said, snapping her fingers.

"You're Tiffany?" he asked the younger woman.

The assistant nodded and passed the phone to the author.

"Yes. She's my assistant," Windsor barked. "Here, these are pictures of the antiques I use in my presentations. This dagger, that hairclip, the pin, and that tatting shuttle have vanished. Oh, and one of my favorite broaches."

Charles scratched away in his notebook. Without looking up, he asked, "And you're sure these were packed and ready for today's presentation?"

"Yes, of course," Windsor said. "Tell him, Tiffany."

"I, uh, unpacked all the items this morning, and I laid them out across the table."

"Can you verify that these items were in the suitcase?" he asked, staring at the younger woman.

"I think. I mean, I didn't take a picture or anything. I laid them all out like I always do. It didn't look like anything was missing to me. But I was really busy. Ms. Abernathy needed a lot of things this morning. I, uh, kept getting interrupted."

Charles nodded. "Anyone you suspect of stealing from you?"

Windsor made a harrumphing noise. "When you're in the public eye, there are always stalkers and overly aggressive fans, but I've never had any issues in the past. I wouldn't put it past some of these authors. Some are very jealous and would probably gleefully sabotage the others."

"Anybody in particular I should talk to?" he asked.

"That Phoenix Abbott. She's always sticking her nose where it doesn't belong. And she seems bitter. She's not happy with anyone more successful than she is."

"Thank you, Mrs., uh…"

"My pen name is Windsor Abernathy. I'm Joyce Jones on official documents. Tiffany, give him my contact information. And anything else he needs to find the culprit."

Tiffany pulled out a bejeweled card holder and passed a business card to the deputy.

He smiled and handed her his. "That card has all my information. We'll investigate your claim. Anything else I need to know? Can you send me the link to that website with the pictures?"

"Done," Tiffany said, letting a slight smile creep across her face. "And don't hesitate to call if I can help you. I made a list of the missing items in the email I sent you."

"Thanks," Charles said as a flush rose in his cheeks. "I'll be in touch." His black sneakers squeaked on the industrial floor.

"Uh, Charles," Elaine called after him. "Aren't you checking out the places Ms. Abernathy has been today with her antiques?"

"Uh, sure," he said.

"I'll show you," Tiffany said.

"Yes, this way. Follow me," Windsor said. "Tiffany, my bag."

The younger woman returned to the table for the suitcase and followed Windsor and the deputy around the corner.

When they were out of earshot, Elaine said, "Well, I guess we'll all be on the lookout for her stolen items. I wonder if she even packed them. This whole thing could be a goose chase. We'll let the deputy sort that out, I guess. We've got to get ready for the fashion show and meet and greet with the models. Let me go check in with Elizabeth. Reach out if you need anything."

"I think I'll head out, too if you don't need me for anything else," Jules said, rising.

"Nooooooo," Kim said, gently pushing Jules back in her seat. "We need you to hang around for a bit."

Chapter Eleven

Thursday

Puzzled by Kim's reaction, Jules said, "Okay. I can stick around for a while." She pulled out her phone and sent Roxanne a text that her return would be later than expected. Looking up, she asked, "Hey, Kim, what do you need me to do?"

"For now, we can take turns getting lunch before the panels end and the guests flood the food trucks. They'll have an hour before the fashion show starts. So, we'll answer questions and then move down to the cafeteria for the afternoon meet and greet. Here's a ticket you can use at any of the lunch trucks." Kim paused and glanced down the hallway. "You can go first if you want. The trucks are parked in the circle out front by the flagpole."

"Be back in a flash." Jules wandered up and down the rows of brightly colored food trucks and landed on one that specialized in pitas and wraps.

Taking her veggie wrap and bottled water back inside, she sat down next to Kim and rubbed her hands together. "There's a huge selection out there. I can cover things here while you get your lunch."

"Not too much action yet. But I'm sure it will get livelier later. I'm starving," Kim said. "Your wrap looks scrumptious. I'm hoping the taco truck's out front. I could go for some spicy fish tacos."

Elaine and Elizabeth breezed by on their way outside. "Oh, Jules. I'm glad you're still here. After lunch, we'll need help in the auditorium. Can you shepherd all the guests down to the cafeteria in an orderly fashion for the final part of the program? We can't have a rowdy stampede to the autograph session," Elaine said, tapping her foot.

"Of course. Let me know what you need," she said, wiping mustard that oozed from her turkey wrap off her chin.

Jules gathered her trash as Kim slid behind the table with a paper container of tacos and a large soft drink.

"That smells heavenly," Jules said.

"I missed breakfast. The dog or a raccoon got in the trashcan this morning, and there I was on the curb in my bathrobe and fuzzy slippers picking up the mess. So, needless to say, I was late. Ummm. This tastes wonderful."

A woman in a pink tracksuit wandered to the table as Kim took a bite and wiped her hands on a napkin. She chewed faster.

Jules patted Kim's arm. "Don't rush. I've got this." Turning toward the woman, she smiled and said, "Hi. How may I help you?"

"I'm looking for a schedule for this afternoon."

"Here you go." Jules handed her the trifold.

"Thanks." The woman turned and then paused. "I found this in the hallway back there. I'm not sure if anyone is looking for it." She reached in her pocket.

Jules's heart rate increased. *I wonder if Charles is still here.*

The woman pulled out a smartwatch and set it on the table.

The excitement that surged through Jules dissipated as quickly as it appeared. "Thank you. We'll put it in the lost and found in case anyone claims it." *Dern. I thought it might have been one of Windsor's pilfered items.*

"My name is Tammy Stonehouse. If it's not claimed, I'd like it back." The woman stared at Jules. "Aren't you going to write it down?" She repeated her name and added, "And my number is 434-522-1203."

Jules jotted it on the back of a schedule. "Thanks. I'll make sure the director gets this."

The crowd hustled out for lunch and interrupted their conversation. Tammy mixed in with a large group on its way outside. Not many stopped for programs or questions. About fifteen minutes before the fashion show, Elaine bustled up to the table. "'Bout ready, gals? Jules, could you act as hall monitor by the auditorium doors in case there are questions and to keep order if the women get a little crazy? We can never take too many precautions. Have either of you seen the deputy?"

"Not since he went with Windsor to investigate the missing items," Kim said, taking a sip of her drink.

"I don't think we'll have any issues, but you never know. The show should be about ninety minutes. Elizabeth is interviewing two of the models at the end. After that, we'll all head to the cafeteria for autographs and pictures. Let me know if you need anything," Elaine said.

"Sounds like a fun afternoon." *I haven't been a hall monitor since the fifth grade. I'm surprised Elaine didn't provide whistles and reflective vests. Hopefully, it won't get too wild and crazy.*

"Hey, why don't we take turns watching the fashion show? You can go first," Kim said, pointing to the auditorium.

"You sure?" Jules asked.

Kim nodded and pulled out her phone. "You go ahead. I need to check on some emails for work." An impish grin appeared on Kim's face as she stared at her phone.

The guests started trickling in, and then the floodgate opened about five minutes before the fashion show. Jules spent her time greeting guests and answering questions. Her biggest task was helping to stow a stroller behind the half-wall at the back of the room.

Jules tiptoed in and leaned against the back wall as the auditorium lights dimmed. A spotlight focused on Carleen "Red" Tucker as she strode across the stage. The owner of Red's Honky Tonk sported a red and white cowgirl outfit, complete with fringe and a sequined red hat.

"Howdy, y'all," she said as the noise in the auditorium evaporated. "Hey, it's nice to be here today. I'm Carleen Red Tucker, and I own the little joint down the road that caters to all the live music lovers in the area. Stop in and see us. We always have a band or karaoke at Red's. Enough of the commercials. I know what y'all are here to see. We are so fortunate to have cover models and superstars, Steve Sterling and Marcus, with us today. And joining them, we have some locals who'll make their modeling debut on this very stage. And y'all got to see it first in little ole Fern Valley. After the fashion show, Elizabeth Rhoney will do an interview with Steve and Marcus. And then we'll all meet down at the cafeteria for pictures and autographs with our hunky guests. Y'all ready?"

The ladies in the audience whooped and hollered, and Red thumped her large diamond ring on the microphone several times to get their attention.

When the noise had settled down to a dull roar, the music blared from the speakers, and Carleen yelled, "Ladies, this is Marcus. Some stars only need one name, like Elvis and Cher. Marcus has a stellar career, appearing on over two hundred romance covers for a variety of publishing houses. Today, he's here to show off his motorcycle outfit. Marcus loves long bike trips with the right partner, and he has a collection of over ten classic bikes. Let's rev your engines and give a big Fern Valley welcome to Marcus."

After the extremely tall and shirtless Marcus in motorcycle leathers and boots strutted his stuff down the short runway that formed a "t" off the school's main stage, another shirtless model appeared in jeans and a cowboy hat. He tossed long-stemmed roses in the audience as he made his way across the stage. The women scrambled to retrieve the flowers.

"And ladies, now we have Steve Sterling and a bouquet of roses. Be still my heart. Cowboys are always my favorites. Y'all be careful with those flowers. Don't start a stampede down there. And certainly don't put anyone's eye out with those long stems."

When Steve ran out of flowers, he blew kisses to the audience and retreated backstage.

"Now we have some locals for you to meet," Carleen said. "This is Anthony Rizzo. He is a full-time security specialist with O'Rourke Security, and when he's not keeping us all safe, he enjoys long hikes, romantic dinners, and adventure books. We could all use a bodyguard like Anthony. Whatcha say, ladies?"

Jules smiled as her contract security guard strutted down the runway in a black leather outfit. He was shirtless except for a bulletproof vest. She snapped a couple of pictures of Anthony.

When the applause died down, Carleen said, "Next, we have Sawyer Kelley; he's a computer programmer who provides illustrations for graphic novels in his spare time."

Sawyer marched across the stage in jeans and a tight-fitting black shirt. He had a pair of black-framed Clark Kent glasses on and a laptop tucked under his arm.

After Sawyer saluted and made his exit, Carleen continued, "And next we have Jake Evans. He's head of maintenance and security at the Fern Valley Luxury Camping Resort, and in his spare time, he's a fierce karaoke competitor. He also owns a tiny house construction business." Carleen winked at Jake, who walked down the runway in an unbuttoned flannel red shirt, jeans, and work boots. His loaded toolbelt jangled as he showed off for the crowd.

Jules's eyes widened, and she snapped photos. Jake was full of surprises. *That explains his disappearing act this morning and why Kim wanted her to hang out for the show.*

"And last, but not least, we have Red's Honkey Tonk's own chief of security, Gabe Howerton. Y'all feel safe around here, don'tcha with all these hunky security guys? Gabe's been keeping everyone safe at the honkey tonk for about three years now. And when he's not on duty, he likes hiking, camping, and he's an amateur chef. He's also single, ladies." Whoops echoed through the room.

Red continued her emcee duties as the models changed outfits and paraded back through to roars of applause and cheers.

Most of the audience was on their feet or huddled close to the stage for a better view.

When the music ended, Carleen strode to the edge of the stage. "Y'all give them all a big round of applause. The models, professional and guests, waltzed across the stage and took multiple bows as phones flashed. "Thank you all for helping us out today. All of these fine gentlemen will be in the cafeteria at two o'clock for photos and autographs. And Ms. Rhoney's team will have lots of books on sale that feature Steve and Marcus. Speaking of them, we're gonna to switch things up here for a bit, and our own Elizabeth Rhoney, owner of Between the Covers, will be out in a sec." Carleen paused and offered an exaggerated wink. "That's our local bookstore. Y'all get your minds out of the gutter. Anyway, she's got a fabulous interview with Sterling and Marcus planned, so you can get to know them better. Let's give a rip roarin' round of applause for our host and guests."

The women standing three-deep at the stage made their way back to their seats.

The door opened beside Jules, and Elaine tapped her on the shoulder and motioned for her to follow.

Outside in the empty foyer, Elaine said, "Wow. That was a hit. I'm sure the afternoon's meet and greet will be super popular, too. Do you mind coming down there with me? We'll need all the hands we can get to keep some semblance of order. Some of those women were a wee bit unruly during the final part of the performance. We don't need anything unpleasant or any injuries." Elaine motioned toward the empty hallway that smelled like a mix of antiseptics.

Jules had a flashback to her own high school days as their heels clacked on the industrial floor. The only thing missing from her trip down memory lane were the rows of lockers that used to line each side of the hallway. Things have changed, but there was no mistaking that high school smell that sent her memory into overdrive.

Interrupting Jules's thoughts, Elaine asked, "Did Jake surprise you? He would make a great cover model. Very handsome." The older woman wiggled her eyebrows for effect.

Jules felt the heat rise up her neck to her cheeks. "He's always got something up his sleeve. I'll have to swing by and get his autograph," Jules said with a wink. "Anthony, Gabe, and Sawyer looked like they were having fun out there, too."

"We tried to get Sheriff Matt to do it, but he's knee-deep in alligators with that murder investigation. Plus, I don't think even Roxanne could have talked him into it. He likes to fly under the radar. This wasn't his cup of tea." Elaine made a face that looked like she had licked a persimmon. "And then the town manager said we couldn't have municipal employees take part. Anyway, we had a great set of models and a fabulous turnout. And we raised a bunch of money for charity. You need anything before we begin the afternoon's festivities?"

Jules shook her head as they approached the table where Kim Lacy and Darlene Denunzio sat behind a long table near the cafeteria. "Oh, Kim has a smartwatch that was turned in to lost and found if anyone is looking for it."

Elaine nodded. "Hey, ladies, I'd like one of you to watch the table, and the other two of you can come with me inside. We'll be the ambassadors to answer questions, shepherd the lines through, and make sure everyone behaves. We have scads of people to move through here. We don't want bottlenecks or dawdling or people getting too close to the models. Once the women get inside, I'm anticipating that the lines will be long. I'm sure they'll all want to see the models."

"I can do the desk," Kim volunteered. "I should be okay out here by myself. All the action is in there." That sly smile crept across her face again.

"Jules and I can keep the peace in there," said Darlene, owner of Pins and Needles quilting shop. "We can handle this bunch."

"We've got this," Jules said with a wink. "This time, it's a female security force."

"Let's find our places, ladies. Darlene, you and Jules stake out spots on the perimeter and be ready to jump in if there are issues. Keep your eyes peeled for anything that needs attention. They'll be here in a bit," Elaine said, looking at her watch.

Deputy Dempsey strolled in, stirring a large coffee and hitching up his gun belt. "Afternoon, ladies. I'm done investigating the missing items. Sheriff said you needed someone here to keep order."

"Did you find them?" Elaine asked.

Deputy Dempsey shook his head.

"Well, it's nice to see you anyway. I know you all will get to the bottom of Windsor's missing things. We'd also like you to make sure things are orderly out here. And then we may need some help with the traffic outside as people start to leave."

"Gotcha covered," he said.

Jules followed Darlene and Elaine inside the cafeteria. Before they could get settled, Elizabeth swooped in the back entrance with the models.

"Good afternoon, gentlemen. Thanks so much for all your talents. You each have a table with a tent card on it. Get settled and let us know if you need anything. There's water at each station for you all. We'll open the doors in a few minutes to your adoring fans," Elaine said.

Jules raised one eyebrow and gave Jake a finger wave when she caught his attention. His impish grin showed his dimples, reminding Jules of the teenager who used to tease her constantly.

Elaine opened the cafeteria doors, and a line of women rushed inside. Each hurried to find a spot in front of the models. The lines quickly snaked through the cafeteria and out the door. The dull roar of voices gave Jules a slight headache.

As Jules watched what felt like hundreds of women in all age groups file by, one woman's hair caught her attention. Her long henna locks were in a fancy updo, held in place by an ornate comb.

Trying not to lose the woman in the crowd, she scrolled through her phone for a look at Windsor's website. Could the comb be the same one? She needed to get closer to the woman to verify it was one of the missing items.

After dodging elbows and pushing her way toward the woman with the fancy comb, Jules drew close enough to the woman to snap some pictures. Then suddenly, the woman turned and glared at Jules, caught with her phone extended to capture the picture. "Oh, hi." Jules could feel her face redden. "I love your hair comb. It's beautiful. I had to snap a picture of it to show my friend. Where did you get it?"

The woman's stern expression melted as she touched the back of her hair. This was my aunt's. She gave it to me when I turned thirteen. I absolutely love it. She brought it with her to the U. S. when she was a little girl, and her family migrated here. Sure. Go ahead." The woman turned so Jules could capture the photo.

"It is fabulous, uh, Tess," Jules said, glancing down at the woman's name tag when she turned back around. *Tess Davies.*

"Thanks. I've never seen another one quite like it. It has so much sentimental value for me. One day, I hope to gift it to my niece as a family heirloom. And I love how it looks. I always feel like a princess when I wear it."

"It's lovely. I hope you enjoy your afternoon and the rest of the festival. I'm Jules, by the way. I'm one of the volunteers."

"It's so nice to meet you. This has been fun. And I can't wait to meet the models and get my book covers signed." The line for Marcus inched forward, and Tess turned to catch up to the woman in front of her.

Jules disappeared into the crowd and let out a long breath that she didn't realize she was holding. Could the comb be the same one? It was hard to tell from the two pictures. Both pieces were ornate.

Finding a quiet spot out of the fray, she tapped off a quick text to Deputy Dempsey with Tess's name and the picture of the hair comb. She stared at her picture and then Windsor's website again. *I hope I didn't send Bubba on a wild goose chase.*

Chapter Twelve

Friday

Jules sank further into her office chair and stared at the ceiling. Fridays in February were usually quiet. Not today. She had spent the morning fielding questions about the festival's events, booking reservations for the spring and summer, replacing a lost key, scheduling a girls' wine-tasting weekend, and trying carefully to dodge questions about Cinnamon Moon's murder. She had been so busy she had missed the author tea at the library.

Taking a few deep breaths, she started to relax until her phone's ring jarred her from her moment of solitude.

"Hi, Mel. What's going on?"

"Sorry to bother you, Jules. Crystal and I are setting up for tonight's dinner, and one of the authors is here. She has a lot of suggestions about how things should be. Many ideas for changes…"

Jules let out a sigh. "I'll be right over." Disconnecting, she looked at Bijou. "Be right back. Gotta go and see what the authors are up to now. One seems to have suggestions for ways we can improve tonight's event. I need to go help Mel out."

Bijou closed her eyes and snuggled in her bed.

"Glad you're confident that I can handle it," Jules said, slipping out the back door.

Tonight was a chance for the fans to have a cozy dinner and chat with the authors. Different venues around town hosted the dinners billed as "Be Still

My Beating Heart—Dinner with Your Favorite Romance Author." Jules's event featured Echo and Gigi. Jules, Mel, and Crystal had worked hard to plan a fun and elegant meal for the guests with some special surprises in a relaxed setting. The hours of planning covered every little detail from the table settings and decorations to the menu. Jules wanted it to be a different experience. She and Jake had even rearranged the tables for a conversational vibe.

Jules opened the back door to the lodge's kitchen and followed a loud voice to the dining room, where she found Gigi Johnson waving her arms at Mel and Crystal. She took a deep breath and steeled herself before Gigi let loose with another tirade.

"You're not listening. I said that it's important that all the guests have the books at their place settings," Gigi said with one arm planted on her hip. "Echo and I want this evening to be perfect."

"Good afternoon, Ms. Johnson. We do, too. Mel, Crystal, and I have been working on the plan for tonight for a while. We have pulled out all the stops, and it will be a chic affair that your fans will remember. We want an elegant, minimalistic look for each place setting."

Gigi looked around the room and stared at the tables. "The books are the highlight of the evening. That's why we're here. They should be on the table. Front and center."

"I understand your concern, but there will be multiple dinner courses with drinks, butter, salad dressing, and gravy, and we want to make sure the books are protected. We have a personalized gift bag for each guest. It will contain the books from both of you. Everyone likes a pretty gift. And it will make it easier to keep their things and the swag the authors provide together."

Gigi rolled her eyes. "If you say so. But I think the books need to be like chargers on the plates. In full view. The books are the reason for everything. And this is the menu?" The author pointed to the card on each table.

Before Gigi could provide any additional commentary about the food, Jules smiled. "Yes, we have a beef and a vegetarian option with salad and vegetables. And the evening will be topped off by Crystal's fabulous chocolate torte cake. And then each guest will get a bag of chocolate truffles to take with them."

"Sounds fine. I'm not a mixed vegetable fan, but I guess I can eat around them, especially if you included peas. Yuck." The author wrinkled her nose. "And where will Echo and I be?" Gigi scanned the room, counting the seats at each table.

"You both will be at the two VIP tables near the fireplace." Jules pointed to the wall of windows at the other end of the room. "You'll each have a table full of fans."

"And that's the podium. You have a microphone, I presume." Gigi pointed a long aqua fingernail toward the fireplace.

Jules hoped her smile didn't look as fake as it felt. "Of course. The system is all set up at the lectern and ready for your and Ms. Aames's presentations. I'm sure the fans will be delighted to learn about both of you."

"I'm first on the agenda, right?" Gigi glared at Jules and Crystal.

"Elizabeth Rhoney will be emceeing for us tonight. We'll have to check on the order of the talks when she gets here. I'm expecting her about four o'clock. She said that you and Ms. Aames would be arriving about five-thirty to get set up and do a sound check."

Gigi nodded and looked at her watch. "That should give me time for a facial and to get ready. I want that first table up there, please." The author adjusted the strap of her Coach bag and waltzed out the lodge's main doors.

After they heard the door shut, Mel said, "Thanks for coming over, Jules. She blew in here like a hurricane and went from civil to harpy in about ten seconds. Nothing met her expectations. She was rearranging the place settings before I could stop her."

Crystal patted her mom's shoulder. "Some of these ladies remind me of the actors who were here this past fall. Definitely high maintenance. Everything looks lovely. I'm sure everyone will have a wonderful time."

"I'll make sure I'm here early and ready to diffuse anything that pops up this evening. I'm surprised she didn't ask me how many tickets were sold. I saw her counting chairs," Jules said with a half-smile. "I'll give Elizabeth a heads up when she arrives. I'm sure she'll be thrilled to receive all the helpful hints."

"We'll be ready. Jake and Lester helped with the setup. We'll have one final meeting with the part-time waitstaff and Emily when they get here," Mel said.

Jules smiled at the mention of Emily Owens. She had worked part-time at the resort through her high school years. "I think the place looks great. Elizabeth and I will be here early for registration and to hand out the gift bags. And keep the peace. We don't want to have any dust-ups."

Jules spent the rest of the afternoon on future bookings. If this continued, they were in for another banner year. She smiled after a glance at the year-to-date numbers.

"Come on, Bijou. We need to get a move on. Big dinner plans."

After walking around the resort and ensuring Bijou's dinner bowl was full, Jules showered and dressed in record time. Nixing her stiletto black boots for a comfortable pair with a chunk heel, she patted Bijou on the head and made sure the living room and outside floodlights were on. "You're on guard duty, kiddo. Be back after we clean up tonight."

The hours of daylight were getting a bit longer as the calendar inched toward spring. However, the chilly breeze reminded her that winter hadn't completely surrendered yet. Jules hustled the short distance from her cabin to the lodge.

Once inside the industrial kitchen, she stowed her coat in the tiny office next to the pantry that Mel and Crystal shared.

When Crystal popped into the kitchen with a cart full of coffee carafes, Jules said, "Hey, there. What do you need help with?"

"I'm wrapping up the setup. Mom will be here in a few, and we'll start working on her checklist. Most of the food is already prepped. We should be good to go. I know she wants to do a quick walk-through with the waitstaff. Other than that, we're on track."

Crystal made her way to the massive workspace next to the industrial refrigerator.

"I'll be over there. I want to check on the place settings and the registration table. It looks like we're all ready for a fun evening. Holler if you need me,"

Jules said.

Jules buzzed around, adjusting name cards and centerpieces, making sure everything was set at the registration table, and stoking the fireplace. Inside the dining room, Jules heard a faint tapping, and she followed the sound to the kitchen door. Elizabeth Rhoney and the two authors stood on the cement stoop.

"Come on in," Jules said. "Welcome. We're almost ready here. If you all have coats, we can put them in the chef's office unless you want to keep them with you."

"How cold is it in there?" Echo asked.

"It's toasty. We revved up the fireplace," Jules replied.

The three women followed her to the main room.

"This is lovely," Gigi said, staring out the windows. "But I think I'll keep my coat with me."

"Me too," Echo chimed in.

"Ladies, VIP tables are here at the front. After dinner, Elizabeth will have a short chat with both of you before we open it up to questions and answers from the guests."

"I'm first," Gigi interrupted.

"Yes, you can be first," Elizabeth replied with an expressionless face. Jules noticed a slight twitch in one of the bookseller's eyes, the only hint that Elizabeth was annoyed with the pushy author.

"Okay. No offense, Echo, but it's my turn," Gigi said, waving a dismissive hand.

"That's not a problem. I'll say they saved the best for last," Echo replied coyly. "May I have a glass of water?"

Gigi scowled and turned her head.

"Sure. Would either of you like one?" Jules asked as Echo shook her head. *I'm not sure I should leave those two alone together. At least Elizabeth is here to send them to opposite corners if they go at each other.*

Before Jules returned with the drink, Elizabeth bustled into the kitchen and whispered, "Jules, this night cannot end fast enough. I'm not sure how long I can take the sniping and rudeness. You may have to bail me out if I get arrested."

Jules cracked a smile and patted her friend on her arm. "It'll be okay. I've got your back. We better get in there before the claws come out." Jules pushed the swinging door open to find an empty dining room.

I hope they're not out scrapping in the foyer. It's almost time to open the doors and play nice for all the paying fans.

Jules wandered to the lobby. Hearing voices near the public restrooms, she rounded the corner. Pausing outside of the women's door, she heard Gigi say, "I swear. I hope it's sold out" through the door.

"What do you care? They already bought the books," Echo said.

"But they can still return them if there are no shows. This place is pretty, and the food is nice, but we should have been at that bistro in town. I heard they had special cocktails named for the authors at their happy hour. That was the party everybody wanted to go to. I overheard that chubby lady saying that the news crew were covering that one. That's the A-list location tonight. That Windsor and Allegra always get all the perks."

Jules closed her eyes for a second to try to calm down.

"But at least we're not with the bottom feeders," Echo said as the restroom door opened.

"Oh, there you are," Jules tried to pretend she wasn't eavesdropping. "Here's your drink."

"Uh, thanks," Gigi said, taking the glass.

"If you all want to find your seats, I'm going to check with my team, and we'll open the doors in a bit. Your fans are so excited to have a fancy dinner with the both of you." Jules hoped she didn't lay it on too thick, but she was tired of their snark.

When Mel and Crystal gave the sign that they were ready, Elizabeth settled in behind the registration table as Jules opened the main door for the crowd outside.

As the servers brought out the dessert, a gooey chocolate torte cake, Echo tapped the microphone at the lectern. "Good evening, all. I hope you're enjoying this wonderful food and conversation. It has been fun for me to get a chance to talk with everyone. As you enjoy those awesome desserts, I wanted to give you an update on what's next for me, and then Gigi will talk." She shuffled index cards as Gigi popped up from her table and bellowed, "What do you think you're doing?"

All heads shifted toward Gigi, who waved her arm and darted toward one of the side tables. Jules tried to figure out her target as she made her way toward the animated author. It felt like all eyes in the room were on her. Echo tapped her ring on the microphone to divert the audience's attention as Jules followed Gigi through the maze of tables.

Jules almost plowed into the back of Gigi as she stopped short near a table by the kitchen entrance. "What do you think you're doing here? Poaching is not allowed. This is my event. Why aren't you at yours?" Gigi demanded, waggling her finger inches from Phoenix's nose.

"We wrapped up early at the library. I saw the lights on here, and this wonderful table invited me to join them." Phoenix smiled broadly and opened her arms like she was reaching to hug someone.

"Oh, no, sister. You had your event. This one is mine. You're always horning in and inviting yourself where you're not wanted. She doesn't have a ticket. I want her removed. Just cause her event tanked doesn't mean she can crash ours." Gigi harrumphed and planted a fist on her right hip.

Before Jules could intervene, Echo said loudly in the microphone, "And that's about it for me. Gigi, it's your turn. Folks would love to hear about what's next for you."

The tallish author whipped her head around toward the stage and softened her sneer. "Of course. My public awaits." She turned and flounced to the front of the room. "And you," she aimed a bony finger at Phoenix. "I better not see you anymore this evening, or you'll be sorry."

Ignoring the comment, Phoenix squeezed into the empty seat between two women in matching Echo Aames's T-shirts. "There is always drama with romance writers. Don'tcha just love it? Uh, could you get me some coffee and a dessert? And a fork?" she asked Jules.

Vowing to keep an eye out for any other author eruptions, Jules headed to the kitchen to fill Phoenix's order.

After all the guests had left and the team finished clearing the tables, Jules asked, "Anybody want anything to drink?" When no one responded, she slipped into the kitchen for a glass of ice water. Seconds later, she sank into a nearby chair in the dining room and stretched her legs.

"Despite the authors with 'tudes, I think it went well," Elizabeth said. "You and your team outdid yourselves on the decorations, food, and gift bags. I know the guests had a great time." When Mel walked by, she said louder, "Mel, you and Crystal did a fabulous job. The meal was exquisite."

"We had fun with the event planning." Mel beamed. "I'm glad everyone had a pleasant time."

After they restored order to the dining room and kitchen and locked up, Jules slipped into her coat and turned out the lodge's lights. She followed the meandering path to her cabin. The quiet of the cold night felt serene. It was refreshing to breathe in the mountain air and to enjoy the peacefulness.

Jules hadn't taken three steps before a shriek pierced through the night air and jolted her from her thoughts.

Zeroing in on the direction of the noise, she darted off toward the vintage campers. Rounding the corner at the first row of trailers, she paused. Just silence. *I know I heard a shrill noise.*

A twig snapped. Jules slowed her pace and crept to the edge of the trailer. She paused to listen for any other noises.

"What a disaster," Gigi said. "I'm telling you. I'm getting too old for all this smiling and glad-handing. Some of these readers are so flippin' nosey. They act like they know you because they read your books. I'm not here to make friends. One old broad had the nerve to tell me there was a typo on page forty-nine of my book. Sheesh. And that beef was a little tough. I'm so tired of the food at these things."

"I don't know about you, but the dessert was excellent. And I kinda like talking to readers. I get a kick out of how engrossed they get in my characters' lives," Echo said. "I always meet interesting people."

"Most of 'em need to get a life. I'm still ticked that we got stuck with the B team. Uh, no offense." Gigi rustled around and continued, "Maybe we should be careful out here. Isn't this where Cinnamon was kidnapped, and you know…"

"Who knows?" Echo said. "I thought the sheriff said it happened in her trailer. I guess you can never be too careful. You never know who to trust."

"I don't trust anyone. I've had way too many people act all nice to my face and then try to mess me up." Gigi's voice faded to where Jules had to strain to hear her.

Jules made a noise and popped around the corner. "Hello, ladies. Is everything okay? I heard a squeal."

"That was me," Echo said. "These shoes weren't meant for hiking, and I stepped in a hole."

"Are you okay?" Jules asked.

"She's fine. We had a lovely evening. The food was to die for. Can't wait to attend the rest of the festival events," Gigi said.

Jules wished there had been more light. She would have loved to see the woman's face as she had a sudden change of heart about the event.

"Well, bless your heart. Thank you so much. I'll pass that on to the team. They will be thrilled, especially coming from famous authors like you two." Jules was glad they couldn't see her toothy grin. "It's getting late. You ladies let me know if you need anything at all." Jules turned toward her cabin. She hoped her brisk walk would burn off some of the tension these two created.

Chapter Thirteen

Saturday

"Hello. Did you eat lunch yet?" Roxanne asked, putting her red Coach bag in the desk across from Jules. "And hello to you too, Bijou." The little dog stood at her feet, pawing for one of the treats hidden in the desk drawer. "Of course, you've been an excellent fur baby. I don't even have to ask. Let's find a little snack to hold you until dinner." She scooped up the wiggly dog and kissed the top of her head.

"Nope. I missed lunch. Are we still on for the book talk and dinner tonight?" Jules looked up from her laptop.

"Of course. Sounds like fun. It'll give me a chance to get some autographs while the authors are still in town. I haven't had time to get any books signed. Whatcha feel like for dinner? Pop's is always a winner. I'm kind of in the mood for one of his thick burgers. I've had enough rabbit food this week. Bijou, I've been a good girl, too. How are things here?"

"Yum, Pop's. Let's see, I had ten new check-ins this morning. Only two campers checked out. They were here for the first week of the festival."

"After I get settled, I've got some bills to pay. Anything else you want me to work on? Expecting more check-ins today?" her aunt asked.

"Nope, everyone arrived early. We are done with check-ins for this week."

Before Jules could return to her spring newsletter, her phone vibrated on a stack of files on her desk. "Hi, Pixel. What's up with you?"

"Hey, girl. I've been meaning to call you, but time keeps getting away from me. Do you have a minute or two to talk?"

"Sure. What's up?" Jules asked.

"Work has gotten crazy, but I'm loving it. I was trying to find a day to meet you for lunch for a week now, but stuff keeps popping up. Did I tell you that I was having the time of my life with my new gig? The FBI has such cool toys. Anyway, I digress. I found some stuff on your authors that I wanted to pass on to you."

A charge of excitement caused Jules to sit up straighter in her chair. She picked up her notebook and a pen. "Whatcha got?"

"Let's see. We'll start with the victim. Cinnamon Moon or Amy Bishop was super popular, and her fans are rabid. They're all still mourning her loss. It's sad that she won't get to see her series made into a TV show, but I'm sure her death will make it an overnight classic. The dirt I could find on her was some accusations about fifteen years ago. She was in a critique group with Tammy James, aka Echo Aames, but she was known back then as Tamara Scott. Anyway, she accused Amy of stealing her idea of a Western romance set in New Mexico from discussions at their critique group. And by the way, guess which series was optioned for TV. I'm wondering if Echo, a.k.a. Tammy, will dredge up her old claims again when the show hits the airwaves."

"Hmm," Jules said. "How much truth do you think there is to the story? You'd think if someone plagiarized your work that you'd file a lawsuit or something."

"You'd think, especially if it was a valuable idea. That's how you recoup money. Not by ranting on the internet. But she seems to air all of her grievances on social media. I couldn't find anything about any lawsuits. Just lots of online whining and tirades." Pixel paused and tapped something in the background. "That was pretty much all I found on Echo or Tammy, or whatever her name is. Oh, this is juicy. Phoenix Abbott or Tracey Davis is really big into her social media platforms. There are tons of stuff out there on her. She seems to jump on everything that comes along and promises to make you a best-selling author. Recently, she's started publishing her own and others' books, and she offers a variety of services to authors. Her latest idea is to put together these boxed sets from a variety of authors, promising those who pay to be in the set a chance to hit the best-seller lists. There have been some online complaints about how she cheated people and how some of the authors feel they didn't get the royalties they deserved. I couldn't find any lawsuits, but she does have a ton of unhappy clients. She rants on her blog and TikTok frequently about how indie authors are treated unfairly. She seems kinda bitter. I thought romance writers were all roses, chocolate, and steamy love scenes."

"Now that you mention it. She's not that friendly in person either. Some of these authors are lovely and spend time with their fans. Phoenix has an edge to her."

"Hmmmm. Let's see, what else did I find? Margaret Allegra Rhodes has been on the scene for a while. She used to write for a popular soap, and the fans love her, too. I couldn't find any dirt on Windsor Abernathy either," Pixel said.

"Did I give you her assistant's name?"

"Nope. What is it?" Pixel asked.

"Tiffany Blake. Windsor bosses her around all the time. It's on my to-do list to try to catch the assistant alone to see what she'll tell me. She always seems kinda sad," Jules said.

"I'll see what I can find. Let's see who's next. Carrie Shultz, the literary agent. She worked in several of the publishing houses in a variety of jobs prior to opening her own firm. She represents a whole stable of authors. I didn't find anything on Lynnette D'Angelo. Not even a speeding ticket. She's squeaky clean. Lynnette does have a huge social media presence and seems to be able to spin anything. I guess that's why she's a publicist. Her website lists a ton of awards for her work with her clients."

"Interesting. You're always a wealth of information. Thanks for looking into this, even when you're so busy," Jules said.

"My pleasure. You always have interesting things happen at your place."

"Hey, dinner's on me when you can tear yourself away from the FBI and all their action, which I'm sure makes everything that happens here in Fern Valley pale by comparison. I am so excited for you. Can't wait to hear about your adventures, or at least the ones you can tell me about."

Pixel laughed. "My schedule should calm down soon. I'll text you some dates for dinner. We are past due for a girls' night out."

"Sounds good. I can't wait," Jules said, disconnecting the call.

"Hey," Roxanne said. "What are you wearing tonight? Just trying to figure out if I need to run home and change."

"You always look nice. I was going to wear this. It's casual. They're doing author talks and book signings. I need to take Bijou for a walk and get her situated at home."

"I'll lock up here. Meet me at my car when you're done. I can drive," her aunt said.

Jules packed up her laptop and notes. Today, the little dog wanted to smell every blade of grass between the office and their cabin. By the time Jules got her settled and fed, Roxanne zoomed up Jules's driveway in her white Mercedes.

Jules locked the door and trotted down the driveway to Roxanne's car. "Sorry. Bijou was not in any hurry to head home."

"No problem. I figured I'd save you some steps. Do you want to eat now before the thing or afterward?"

"It's not over until after eight o'clock." Jules slid into the passenger seat and set her purse on the floor.

"I'll be starving by then. Let's eat now." Roxanne backed out of the driveway faster than Jules expected. She clicked her seatbelt in place as her aunt did a three-point turn with an acceleration move that rivaled NASCAR. Roxanne broke the sound barrier on her way to town. It was a good thing Bubba didn't have his speed trap set up.

"Here we are," Roxanne said, pulling into an empty spot near Pop's shiny front doors. "Looks like we beat the dinner rush." She flipped her purse strap over her shoulder and clicked her key fob to lock the doors.

A teenaged Bobby Soxer directed them to a booth in the Elvis section of the restaurant. Before they had a chance to glance at the menu, a thin waiter with a pompadour appeared with silverware and glasses of water.

"Hello, ladies. I'm Tomas. What can I get you to start with tonight? We have a special Valentine's Day menu on the pink sheet to help celebrate Heart Day and the romance festival that's in town."

"Oh, nice," Roxanne said. "I'll have the Black and Bleu Burger with fries and water. That doesn't sound romantic, but I'm sure it tastes great."

"And I'll have a mushroom and Swiss burger with the fries," Jules said, handing the junior Elvis her menu.

When he was out of earshot, Roxanne said, "I wonder where Marsha is. She's always here." She pulled out her phone and tapped something on the screen.

"Maybe she's got a hot date or at least a day off. Speaking of hot date, did you get to go out for Valentine's Day? And has the sheriff said anything about the murder?"

"Not a peep. And we took a raincheck on the Valentine's celebration. He and his team have been pulling long shifts during this investigation. I got the sense that he's not getting anywhere. Maybe you need to do more poking. You always seem to be able to uncover the bad guy or gal. I'm sure he could use all the help he can get. You have a knack."

"These things keep happening around the resort. Plus, people always tell me things," Jules said.

"That's why you're the perfect sleuth. No one suspects you of ferreting out information, and you have a knack for uncovering things. Down deep, Sheriff Matt is glad for the help, even though he'll never admit it. You keep being Nancy Drew," Roxanne said.

The waiter interrupted and set down their plates. "I'll be back in a minute with refills," he said. "Can I get you anything else?"

"This looks fantastic," Roxanne said, eyeing her giant burger and steak fries.

"Mmm." Jules took a bite of her mushroom Swiss burger. "So, any news in the Fern Valley grapevine about Cinnamon's murder?"

Roxanne dabbed her lips with a paper napkin. "Nope. After the press coverage died down, people seemed to have moved on. Was Pixel able to find out anything? I'm guessing that if there's any chatter out there, it's on the internet. I was surprised to learn that these romance fans are seriously dedicated readers. I was talking to some of the guests, and they said they read three or four books a week. Whew!"

Jules's eyes widened. "Pixel mentioned some rumors she dug up." Jules lowered her voice and swished a French fry in ketchup. "There are stories that Phoenix cheated some authors out of royalties with her get-rich-quick schemes. And she found another accusation where Echo insinuated that Cinnamon stole an idea from her for a story. The one that was optioned for TV."

Roxanne's eyebrows shot up about an inch. "Money makes people do crazy things."

"There were no lawsuits to support the accusations. Winsor and Allegra have been in the business for a while. Pixel didn't find any dirt on them."

The waiter breezed by the table again. "Ladies, do you need anything? Dessert?" When they shook their heads, he set the check on the edge of the table. "I'll be back for this whenever you're ready. No rush."

Roxanne grabbed the receipt from Jules. "I've got this. We rarely get a chance to go out and relax. You can get it next time. Tonight's my treat. We better wrap it up if we want to get to the library before the thing starts."

Fifteen minutes later, Roxanne and Jules found seats midway back in the conference room. Jules shimmied out of her coat and settled in on the metal chair. They had enough time to wave to friends and for Roxanne to offer her a mint before Elaine thumped her plump finger on the microphone. The thunks echoed from all the speakers in the ceiling, and an electronic squeal elicited groans from the audience and squelched the conversation.

"Good evening, all. If you all in the foyer and the aisles will take your seats, we'll get started shortly. There are still some chairs on this side of the room." Elaine waved her hands like a flight attendant helping people to find the emergency exits. After some people took seats or slid over to make room for others, Elizabeth led Gigi, Phoenix, Echo, Allegra, and Windsor inside. The women filed in behind the long table covered in a black cloth.

After a quick inspection of the authors, Elaine said something to Gigi and Phoenix and pointed to the lone microphone between the two of them. Gigi gave Elaine a dismissive wave while a dark look crossed Phoenix's face.

Returning to the lectern, Elaine said, "Good evening, authors, readers, and fans. Welcome to Fern Valley's Love is in the Air Book Festival. We're so excited to have you here tonight, and many thanks to the library staff and our sponsors." She pointed to the banner on the front of the table. "Tonight, we are so fortunate to have these amazing authors here to talk about their books and to answer your questions. But before we get started, I have some housekeeping details for you. I'll ask the authors some questions that they will respond to, and then we'll save the last half hour for your questions. When we break, Elizabeth Rhoney, owner of Between the Covers bookstore, has books available out in the foyer, and these ladies will be here until eight to sign and chat. Let's get started."

Elaine introduced each author, and Gigi made a big deal of pulling the microphone toward her when it was her turn. Phoenix yanked it back when she was ready to respond. *I hope this isn't a sign of how the evening is going to go.*

Most of the crowd didn't seem to care about the microphone scuffle at the end of the table, but Jules noticed that a couple of people were recording it. *Elaine won't be happy, especially if it goes viral.* Jules glanced at Elaine, who glared at the authors.

Jules's anxiety faded as the program continued. The authors answered Elaine's questions and engaged the audience. No more microphone fights. The audience asked lots of questions and kept the discussion focused on Windsor and Allegra. Phoenix and Gigi used every available pause to jump in with a comment about their books.

A woman in the front row asked any of the authors to talk about their first real love, and Phoenix grabbed the microphone that Gigi was holding and pulled it closer to her. Gigi's eyes flashed, and her cheeks reddened as Phoenix launched into her story. Gigi let out an exaggerated sigh. Then she slammed both fists on the table and rose. Jules closed her eyes for a brief moment. So much for a calm event.

"I will not be treated like this," Gigi said before storming out. Elaine opened her mouth and closed it quickly as Phoenix continued her story about teen love like nothing happened.

When she finished, Elaine said, "Thank you all so much. This has been a very entertaining evening. We wish we could keep this going, but we need to save time for book signings and the meet and greets. But you'll have lots of opportunities to talk to the authors this week. There are flyers on the table about our upcoming events. If you'd like to pick up books, the bookseller is in the lobby outside these doors." Elaine waved both hands toward the doors to the foyer. "Thank you, ladies, so much. We enjoyed your talk this evening. Let's give them all a hand. And a hand for all our volunteers who make events like this happen."

When the applause died down, the audience picked up coats and purses and shuffled to the lines forming at the table for autographs.

"Be back in a jiff. I want to get some books. Be back as soon as I get them signed," Roxanne said.

Before Jules had a chance to move, Elaine swooped in and touched her on the shoulder.

"Wow, that was draining. Those two authors better behave from here on out. They looked like petulant children up there." Elaine closed her eyes and shook her head.

"We have some divas here," Jules said in a low tone.

"Divas who signed contracts for these events. I don't want to have to remind any of them of their responsibilities, but I will. I'm going to give that one the night to cool off and then see if she shows up tomorrow for the workshops. This petty behavior is unbecoming. She seems oblivious to our code of conduct."

Jules stole a look over Elaine's shoulder. Gigi's coloring had returned to normal as she found a seat at the long table to sign autographs.

"Looks like you've got it all under control. Let me know if I can help with anything," Jules said.

"Who would have thought two grown professionals would fight like six-year-olds for the microphone? Sheesh."

Jules shrugged a shoulder. "We all turn into children when there is a cool toy."

Elaine made a harrumphing sound. "We'll see how tomorrow goes. I expect some improved behavior." Elaine, who is as wide as she is tall, turned on her sensible shoes and disappeared into the crowd.

Could petty squabbles lead to something deadly? It seems that at least two of them had axes to grind, and the resentment and anger were building. *I hope we haven't reached a boiling point.*

Chapter Fourteen

Saturday Night

"Well, that was fun. And a little dramatic," Roxanne said, stopping suddenly in Jules's driveway.

"Thanks for driving and dinner. Let me know if you hear anything from the sheriff," Jules said, climbing out.

"Will do. But don't expect a lot of info. You know how he is when he's investigating something."

Roxanne waved and then floored it down the maintenance road. The taillights of the Mercedes disappeared through the resort's entrance.

She barely had the front door open before Bijou bounced out like a ping-pong ball. "Okay, puppy. I know it was a long time. Let's get your leash and go for an evening stroll." Jules dropped her purse inside and pocketed her keys and phone. "Come on," she said, but Bijou was already out the door.

They trekked around the cabin, following the tree line along the woods away from the lodge. An owl hooted in the distance, and Bijou froze. Moments later, she returned to her mission of smelling every blade of grass and pebble she could find.

The ambient light from the resort started to fade. Jules tugged on the leash, trying to guide the Jack Russell terrier back toward the cabin, but Bijou had other plans. Some scent had caught her attention, and she wasn't ready to move on.

A shrill shriek echoed across the field, and this time, Jules and Bijou froze.

A second squeal made Jules wish she had brought her pepper spray with her. Scooping up Bijou, she walked gingerly toward the noise. As the pair crept closer to the barn, Jules spotted a figure in white waving its arms and cackling at the edge of the woods. Bijou let out a low growl, and Jules hugged her closer.

The figure did some sort of shaky dance and disappeared behind a tree. Jules paused.

Then, the person in white stumbled out and fell forward, letting out a string of curses and another cackle. Rolling over to a seated position, the person laughed again and let out another stream of curses.

"Gigi?" Jules whispered, walking closer to the figure, still seated in the grass. "Gigi, is that you? What are you doing out here?"

"Yep, it's me in all my glory," she said with a nervous laugh. After a couple of tries, the author stood and wobbled.

"Are you okay?" Jules asked.

"I'm fine," Gigi hiccupped. "I tripped over some stupid tree back there and broke my heel. Stupid tree. Stupid shoe."

"Let's get you back to your camper. It's cold out here. What are you doing in the woods this late at night without a coat on?" Jules asked, helping the woman to her feet.

"I needed some fresh air. My camper was hot. And I didn't feel like sleeping. A nice ol' walk clears one's head and gets the ticker thumping. Plus, it's a free country, I can walk around ooooutside if I want to," she slurred.

"I wanted to make sure you're safe. Occasionally, we have foxes, coyotes, and bears around here. I wouldn't wander too far into the woods with no flashlight. And those really don't look like hiking shoes to me. Let's get you back to your bed. You'll feel better in the morning."

"I feel fine. Just let an old coyote try and come after me. I'll show him whose boss. I used to love those old cartoons. Beep. Beep." Gigi jerked away from Jules and toddled in the grass.

"This way," Jules said, lighting the way with her cell phone. Gigi hobbled along behind her toward the trailers.

"Here we go. Do you have your key?" Jules asked as they approached the patio of the small trailer.

"Door's open," Gigi said. "I might be expecting company later. Shhhh. It's a secret."

"Okay, but be careful." Jules held the door for her as the woman teetered on the three small steps. "It's always a good idea to lock your door."

"I'm fine. I'm collecting information. And when I have it all, I'll call the sheriff and tell on the killer. It was sad that someone got Cinnamon. She was a nice lady. But I know who did it, and I will tell everyone. Hey, I might even have a press conference. That'll show them. And I'll finally get to brag. Shhhhh. Don't tell anyone I know." Gigi stumbled into the trailer and plopped down on the couch across from the door.

"Who killed Cinnamon?" Jules asked.

"You have to wait for my press conference. I might even write an article or do a blog. Ha! It's for me to know and you all to find out." She reached down and tried several times to take off her shoes. "I know a secret. And somebody's not going to like it."

"Okay. Time to get some sleep. Let me know if you need anything else this evening."

"I told you I'm fine," she slurred again. "Time to work on some chapters before I hit the hay. Hey. Hay and hey. That's funny," Gigi rambled. "The news shows will want to interview me about what I know. Big story. Big reveal. I gotta get to work. Everybody will know who I am after that. Maybe I should write true crime. I could do a podcast," she hiccupped.

Jules shut the door and backed down the stairs.

Once inside her own cabin, she sent a text to Elaine and Elizabeth in case Gigi didn't show up for tomorrow's event. Elaine may have to track her down in the morning if Gigi decides to sleep it off.

Then she tapped a text to the sheriff.

Not sure if this is important. I found Gigi Johnson wandering around under the influence of something in the woods. She claims she knows who killed Cinnamon, but she's not revealing the name until her press conference.

Her phone dinged with a reply almost instantaneously. **I'll swing by and check on her tomorrow. I'll take any leads I can get right now.**

Chapter Fifteen

Sunday

As Jules flipped on the lights in the office, she heard shuffling on the store's front porch. A knock sent Bijou into attack mode until she saw that it was Sheriff Hobbs, and she wanted to play.

"Good morning, Jules," the sheriff said, reaching down to pet the wiggly dog. "And you, Bijou."

"What brings you by this early in the morning? And can I offer you brunch at the lodge?"

"I wanted to stop by and talk to Ms. Johnson this morning before she gets busy with the festival. Let's swing by her trailer, and then we can check out what Mel and Crystal have on the menu," he said.

Jules raised one eyebrow. "Not sure what kind of condition Gigi'll be in this early. She was chatty and a little scatter-brained. She didn't make much sense. I found her wandering around at the edge of the woods in her pajamas. She was a bit unsteady on her feet. As Lester would say, she was in an onery mood."

"I'm sure she'll be all sweetness and light this morning, especially if she has a hangover, but I'm trying to catch her off guard to see what she knows about the death of Cinnamon Moon. Can you show me her trailer?"

"Sure, she's in the pink Barbie camper. Speaking of that. What do you want me to do with Ms. Moon's belongings?"

"Can you box them for me, and I'll have someone pick them up?"

Jules nodded and slid into her puffy jacket. "Bijou, you're on guard duty until I get back." Jules made a mental note to send an update to Cinnamon's agent.

"We're checking every lead we can find. I'm waiting to get the data from Cinnamon's phone records. That will give us more to go on. Let's go see what Miss Gigi will share this fine morning." Sheriff Hobbs stepped toward the back door.

Jules followed the sheriff toward the trailers, and they passed guests on the path to the lodge. Everything looked like a normal Sunday morning.

Sheriff Hobbs strode up the steps to the pink trailer and pounded on the door. After several seconds, he repeated the knocking with no answer. "I'll try contacting her later. If you happen to see her, let me know."

Before Jules could answer, a sharp trill sounded. "Hobbs here…..Yep….Okay, be there in a bit." Pocketing his phone, he looked at Jules. "Looks like I'm going to have to take a raincheck on breakfast."

Jules did a drive-by of Mel and Crystal's brunch buffet and returned to the office with biscuits and gravy and a fruit parfait. Bijou sniffed the air when hints of sausage gravy wafted from the to-go container.

A noise near the back door diverted Bijou's attention from hopes of getting a breakfast snack. Her guard dog growls turned into wiggles when Lester popped into the office.

"Howdy, Jules. Hey, puppy. I hope y'all are doing well."

"Good morning. We're finishing up Mel's great breakfast this morning. Did you get brunch?"

"Nope. Sunday's oatmeal day for me. I was checking out the grass to see if it needed a clipping today. I was over by the tiny houses, and I spotted something shiny in the grass."

He reached into his pocket and handed the contents to her. "I'm not quite sure what it is. Maybe some hair thingymebob? It looks fancy."

Jules turned over the filigreed metal in her hands. The football-shaped item was crushed on one end. A bent, tiny hook jutted out from the mangled end. "I'm not sure what this is either."

"I heard a zing as I was bopping along on the mower. Then I spotted this thing glinting in the sun. I hope it wasn't that valuable. It looks a little mangled now."

"Hmm. I'll check around to see if anyone has lost anything. How's the buzz on your police scanner?"

"It was hopping right after we found that author lady in the barn, but it has calmed down considerably. Not much over the last couple of days. Twila Jackson's cat got stuck in a tree, and the fire department had to help it down after a couple of days. Oh, there was some vandalism at the high school. Somebody spray-painted the dumpster. But that's about it. I've got some more chores to work on this morning, so I'll be in the barn if you need me." Lester saluted and headed out after one final pat for Bijou.

"Interesting. What is this?" Jules asked. Bijou didn't even attempt to feign interest. She headed for her bed and a morning nap.

Snapping a picture of the damaged thing, Jules repeated her question to Google. The list of responses filled five pages that included everything from medical devices and hairclips to a shuttlecock.

"That might be it." Jules tapped her bottom lip with her finger. "I wonder…." Her voice trailed off as she pulled up Windsor Abernathy's author page. "Bingo!" she said forcefully enough to startle Bijou. "Sorry, puppy. I think Lester found one of Windsor's missing items. But what was it doing in the grass?"

Jules tapped a text to the sheriff. "This proves that Windsor was right, and some of her items were missing. That day at the high school, her assistant couldn't remember if she had packed and unpacked everything. That lady's hairclip might not have been Windsor's, but this thing was," she said to Bijou.

Save it for me. I'll pick it up in an hour or so, Sheriff Hobbs replied.

Jules put the damaged item in an envelope and laid it on Roxanne's desk. She scrawled "for the sheriff" in black marker.

Not interested in the Victorian tatting shuttle or any of the missing items, Bijou closed her eyes again.

Before Jules could return to resort work, her phone dinged again.

Whatcha doing today?

Waiting for the sheriff to swing by. What's up? She replied to Jake.

Gonna work on the tree house today. Wanna help?

Sounds like fun, she texted with a string of trees and heart emojis. **I'll be over in a while.**

See you soon. XXOO, he replied.

Not wanting to leave evidence unattended on the porch, even if it was in an envelope, Jules spent the next half hour on her next newsletter.

At about the time she was thinking about a second cup of coffee, she heard footsteps on the porch. Bijou, in full attack mode, bolted through the doorway and greeted the sheriff.

"Morning again, Jules. Whatcha got for me?"

"Hey. Thanks for coming back. Lester was out on his mower this morning, and he found something shiny." She dumped the crushed piece of metal into his palm. "It's a little damaged, but it's a tatting shuttlecock. There's a match for it on Windsor Abernathy's webpage."

"If you say so. It looks beyond repair. Where is she staying?"

"In the Beatrix Potter tiny house. It's the one that looks like an English cottage with the rabbit statues in the flowerbeds."

The sheriff, who filled almost all of the doorframe, nodded. "I'll take a walk over there. Thanks."

Jules waved and locked the door behind him. "Come on, Bijou. Let's wrap things up here and go see what Jake's up to."

The little dog pranced to the back door and waited patiently for Jules to gather her things.

After a quick stop to drop off her laptop and Bijou at the cabin, Jules changed into an old coat and work boots. There was no telling what fun tasks Jake had planned.

Chapter Sixteen

Monday

"Greetings and salutations," Roxanne said, dropping a shopping bag and her purple Michael Kors bag in the desk chair. "What's shaking around here?"

"All's pretty quiet for a Monday morning. No issues. Yay. When you get settled, I'm headed over to the Elvis Airstream to pack Cinnamon Moon's belongings," Jules said. She stood and stretched, trying to ward off the sore muscles from helping Jake with the tree house yesterday.

"Sounds like a plan." Her aunt's smile faded. "Sorry, you have to do that again." Roxanne busied herself with straightening the file folders and the small stack of bills on the desk.

Jules pulled two empty boxes from the supply closet and located the key to the author's trailer. "Be back in a bit."

Piling the boxes in the backseat of the resort's golf cart, Jules tooled over to the camper village. The only sounds were twittering birds that didn't migrate to points further south. Definitely a quiet morning, which was better than one filled with drama, especially from some of the authors. Jules reminded herself to check with the sheriff about what happened to Gigi. She was curious about who she thought killed Cinnamon. Climbing the two aluminum steps to the trailer, Jules was surprised when she opened the door. A suitcase and a purse sat on the fold-out couch. Besides the gray smudges from the fingerprinting, the camper didn't look like it had been slept in. Even the queen-sized bed in the back bedroom was made. She was either overly neat or had plans to leave soon. *Her killer wouldn't have taken the time to pack her things and clean up. This is odd.*

Jules did a quick walk-through, checking the closets, nightstands, and drawers. It didn't seem like Cinnamon had unpacked anything during her brief stay.

She dragged the empty boxes back to the golf cart and then made a return trip for the author's purse and suitcase. Plopping down on the front seat of the cart, she sent a text to Carrie Shultz to let the agent know that she was sending Cinnamon's belongings to the sheriff's office.

Before Jules could head back to her office, her phone alerted with a text from the agent.

Thanks. Only a purse and suitcase?

Yes, Jules tapped on her phone's screen. **Everything was packed, and the bed was made.**

That doesn't surprise me. Cinnamon was very organized and particular about everything. I'll let her family know the Sheriff's Office will contact them. Thanks.

A shriek echoed through the quiet campground. Jules paused and looked around, trying to find the source. She put the golf cart in gear and drove toward the noise.

"Oh, no, you don't," and a string of shrieks came from behind a nearby trailer.

Jules stopped the cart and watched Deputy Mario Caswell try to handcuff Gigi. It looked like the pair were practicing some weird dance. Gigi writhed and dodged every time he tried to secure her wrists.

Before Jules could say anything, Sheriff Hobbs appeared behind the pair and clutched both of the author's wrists. "Stand still before you get hurt," he commanded.

"You've got the wrong person. I don't know what this is all about. This is so unfair. And I have a presentation to do this afternoon," Gigi whined. "What is this all about?"

"Ms. Johnson, I told you when I arrived what the charges were, and I read you your rights. We need to take you down to the station to question you about the murder of Cinnamon Moon. We'll get it sorted out at the station. Do you understand what I've explained to you?" Deputy Caswell said louder.

"Yes. But you still have the wrong person. You've made a terrible mistake," Gigi wailed. "There is no way I could have killed anyone. I've been in my trailer most of the week working on my book. I want to call my lawyer. You have made a ginormous mistake. You're going to be soooo embarrassed about this." Gigi dropped to the ground and sat at the deputy's feet.

"Ms. Johnson, we are taking you to the station. You can walk out of here, or I can carry you. But either way, you're going," Deputy Caswell said. A pained look crossed his face as he hoisted the author back to her feet.

"I want my lawyer. You can't do this. You have no right. You're hurting me!" Gigi yelled.

"You can call your lawyer from the station," the deputy said, leading her past a small crowd that had formed near the trailer. Jules cringed when several held up phones to record the scene.

Gigi's wail faded as the deputy led her away to the parking lot.

"Morning, Jules. Sorry to disturb the peace this morning. We wanted to talk to Ms. Johnson before she started her day. I didn't realize she would raise a ruckus," the sheriff said.

Jules shrugged her shoulder as the crowd started to dissipate. "While I've got you here, I packed Cinnamon Moon's things. Do you want me to drive them over to your squad car?"

"What've you got?" Sheriff Hobbs asked, stepping toward the cart.

"Her purse and her suitcase. The boxes are empty."

"I can get those. Thanks for packing them up," he said.

"I didn't have to do much," she said. "The trailer looked barely lived in."

As Sheriff Hobbs pulled the two bags from the cart, Jules continued, "So, Gigi is your gal?"

"Looks like it. We got an anonymous tip. When we checked into it, we found packaging and one knitting needle under her trailer. It wasn't an antique. And her alibi has as many holes as a slice of Swiss cheese. The forensic team will be here in a bit to go over the area. I'll make sure everything is locked when we're done."

"Can I get you anything, coffee or tea?"

"I'm good. Thanks, though." The sheriff picked up Cinnamon's things.

"Holler if you need any help," Jules said, climbing into the golf cart.

Not ready to head back to work, Jules drove around the property. She hoped that nature and the serenity of the mountains would help her gather her thoughts. Gigi's arrest was a surprise. Why would Gigi kill Cinnamon? Abrasive and brash, yes, but did she have motive to kill? The sheriff must have had information than what he was sharing. Could an anonymous tip and a discarded knitting needle be enough to charge her with murder?

She parked the cart and stared off at the mountain ridge. The scenery here always filled her with calm. She breathed in the frosty air until she felt a calmness wash over her. Jules put the cart in gear and hurried back to the office for her laptop.

When she stepped through the back door, Roxanne asked, "What's got you all focused?" She put a mug under the coffee maker's spout.

"Well, first the sheriff and Mario arrested Gigi."

"For what?" A crease formed between Roxanne's eyebrows.

"For Cinnamon's murder."

"They think she did it? Matt must have his reasons," her aunt said, continuing to frown. "Interesting. Let's see if I can find out anything." Her aunt pulled out her phone and tapped what sounded like a barrage of texts.

"And earlier, when I went to pack Cinnamon's things, the trailer looked a little odd. I wanted to do some more poking to see what I can find about her."

Roxanne' raised one eyebrow and made a face. "Define odd. All of these authors are a bit interesting if you ask me."

"Her purse and suitcase were packed on a made bed. Her agent described her as a bit fussy, so it might be nothing. It struck me as strange. It looked like she had never stayed there."

Jules pulled out her phone and sent a quick text to Pixel about Gigi's sudden arrest for Cinnamon's murder. *Something is bugging me about all of this.*

Be glad to look into it this week.

You're the best. Something's fishy, Jules replied.

Jules set her phone down on the desk, and it alerted again. **Couldn't find much on CM. She was squeaky clean. We'll see what I can turn up on Gigi.**

Jules responded with a string of broom emojis and a smile. A clean report matches her overly neat accommodations.

After about an hour of visiting what felt like hundreds of romance websites and fan pages, Jules had to agree. She couldn't find anything, including a single bad review about Cinnamon, and now, since her death, she had been elevated to almost sainthood. Rubbing her eyes, she gave up on her search and decided to wait to see what Pixel could find.

Maybe some fresh air would clear my head. "Roxanne, I can't seem to concentrate today. I'll be back in a bit."

"See ya when I see ya," floated in from somewhere in the store.

Jules drove the golf cart past the amphitheater, used mostly for concerts and movie nights, but it had served as the site for weddings and memorial services over the years. Still not ready to head back to the office, she drove down the wooded path to the meadow, the area used for tent camping or private groups with RVs. She parked and scanned the woods. The leaves would be popping out in a couple of weeks, and the wildflowers would be close behind. Spring in the Blue Ridge Mountains was her favorite time of the year.

Taking in a deep breath of the crisp air, she put the cart in gear and traveled back to the other side of the resort. Backtracking her path, she zipped past the barn and the lodge. Instead of turning toward the office, she did a quick tour of the tiny house village.

All quiet around the four houses that ranged from four hundred to almost twelve hundred square feet. These dwellings were perfect for guests who wanted a unique vacation experience or to try out tiny house living. Jake also used them as models for his side business. The tree house would be a popular addition to the little neighborhood.

Rounding the corner to return to work, Jules slammed on the brakes at the tree house site. She and Jake had recently worked on framing the part that sat on the ground at the base of the trees. Around the worksite, a couple of bags of quick-drying cement had been ripped open and were strewn about. Boards were also thrown around. She snapped several pictures and called Jake.

"Hey there," he said, answering on the first ring. "What's up?"

"Hi. When was the last time you were at the tree house?"

"Yesterday afternoon. I did some framing before I helped Lester with the tractor's tune-up. He noticed that the blade had been bent, and we took it off and repaired it."

"From the, uh, incident with the body?" she asked quietly.

"Probably. What's up?"

"After cleaning out Cinnamon Moon's camper and watching Gigi get arrested, I drove around the resort for some fresh air."

Busy morning," he said.

"It's always something. Anyway, on my ride back, I stopped by to take a look at the tree house. Two or three cement bags are torn open, and boards are strewn about."

"Be there in a minute. Does it look like an animal?" he asked. She heard shuffling sounds in the background and a door slam. "I made sure not to leave any food or trash there."

"I think it was the two-legged kind with a pocketknife," Jules said.

"I left construction stuff there. And I didn't notice anything unusual when I made my rounds yesterday."

Her head turned when she heard footsteps. Before she could comment, Jake walked up behind her. She clicked off the call as he put his hand on his shoulder.

"Nope. This isn't how I left it. It looks like some kind of prank." Jake stepped over the mess and looked at the house's framing. "The house looks okay. I don't see any damage besides the wasted supplies." He hoisted himself up on the roof of the first floor and looked around. "Nothing wrong up here," he said, shimmying down to the ground and wiping his hands on his jeans.

"It doesn't seem like it fits with the murder. I would guess that it's some kids trespassing. Let me see if the sheriff can talk. He may be busy with Gigi." She clicked her contact.

"Hey, Jules. What's up?" Sheriff Hobbs asked. It sounded like the window was down in his car.

"Jake and I are over at the tiny houses where he has a new construction site. Some of the supplies have been vandalized and strewn about. I'll send you some pictures in a sec."

"Maybe kids goofing off."

"We'd thought we'd let you know. In case it might be important. It's probably a prank. No major damage. But we have had the other stuff going on around here lately."

"You got any cameras you can put over there? Might be helpful in case they come back. Send me the photos, and I'll get someone to look at them."

"I've got a camera that I'll get Jake to install for me. We'll keep a watch on it."

"Let me know if you get wind of anything else," the sheriff said.

"Thanks. I seem to have you on speed dial. Hopefully, the next time I talk to you won't be about a crime," Jules said, disconnecting.

Jake enveloped her in a bear hug. "It'll be okay. I'll get it cleaned up. No harm. No foul." He kissed her on the head.

"You plan to be here for a bit? I need to run back to the office and get that extra camera. Can you install it for me?"

"I'll get my toolbox and meet you back here."

Jules drove to the office and rummaged through the closet for the camera. After activating it on the mobile app, she checked the battery life.

"What's up?" Roxanne asked, breezing into the back room.

"Someone trashed some supplies at Jake's build site. He's going to put up a camera for me in case they come back for more trouble."

"Kids?"

"More than likely." *But what if was related to the murder? Why would the killer of a romance writer trash a construction site?* "I'll be back in a bit." Jules made the return trip and handed Jake the camera.

He paused and looked around. "I think I'll mount it on that tree over there. It should give you a wide enough view of the tree house and the surrounding area. Plus, there are no low-hanging branches to set it off." He dragged his ladder over and screwed the camera mount on the bottom of a heavy branch.

Jake climbed down and dusted off his hands. "That should work for now."

"You need help cleaning this up?" she asked.

"Nope, I need to do some work around here before the sun goes down. The camera will let us know if any unwanted visitors happen by. We'll see if they're dumb enough to come back."

Chapter Seventeen

Monday Afternoon

Jules returned to the office, lost in thought. Did the vandalism have anything to do with Cinnamon's murder? It felt like two separate things. *I hope the new camera will show any other trespassers, and it will also be a way to see the progress that Jake was making on the build.* She clicked on the app and watched Jake on the roof. *Maybe I can make a Reel or a TikTok with some of the footage for the website.*

"Hey, Jules. You may want to see this," Roxanne yelled as she stuck her head in the doorway. "Your girl is having a press conference. I'm sure Sheriff Matt is not happy about this. Elaine's probably hyperventilating, too." She waved her phone in front of Jules.

"What's going on?" Jules craned her neck to see better. Gigi Johnson and a man in a gray suit stood in front of the sheriff's office.

Roxanne pushed the volume button. "I am innocent. I had nothing to do with Cinnamon Moon's murder. Why would I kill a fellow author? This makes no sense. I am very thankful for my family, fans, and lawyer who believe in me and made it possible for me to walk out of jail and be with you here today as a free woman. I am traumatized, and it will take me some time to recover from the shock of my unlawful arrest. But have no fear. I will be back to my writing here soon. You all can expect the next book in May. It's called *Dawn's Delight.*"

The burly man beside her reached for the microphone and cleared his throat. "I'm Attorney Douglas Burgess. I will be filing lawsuits on behalf of Ms. Johnson to protect her reputation and ensure that justice is served for our other victim, Cinnamon Moon."

Before he could finish, Gigi leaned forward and said, "I am innocent. And my accusers will pay for the emotional and reputational damage they have done to me. Are there any questions from the press about today's events or my upcoming books? Don't forget to come and see me at the Fern Valley Romance Festival. I'll be there the rest of the week signing copies..."

Several reporters, including Jane the Pain Jenkins, fired off questions and drowned out Gigi. In every response, Gigi defended her innocence and made her case about how poorly she had been treated.

"Uh, oh. Matt's not having a pleasant afternoon. I'm guessing we may have to reschedule dinner again," Roxanne sighed. "I'm sure he, the town manager, and Elaine are on edge until they get this solved."

Before Jules could comment, her phone alerted with a series of texts. The rapid-fire ones were from Elaine.

Did you see the news? Gigi plans to sue everyone and his brother.

Do you think we should remove her from the program?

Maybe we need an emergency board meeting. We've got damage control to do.

Jules let out a long puff of air that fluttered her bangs.

"You okay?" Roxanne asked.

"Elaine's on a tear. Maybe a rampage. She's having fits of apoplexy."

"I guess she saw the press conference," Roxanne cracked a wry smile.

Jules punched in Elaine's contact. "I may have to talk her off the ledge."

"Jules, how are you? Did you get my texts?" a breathless Elaine said before Jules could offer any greeting.

"I did. And I saw part of Gigi's press conference."

"All of the authors signed a code of conduct when they agreed to participate in our event. This is not the behavior we want to promote. I think the rest of her events need to be canceled. This is not the sweet Valentine's Day event that we all wanted. How could it go so wrong?"

"Have you talked to Tom or the Sheriff?" Jules asked.

"No. Events have been unfolding before our eyes this afternoon. You think we need an emergency meeting? Maybe it's a good idea to call Tom. He may want to pull together his advisors and outside counsel."

"Maybe not. Hear me out. If this woman and her lawyer are sue-happy, canceling her will fan the fires. She'll find a pulpit with the media or on social media and do even more damage. As painful as it may be for us, we should let her continue her events. Make it clear that our festival is not a platform for her innocence campaign. Sadly, all the drama will probably make the festival more popular."

Elaine let out a harrumphing noise. "It's not my preferred method of action. Do you think it will work?"

"I wouldn't feed into her narrative. Stick to the book festival and the plan. People are fickle. They'll move on to a new, hot story by the next news cycle. This will be all but forgotten by next week," Jules said.

"I hope you're right. I feel like Tom, as town manager, needs to make a statement and enforce our code of conduct." Elaine let out a sigh that sounded like a whimper. "I think we need to be decisive and firm."

"I would check with Tom Berryman. He'll give you guidance and maybe some talking points. We don't want to cause a stir," Jules said.

"Jules, you are always so level-headed. I appreciate you. I'll give Tom a call. Knowing him, I'm sure he won't want to make waves. Gotta run. I've got to make sure the library is set up for tonight's event. And if Gigi decides to participate, I'll ask the sheriff to send some extra security. Thanks. I will see you tonight, right?"

"Of course. I wouldn't miss it," Jules said, disconnecting.

"Oh, I wouldn't miss it for the world either," Roxanne added. "Matt took another raincheck on dinner, so I'm hoping the author panel will be entertaining. Sit by me. I'll bring snacks, and we'll watch the fireworks."

Jules cracked a smile. "I think I calmed Elaine down. We'll see how long that lasts. I hope tonight goes smoothly."

"Between the diva authors and our worrywart Elaine, what could go wrong? I need to head out in a bit. I've got a couple of errands to run before tonight. See you at the library." Roxanne waved over her shoulder.

"Bye," she said as her aunt zipped out the front door. "Hey, Bijou, how about a walk before I have to leave."

Headed to the library soon. Wanna go? She texted Jake.

Have fun. Still working on the tree house. How about dinner tomorrow?

She replied with a string of hearts, forks, and spoon emojis.

Jules guided Bijou toward the vintage trailers to see if Gigi had returned to the resort yet. They walked past the pink trailer with all the blinds pulled. No sign of the author. All quiet on this side of Fern Valley. "Let's hope the author talk goes off without a hitch," she said as Bijou trotted toward home.

After adding some kibble to Bijou's bowl, Jules made her way to the bathroom for some mascara and lipstick. She pulled her windblown curls back in a scrunchy and fluffed her ponytail.

Grabbing her coat and purse, Jules said, "Be back in a bit. You're in charge while I'm gone." Bijou yawned and found a comfy spot on the lap blanket on the couch.

Leaving the porch light on, Jules jogged down the steps to her Jeep as the remaining soft rays of sunlight peeked over the mountain.

"Uh, oh," Jules said to herself when traffic ground to a halt about a block from the government center. "This will give Elaine apoplexy. At least there will be a full house for the event."

Jules's Jeep crept toward the library. Not finding any parking in the nearby lots, she found an empty space in the grass. Checking her look in the rearview mirror, she floofed her bangs and headed to the government center, where throngs of people waited outside the library's main doors. She blended in and scooched closer to the line of people to block the chilly breeze that whipped around the building.

Jane the Pain, with her camera and big coat, bounced from one foot to the other near the door. Jules waved, but she wasn't sure if the reporter noticed her. Eavesdropping on the conversations around her, no one seemed to be that interested in the murder or Gigi's arrest. Most of the talk was about new books and meeting the authors. Jules felt some of the weight lift off her shoulders. Maybe the murder wouldn't be front and center tonight.

As soon as the doors opened, everyone filed in and found seats in the conference room. It didn't take long before it was standing room only, and someone propped open the exit door for fresh air.

Promptly at seven o'clock, Elaine led the panelists to their seats at the long table in the front. Gigi filed in between Echo and Allegra. Windsor rushed in, fashionably late.

Jules scanned the audience full of fans and guests with some townies sprinkled in. Not seeing Roxanne, she tried to get comfortable in the plastic chair. Minutes ticked by, and no sign of Roxanne.

Where are you? she texted her aunt.

Sorry should have told you. Got a slight headache. Decided to stay home. Have fun and let me know if anything juicy happens, her aunt replied.

Feel better, Jules tapped into her phone.

Elaine opened with long introductions of each author, and finally there was some discussion from the panel. The polite crowd, even during the question and answer session at the end, never mentioned the murder or Gigi's wild press conference. Most wanted to talk to their favorite authors and to find out what's next with their series.

After rounds of applause and author bows, the crowd rushed the table for photos and autographs. Deputy Dempsey scanned the crowd. He nodded at Jules's wave and returned to his phone.

Elaine swooped in and cornered Jules. "Thanks for coming. It was much more pleasant than I imagined. So thrilled that everyone stuck to the agenda and that the press didn't use this as an opportunity to hype their stories or hijack the evening for another press conference. This could have gone wrong so easily. I'm counting my lucky stars that it went off without any chaos."

"I saw Jane the Pain. Were there other reporters? I didn't see any TV trucks outside. Maybe the hubbub has already died down."

Elaine shrugged her shoulder. "Who knows? I hope the rest of the festival goes this smoothly. I don't know how Elizabeth deals with all the demands and special requests. I'm sure some of these ladies see themselves as rock stars or something."

Jules smiled, but before she could comment, Elaine continued, "At least we made it through today. We only have until Saturday when this wraps up. I definitely need a vacation before our spring events start."

"Sounds good," Jules said, patting Elaine's arm. "You deserve a break. I'm headed home. See you later this week. Let me know if you need anything."

Jules picked up her purse and followed the stragglers out of the library. The lone streetlight shone on the remaining cars in the lot and nearby grassy field.

An ear-splitting squeal pierced the quiet of the evening. Tiffany stood near the library's side door under the floodlight. Her hands squeezed into fists, and her face matched her red ski jacket. "I had nothing to do with the missing items, so I suggest you keep your mouth shut. You have no proof. And you, of all people, should be a little more understanding. I mean, you know what it's like to be accused of something you didn't do." Tiffany Blake set her jaw and stamped her foot.

"I'm saying that there's a lot of weirdness around here. And I don't want to be a victim again. You need to watch yourself and your sassy mouth. I'm not sure Windsor would appreciate how you act when she's not around." Gigi glared at the younger woman.

"Hello, ladies," Jules interrupted. "Is there anything I can help you with?"

Gigi slammed her hand on her hip and glared at Jules. "This doesn't concern you."

Tiffany took advantage of Gigi's laser-focused attention, shifting to Jules to take a couple of steps back. The younger woman scooted behind Jules.

"I'm sorry to interrupt. I wanted to make sure you all were okay." When no one said anything, she continued, "Well, then. Good night." Tiffany fell in step beside Jules.

When they were far enough from Gigi, Jules asked, "Are you okay?"

"I guess. It makes me wonder if this job is worth all the hassle and the stress. I thought it would give me an in with the publishing world, but after being at her highness's beck and call all day, who has the time or the energy to work on a manuscript. I don't have enough time to do all her stuff, much less the stuff I want to do." The personal assistant paused and looked toward the parking lot. "And now I've kept you-know-who waiting in the car far too long. I'll get an earful on the ride back about punctuality and commitments and every other sin that I've committed," Tiffany said. She offered a slight wave and jogged off toward a car in the distance.

Chapter Eighteen

Tuesday

Jules poured over her notes. The authors and the fans would be leaving this week, and she was no closer to figuring out who killed Cinnamon than she was a week ago. She reached for her phone when it trilled.

"Hey, girl. You busy?" Pixel asked.

"Nope. What's up?" Jules rubbed her eyes, trying to ward off the headache that made her face feel like it was in a vice.

"I found a few tidbits I wanted to share. Let's see, Virginia 'Gigi' Jones has had some tax problems and a bankruptcy. So, if money is a motive, we can look further into her life. Margaret "Allegra" Rhodes is the darling of the romance world. Everyone loves her, but you already knew that. I did a little digging and found another thing." Pixel paused and tapped on her keyboard.

"Okay, don't keep me in suspense," Jules said.

"Sorry. I got distracted by an email. It seems she had an affair on the set of that soap in the eighties. It broke up her marriage. She didn't stay with the boyfriend after that. He chose to stay with his wife. It hit the tabloids for about ten seconds, and then nobody really cared. Though she did tend to date men years her junior after that. A cougar before that term was popular. I couldn't find anything else on her. Not even parking tickets."

"Interesting." Jules reached for a pen.

"But wait. There's more," Pixel said. "I told you about Tracey Davis, aka Phoenix Abbott, and her bad reviews and postings about how she cheated authors out of royalties or overcharged them for book promo services. It seems she's changed the name of her company twice in the thirteen months. She may be trying to dodge legal troubles."

"Money and power," Jules muttered.

"Yep. Always motivators for murder and revenge. And then, we have Carrie Shultz. I already told you that there is no love lost between her and Phoenix. This isn't criminal. It's telling and kinda funny. I found a copy of an old video where someone asked her if she ever represented Phoenix, and she spoke candidly for about ten minutes about associating yourself with talented people."

"Did she represent her? Jules asked.

Pixel laughed. "The interviewer tried to wrap up the discussion by asking that same question, and I quote, her answer was 'Nope.' Oh, I found something out something else related to Carrie. I went to some dark corners of the web and found a social media war where someone was blasting Shultz's social sites and her website with an attack about skimming profits from the authors she represents. This was about three years ago, and then it suddenly stopped. But as you know, nothing is ever deleted on the internet. Here's the juicy part." Pixel hesitated, and it sounded like she was chewing on something.

"You are building up tension today." Jules laughed.

"Sorry. Powerbar for lunch. Anyway, the posts came from Miami Dragon."

"Wait, which one of them is from Florida?"

"Yep. You're exactly right. It seems Miami Dragon is none other than our own Phoenix Abbott. And it looks like she devoted her life for a while to harassing the literary agent. Until one day, it stopped. I'm still digging to see if Shultz sued her or took out a restraining order. I'm curious about why the nastiness and the barrage of posts and comments came to a screeching halt. It also appears that Phoenix has a series of accounts that she uses to do reviews for others and herself."

"It's bad enough that she bullies others online, but she fakes reviews, too?" Jules asked.

"It looks like it," Pixel said. "Lots of odd and unethical behavior on the big wide web."

"Speaking of odd behavior, could you add a Tiffany Blake to your cast of characters? I'm not sure if you were able to find anything on her. She is the personal assistant for Windsor Abernathy. She always seemed overworked and a little on edge like she's on the verge of tears."

"Got it. You mentioned her before. Sorry I left her off my list. I'll see what I can find. Anything else that makes your antennae twitch?"

"Did you find anything on Lynette, the publicist? I haven't seen much of her since she checked in."

"She's a busy little bee. The woman must never sleep. She is always on social media. She has to schedule some of the posts. There is no way anyone can be on her phone that much and hold down a regular job. Her daily volume is massive. Or she has help from staff."

"Interesting," Jules said. "Maybe I can stalk her accounts and learn some things for the resort."

"She is on all of the sites all of the time. According to her website, she posts regularly for her clients on their sites. Her website is top-notch. She is focused on her company. I couldn't find much on her personal life. She lives with her two cats in New York. She's divorced, and occasionally, she posts ski pictures with friends." Pixel paused to catch her breath. "So, I poked around in some places that regular people don't visit. Lynnette's record is squeaky clean. She doesn't even have a driver's license. I'll try another search, but it looks like she's devoted her life to her clients."

"Thanks. I'll let you know if I think of anything else. You're a wealth of information. You're always able to access stuff that the rest of us mere mortals can't. I'll let you know if I can think of anything else," Jules said.

"Aww. You make a girl blush. I'm happy to help. Plus, I still owe you for getting me VIP access to *Fatal Impressions* last fall. That's still worth tons of free research."

"You are the best. I'm hoping we can figure out who killed Cinnamon before anything else happens around here."

"Catch you later. Lunch soon," Pixel said before she disconnected.

"Who is responsible for this?" Jules asked aloud.

"I have no idea. But you and Sheriff Matt will figure it out," Roxanne said, heading for the kitchenette.

"It's time for a quick walk if you're okay here." At the magic "W" word, Bijou jumped up and zoomed around the back office. She calmed down when Jules pulled out the leash. "All right, puppy, let's go see what we can see."

After a lap around the field and the barn, the pair skirted the back row of trailers. A loud voice made Bijou bark and dart into the trailer village.

"I'm not going to tell you again. When you're working for me, you're on and present. I need you to pay the utmost attention. There's too much dilly-dallying and too much chitchat on your phone. If it doesn't stop, you'll need to find other opportunities," Windsor said.

Tiffany looked up from her phone, and her glance bounced from Windsor to the barking terrier. A crimson blush flooded the personal assistant's face. "I was checking your schedule and your social media sites. I hardly have time to eat or breathe, much less dilly-dally. I didn't know this was a twenty-four-seven job. Maybe I do need to look for other opportunities." Tiffany pocketed her phone and stormed off toward the tiny houses.

"Well," Windsor said, following the younger woman. "Wait, Tiffany. I need you to send some documents for me and get lunch before we head to the bookstore. Come back here."

When they were out of earshot, Jules said, "That was odd. Not sure about that relationship. It isn't working on so many levels. Maybe Pixel will uncover something about Tiffany. And what were they doing over here at the campers?" Ignoring Jules, Bijou sniffed around the campers and yipped at a bird.

A flash of teal caught Jules's eye. She stepped around the camper for a better look. Carrie Shultz set a rolling suitcase near her trailer's door and then disappeared back inside. Bijou barked and led the way to where the agent's case sat on the small cement patio.

The aluminum door swung open, and Carrie made her way gingerly down, holding two boxes that blocked her view.

"Hi, there," Jules said as she approached. "Do you need some help with that?"

"Oh, hey," the literary agent said, pausing to readjust her grip on the boxes. "I need to put these in my car. Echo's publisher sent some of her freebies to me. So here I am, toting her stuff and all my agency stuff. You never know when you'll bump into someone who's looking for representation." Carrie paused and looked around.

"Here, let me get those. I'm Jules Keene. I don't think we've had a chance to say more than a couple of words to each other. Welcome to the resort."

"I've been so crazy busy since I got here. This festival has been nice. If you could wrangle that suitcase, I've got these."

Hoping to keep the conversation going, Jules said, "I'm so sorry to hear about Cinnamon. That was tragic."

"If it's not one thing, it's another. I've never had a client die or well, get murdered before. I've been fielding phone calls around the clock. Cinnamon will be missed. I've only been her agent for two or three years, but I'll miss her. She was such a lovely person. Her first agent, who had been with her from the start, passed away, and I picked up some of his clients." The agent took a few steps and paused. "Just between us girls, I checked Cinnamon's sales numbers this morning, and they've spiked since what happened. I even got a call from the production company. They want to move up the date for the launch of her new series and talk about optioning several of her other novels. This will keep her memory alive for a long time."

Jules's eyes widened. Willing for the conversation to go on as they approached the parking lot, Jules said, "Well, that's profitable news for her estate."

"And for me," Carrie said with a nervous laugh. "Here I am," she said as she fished in her pocket for her key fob while balancing the boxes against a blue minivan. After a beep, the side door slid open. Carrie tossed the two boxes on the floor and reached for the suitcase."

Bijou hopped inside the van.

"Hey, puppy. We've got to go back to work. Down." Jules pointed at the pavement.

Carrie leaned over and patted the little dog on the head. "You don't want to go with me. It's a boring author talk. They're all alike after a while." After Bijou hopped out, Carrie tossed the suitcase in the backseat and dusted her hands. "Well, thanks." Carrie clicked the key fob again, and the side door slid shut.

"Uh, any idea who would want to harm Cinnamon?" Jules asked.

The agent's countenance darkened, and she hesitated for a beat or two. "No. Not really. She didn't have problems with anyone, and she was making gobs of money. Thankfully, Cinnamon was amazingly prolific. There are three new manuscripts that are ready, so her fans will still get new books for the next couple of years. Her heirs inquired about selling the rights to her name to another author. If that happens, the books will continue on. Sorry. I can't help you with any theories unless it was some crazy stalker fan. But I didn't have anything to offer the police either. See you around." She waved and headed around toward the driver's side of the minivan.

"Come on, Bijou." Jules tugged on the leash as the minivan pulled out of the lot. "I'm not so sure that I'd be announcing that I profited from one of my client's deaths," Jules whispered.

Bijou turned her head and lunged after a bird in the grass. The leash slipped out of Jules's hand, and the Jack Russell raced toward the tiny houses.

Jules paused to catch her breath near the Baum house. When Bijou stopped to smell around the front steps, Jules picked up the leash. "You wanted me to get some exercise, huh?"

The dog turned her head and barked. Then she dashed off again, pulling Jules toward the tree house. Bijou, standing with two paws on the trunk, barked at the tree.

"Shhh, puppy. We have guests in the houses." Jules looked around to see if anyone was outside.

Bijou let out a low growl. Jules picked her up and heard a groan.

She paused. There it was again. Definitely a groan.

Standing on her tiptoes, she couldn't see anything, but she knew she heard a noise on the tree house's platform.

Jules pulled out her phone and called Jake.

"Hey…" he said.

Before he could continue, she interrupted with, "Where are you? Something weird's going on at the tree house."

"Again? I'm in the barn with Lester. What's up?"

"Bijou started barking at something, and then I heard weird noises. Can you bring a ladder?"

"Sure, Boss. Be there in a sec."

Jules pocketed her phone and strained to hear any other sounds. She took a step backward, trying to see if she could spot the source of the groans.

Chapter Nineteen

Tuesday Afternoon

Minutes ticked by before Jake arrived with the aluminum ladder. He hurried over, and she pointed to the tree.

Before he reached the top rung, he yelled, "Call 9-1-1."

"What is it?" Jules's voice cracked.

"It's one of your authors. She's up here without a coat or shoes. Tell the dispatcher that she's cold to the touch, but she's breathing faintly."

When the call connected, Jules relayed the current situation to the dispatcher.

"Do you know who it is?" the dispatcher asked.

Jules covered the phone with her hand. "Jake, what does she look like?" Returning to her call. "Sorry, she's on a platform that we're building for a tree house. My boyfriend is up on a ladder. I can't see her from here."

"Kinda small with short gray hair," he yelled. "I think she's the one that used to write for that soap opera."

Jules nodded. "We think it's author Allegra Rhodes, but that's her pen name. Tell them to hurry. I'm not sure why she's outside in February with no shoes or coat."

"They're on their way. You should hear them soon," the dispatcher said. "Any sign of blood or trauma?"

"Any blood," she yelled up to Jake.

"None that I can see. She's on her stomach. I didn't flip her over. But she is breathing."

"Did you hear that?" Jules asked the dispatcher.

"Got it. The ambulance is on Baker Road. They should be at your place soon. Where are you on the property?"

Come through the gates and stay on the maintenance road. We're on the left near the tiny houses. It's before you see the campers."

The dispatcher relayed the information as Jules heard a faint siren.

Jules took several deep breaths to calm the bile that was rising in her stomach. Who was targeting these authors? Or did she wander over here by accident? Either way, how did she get up on that platform without a ladder? All the questions bouncing around caused Jules's head to pound.

An ambulance, followed by Sheriff Hobbs's car, flew down the maintenance road and kicked up a small dust storm in their wake. Three EMTs rushed over, and one climbed the ladder that Jake had vacated.

Jules picked up Bijou and hugged her close as Jake slid behind her and laid his hand on her shoulder.

Sheriff Hobbs shuffled over. "What happened?" He asked, keeping one eye on the activity on the platform.

"Bijou and I were out for a walk, and something caught her attention at the tree house. I heard noises and called Jake to get a ladder. We think it's the author Allegra Rhodes." At the mention of her name, the little dog turned her head and stared at the sheriff.

"She's up here on the platform for the tree house," Jake added. "It looked like she's sleeping, except she's not dressed for the weather."

Remembering the new camera, Jules set Bijou down and tapped on her phone to pull up the feed. Scrolling back through time, she stopped when she saw herself and Bijou on their walk. Nothing looked out of place. She kept moving back in time. A little after four in the morning, two figures walked into the frame. The second person, in what looked like some kind of long-flowing, hooded cape, shoved the first person. The smaller figure fell to the ground and smacked her head on the dirt. The caped figure kicked the woman on the ground, who curled up into a tight ball. Jules's free hand covered her mouth. Why would someone attack Allegra? She seemed to be beloved by everyone Jules talked to. Who would do this? The other figure's face was hidden in all the shots.

Then, several frames later, the person in the cape disappeared. Allegra lay on the ground, not moving. About ten minutes later, the person in the cape drug Jake's ladder to the tree and then hoisted Allegra up by her arms. After a struggle to get the limp author situated, the figure slung the smaller woman over her shoulder and climbed the ladder slowly. In one frame, the hood fell backward, and the figure stumbled on the ladder, trying to keep a grip on Allegra and put the hood back in place. *Too bad there wasn't a better shot of the face.*

The final frames showed the hooded figure taking Allegra's shoes and coat. *Jules gasped. He or she had left Allegra out in the cold since before dawn.* Shaking off the dark feeling that crept into Jules's thoughts, she made a copy of the camera footage and posted it in DropBox for the sheriff.

"So, the attacker took her shoes and coat," Jake said, watching over Jules's shoulder. "I wondered why she was out here in the middle of winter, barefooted."

"It looks like the bad guy used your ladder," Jules said.

"It was at the side of the barn where I always leave it. I've never had anyone bother it before. I guess I'll need to find a secure spot for it."

"Whatcha got on your cameras?" the sheriff interrupted.

"I sent you a copy of the feed. There's a caped figure carrying a smaller woman around before sunrise," Jules said, handing him her phone.

"Hmm. Can't tell if our mystery person is a guy or gal," he said, pulling the phone closer for a better look. "I'll have the digital guys look this over and see what they can do with the lighting and the sound. We'll see what they can get off the recording. The evidence team will be here for a while. Can I get the keys to her trailer?"

Jules nodded. "I'll go get them. She's in the seventy-one Airstream. The one that's decorated like an English Garden. Be back in a bit. Come on, Bijou." The little dog sat down in protest. She wanted to stay where the action was. Scooping her up, Jules headed for the office.

Once inside the warm office, Roxanne and Lester rushed forward, talking at the same time.

"Sheriff's here again." That sentence felt like a weight on Jules's shoulders. *Was she really bringing trouble to Fern Valley?* The pounding in her temples seemed to intensify.

"I heard it on the scanner. They dispatched police and rescue and the forensics team. I heard they were bringing in some backups from the state police." The older man's eyes widened as he talked. "Did it happen again?" Lester asked.

"What happened?" Roxanne asked, planting one hand on her hip.

"We found Allegra Rhodes on the platform of the tree house."

A look of panic crossed her aunt's face, and she sunk down in the nearby chair. "Is she…"

Jules shook her head. She was breathing when we found her. It looks like someone attacked her in the woods and left her there without shoes and a coat."

"Oh, my stars. She's close to seventy, if not older. Who would want her to freeze to death? And who would go to all that trouble to drag someone up a tree house? None of this makes any sense. It's definitely got to be a crazed killer."

"I couldn't tell much from the video. It was someone in a hooded cloak thing. Not sure if it was a man or a woman."

"Allegra is such a nicc lady. This is incomprehensible." Roxanne sighed.

"If you see anyone in a long, dark cloak with a flowing cape, let Sheriff Hobbs know. The person was fairly tall. A long cape should be pretty easy to spot. To me, it looked like some sort of costume."

"Or the person looked tall next to Allegra. We all know she's a little bitty thing, but don't underestimate her. She wields tremendous power in the romance world. She's a tough bird. I've been reading her stuff for years. She's established with a loyal fan base. Just wait 'til word about this gets out. There will be an outpouring of shock and outrage. She's a grand dame." Roxanne's lips formed a straight line, and she stared down at her nails.

"I need to take her trailer key over to Sheriff Hobbs. Can Bijou stay here with you?"

Roxanne nodded, picked up the terrier, and patted her head. The dog snuggled close for a cuddle.

After locating the camper key, Jules pulled out to-go cups and four pods of strong coffee. While the first one brewed, she looked around for a box or a tray to transport them to the tree house.

When the coffee maker spewed out the final drips of the dark coffee, Jules pushed the lid in place and put the cup in with the others in her box top. "I think I'll take the golf cart back over there. Lester, can I give you a lift?"

"Nope. I need to get my steps in, especially if I plan to be glued to my police scanner for the rest of the afternoon. See y'all later. I'll let you know if I hear anything, and you do the same." He saluted and plunked his Nationals ballcap on his head as he slipped out the back door.

"Come on, Bijou," Roxanne said. "We'll see what's buzzing on social media and maybe eat cookies while Jules is gone."

The little dog hopped in her lap, looking around for the promised cookies.

Jules slipped out and set the box top full of coffees on the golf cart's passenger seat. She drove gingerly over the field, trying not to spill any as she bumped along the path to the tiny houses and Jake's construction site.

The ambulance had disappeared by the time she returned to the tree house. She held up the coffee, and the sheriff approached. Deputy Dempsey noticed the drinks and lumbered over to the cart before anyone could speak.

Jules handed a cup and the camper key to the sheriff and a cup to the deputy. "It's the Airstream that has the trellis around it, and the little English garden looks pretty dead right now."

"Got it. I'll head over there with the forensic guys when they're done here. It's going to be a while," Sheriff Hobbs said.

Jules watched the two men on the tree house platform gather samples and take pictures. A third did the same around the base of the tree. Slow, tedious, deliberate work. They took measurements of everything.

Deputy Dempsey broke the silence when he said, "Thanks for the coffee, Jules." He crushed the to-go cup and stuffed it in one of the compartments on his utility belt before pulling out his phone.

Yellow crime scene tape encircled the area and created a somber setting.

The torn ends fluttered in the breeze. Jules closed her eyes for a moment to hold back the flood of bad memories about the recent murders. *At least Allegra is still alive.*

"Anything else you can think of pertaining to Ms. Rhodes?" Sheriff Hobbs asked, shaking her from her thoughts.

Jules shook her head slowly. "Everybody I talked to seemed to adore her. Nothing about her stood out as odd or unusual. Roxanne said that she's been in the romance business for years. She has a huge fanbase."

"I suspect you'll get calls and some TV news inquiries. She's a national figure. They took her to the hospital over in Charlottesville. Charles, why don't you head over and secure her trailer and see what you can find out while you're waiting for the team to get over there. Check on any updates you can get on Allegra's condition. We'll be there as soon as we wrap up here."

"Anybody else I should reach out to?" Charles asked.

"See if you can get hold of her agent. I'd like to talk to her, too," Sheriff Hobbs said.

"Carrie Shultz is her agent," Jules said. "I saw her leave a bit ago. I think she was headed over to today's event." Jules tapped a text to Elaine.

"Elaine will know how to find her," he said.

Her phone alerted with a quick reply, **She left here when she found out about Allegra. She's probably at the hospital by now.**

Reading over Jules's shoulder, Sheriff Hobbs said, "Okay. Charles, I'll be over to the camper in a bit, and we can work out our plan."

The deputy nodded and reached for another cup of coffee. "For the road," he said, saluting with the coffee cup. He trudged off toward the trailers.

"I plan to send any media questions to your office. There's nothing I can tell them," Jules said.

"That's fine. My other deputy is notifying her family. I'll have him track down the agent, too."

Before Jules could answer, her phone pinged with a series of texts. Glancing down, they were all from Elaine.

Had to go with Plan B. Windsor and Echo agreed to fill Allegra's

slot with a talk on mystery and romance. Lifesavers. Running out of substitutes around here. Keep me posted of what you hear.

Will do, Jules replied.

Before she could ask the sheriff any additional questions, her phone alerted again. Another series of texts, this time from Roxanne.

The phones are ringing off the hook.

There are 2 TV crews in the parking lot.

Help!

Be right there, Jules replied.

"I need to go help Roxanne. It seems the media have descended on our parking lot."

The sheriff pursed his lips. "Great. Try to keep them over there," he said, glancing down at his clipboard.

Jules nodded and called Jake. "Hey, are you busy?"

"Nope. Police still around?"

"Yes. I'm in for a long day. I'm headed to the office to help Roxanne with all the media out front. Could you or Lester go block the maintenance road, so they can't get any closer to this side of the property. The sheriff's team needs to work without distractions and questions."

"I'm on it," he said, disconnecting.

What else is going to happen around here? And why was Allegra Rhodes attacked? Again, another author who seemed not to have any issues with anyone was targeted. What am I missing?

Chapter Twenty

Later Tuesday

Jules paused at the edge of the field near the store to catch her breath. She heard voices, lots of them. Peeking around the corner of the wooden building, she spotted a crowd milling near several news trucks.

She turned and hurried toward the back of the office. Roxanne and Bijou rushed her before she had a chance to close the door.

"You better lock that. I feel like I'm under siege. I put the phones on auto-attendant because I couldn't keep up, and I can't tell you how many people have knocked on the door. This is crazy. It wasn't this bad when the Hollywood folks were here."

"Jake and Lester are blocking the paths to the crime scene. I'm sorry I left you with this mess."

"It caught me off guard. They showed up so quickly. I lost count after about the forty-sixth question about what happened," her aunt said, pushing a loose strand of hair out of her eyes.

"Maybe I should make some sort of statement out there and online," Jules mused. She rummaged through the closet and pulled out her bullhorn.

"That'll get their attention," Roxanne said.

"I don't have much more to say besides call the sheriff. I'd like to say get off my property, but that wouldn't go over that well. Otherwise, we stay barricaded in here until they go away. I don't want them disturbing our guests. And I don't like feeling like a hostage at work."

As she headed to the front, Roxanne said, "There are lots of reporters out there with cameras. You're always beautiful, but you may want to do some quick touchups. It looks like you've run a mile recently."

"Gotcha," Jules said, handing the bullhorn to her aunt.

Glancing at the wild hair in the bathroom mirror, Jules sighed. It took a couple of minutes to tame the curls back into a halfway decent ponytail.

"Thanks," Jules said, retrieving the bullhorn from her aunt. "You're always the fashion expert around here. Maybe you should be our spokesperson."

"Nope. You know those vultures. I try to avoid them as much as possible. No thanks. Go get 'em, tiger." Her aunt patted her arm. "Hey, how's Matt doing?"

"He looked tired. Thankfully, Allegra was breathing, and he didn't have another murder on his hands," Jules said, heading to the front. "I guess we should be grateful for small miracles."

A pained look crossed Roxanne's face. "I hope she'll be okay. She's had some health issues recently. I don't want this to be a setback for her. She is such a treasure." Roxanne's face paled. "And being left alone in the cold. That is so cruel."

"First the murder and now this. None of this makes much sense." Jules took a breath and steeled herself. "Wish me luck. Here goes nothing." Jules opened the front door.

When the crowd outside noticed her, they moved toward the porch. In the parking lot, Jules spotted several news trucks from Charlottesville and some nearby cities in Virginia.

Flipping the button on the bullhorn, she cleared her throat. "Good afternoon." She paused as the crowd noise subsided. "Hello. I'm Jules Keene, owner of the Fern Valley Luxury Camping Resort. I appreciate your concern about the police presence on the property today, but I don't have any updates for you. This is an active investigation, and the sheriff's office will have an update later." She paused and scanned the audience huddled near the steps. "I want to direct all media inquiries to Sheriff Hobbs at the Fern Valley Government Center."

Before she could retreat inside, the barrage of questions started.

Jules raised her hand. "I know you have questions, but I don't have the answers at this time. The sheriff's office will have an update for you later about the situation. I want to make sure you all have the most accurate information."

Groans and questions grew louder as Jules retreated inside the store. "Wow," she said, leaning against the door. "That is a sizable crowd. I hope the sheriff's office is ready."

"I let him know. You could say he was less than thrilled about having to do a press conference." A sly grin crossed Roxanne's lips.

"Maybe they'll move on as it gets later and colder. There isn't much to see here," Jules said as she and her aunt peeked out the front windows. Most of the reporters stared at their phone screens. Lester and Jake's barricades must have worked to corral the reporters in the parking area. Most of them look like they're waiting for something to happen. I saw a couple of the cameramen wandering around taking shots of the mountains and the woods."

"Like I said, vultures. Maybe they'll get bored and head out. It's not like the filming of *Fatal Impressions* when there was stuff for the spectators to see. The only exciting thing that happened today was when the ambulance sped away with full lights and sirens. Which that was actually good for Allegra." Roxanne crossed her fingers.

"I want to try to head off some of the questions with some kind of statement on our website. I'll be in the back if you need me."

"Sounds like a plan. Let me know if I can help," Roxanne said, pushing the curtain back for a better view.

Jules let out a little laugh. "I have no idea what I'm going to say. We'll see what I come up with. Can you go through the phone messages to see if there are any real client questions or reservations? Delete any media requests."

"I'm on it. After I get some hot tea. Want anything?" Roxanne asked.

Jules shook her head and settled in at her desk.

As the clock slowly moved toward the dinner hour, Roxanne breezed in the back and headed for the door. "Matt's outside." Her eyes brightened as she opened the door. "Hey, there. Can I get you some coffee?" She pulled him inside.

"That'd be nice," he said. "Sun's about to set, and we'll be here for a while. The forensic team is setting up the generator and lights. Jules, here's the key to your camper. We'll lock it up when we leave."

"Thanks. Any word on Allegra?" Jules asked, reaching for the key.

"Not much. She's breathing. They're treating her for a head wound and hypothermia. She won't be able to tell us much for a while." Sheriff Hobbs leaned against the counter and watched Roxanne prep the coffee maker.

"She's got to be okay," Roxanne said. "I've been on pins and needles all afternoon, and her fans must be in a dither."

"We were flooded with questions. I pointed all media inquiries about today's police activity to your office," Jules said.

He nodded as Roxanne added, "You should have seen the crowd outside. I saw Jane the Pain and a bunch of reporters nosing around. But in the last hour, it looks like the crowd size has slimmed down."

"Temperatures are dropping," he said.

"Do you have all your winter gear?" she asked, patting his arm.

He nodded. "Forensics had some success. We found some blood near her trailer. I'm hoping they were able to find other DNA, too. We'll have to see. I've got the computer forensic guys looking at your video. Maybe they can clean up some of the shots to help us identify the attacker. Thanks." He reached for the mug Roxanne handed him.

"Let me know when you're done with the camper, and I'll get Mel and Crystal to do a cleaning before Allegra gets back," Jules said.

He nodded again. "Rox, I need to reschedule dinner again. Sorry, but it can't be helped."

"Let me know if you need me to bring you anything," she said, watching him head for the door. "Make sure you eat."

He nodded. "Another late night. We need to figure out how this is connected to Cinnamon Moon's murder. Or if it is," he said, pulling the door closed behind him.

Chapter Twenty-One

Wednesday

After a long night of pouring over her notes and then falling into a fitful sleep, Jules dragged Bijou and herself out of bed. The pair trudged to the office as the sun crept over the mountaintops. *I wonder how many voicemails are waiting for me.*

Relieved that there were only a handful of messages, she deleted the ones from reporters and jotted a note to return a call about reservations for a family reunion. She breezed through her resort tasks and then decided to do something for Allegra. Jules opened her supply cabinets and gathered items to make a basket for her guest. She hoped she could get into the hospital to see her later. Pulling out gourmet chocolates, a book about the Blue Ridge Mountains, postcards, a magnet, tea, and coffee, Jules arranged them in a wicker basket and tied the cellophane with a large red bow and a tag from the Fern Valley Luxury Camping Resort staff.

"That should do it," she said as Bijou opened one eye. "At least one of us can sleep today."

"How's it going?" Roxanne asked, dumping a shopping bag and her black Tory Burch bag on the desk across from Jules. "I popped in early to see if you needed any help. Matt didn't finish work until about two o'clock this morning. He said he had a mound of paperwork and emails to deal with when he got back to the office. I wanted to talk to him before he tried to catch a few winks. And now I'm exhausted because I stayed up until the wee hours, and then I couldn't fall asleep."

"We had a couple of calls. Hopefully, the craziness here has died down. Nobody has asked specifically about Allegra, but I'm sure the interest will pick up again as soon as they find out she was attacked here."

"You know about people's morbid curiosity. They're always interested in murders and places where true crimes have happened. Kinda ghoulish. Hey, that's pretty. What's it for?" Roxanne asked, pointing to the basket.

"My plan is to try to see Allegra later. I'm hoping she's doing better."

"Send my best wishes for a speedy recovery. Tell her that her fans want her back in action lickety-split." Roxanne pulled out her phone and started scrolling.

"Will do." Distracted by her own phone, Jules read through a series of texts from Elaine.

Today's author talk and lunch are a go. Windsor and Echo have stepped in to cover. I plan to say Allegra was unable to attend. They don't need to know the details.

Sounds like a plan, Jules tapped into her phone. **I'll let you know if hear anything. Have fun.**

Did I tell you that I'm counting down the days until this event is over? I need a vacation, Elaine replied.

Me too. Jules smiled and pocketed her phone. "Be back in a bit. Call me if you need me."

"I'm hoping for a quiet morning," Roxanne said. "Bijou and I will have a budget meeting and work on the filing while you're gone." She pulled out an aspirin bottle from her desk drawer.

Jules cranked up a classic rock station and the heat in her silver Wrangler for the ride to Charlottesville. Pulling out her sunglasses, she slipped them on to block out the morning sun and settled in for her ride through the valley.

Finding parking in the visitor lot at the hospital, Jules picked up the basket and her purse. The brisk breeze whipped around the building and put a bounce in her step. She hustled to the main entrance in record time.

"Good morning," Jules said as she approached a woman in the blue vest with lots of colorful pins. The woman, who sat behind a semi-circular desk, fingered a smiley face pin near her collar.

"I'm here to see Margaret Rhodes or Allegra Rhodes," Jules said.

"Hello, let's see. She's been moved to a temporary room on the first floor. Here. I'll jot it down for you. Follow this hallway to the third intersection, and you'll see the nurse's station. It's to the left of that."

"By the way," the woman whispered. "I am such a fan of Allegra. I've read all her books. Some twice. Can't wait for the TV miniseries. Wish her well from Alice." The woman held up her nametag for Jules to see.

"Will do. Thank you." Jules repositioned the basket and followed the volunteer's directions down the long hallway. The echo of the heel clicks from her boots on the industrial floor seemed loud in the empty hallway. Spotting the empty nurse's station, she glanced at the people in the waiting room across the hall. After a second or two and no nurses, Jules checked the sticky note the volunteer gave her and walked around the corner, looking for Allegra's room.

Spotting a match, Jules tapped lightly on the open door and stuck her head in. The author, propped up on several pillows, looked almost childlike in the giant bed. "Mrs. Rhodes, I'm Jules Keene from the Fern Valley Luxury Camping Resort. I wanted to stop by and see how you're feeling. This is from my staff."

"Oh, how lovely," the author said. "I'm feeling much better." The author touched the side of her head. "Though I do have this horrible ringing in my ears. And I'm not all that steady on my feet. I'm hoping it will all go away soon, so I can get out of here."

"I am so sorry that happened. Is there anything I can get you?"

"I'll be fine. They're keeping me here for observation. They worry too much about old ladies. I'm a tough cookie, even though I can't remember that much of what happened. Maybe the memories will come back in time, too."

"I don't want to take up too much of your time. You need your rest. Your fans want you back in tiptop shape," Jules said.

"Oh, my. I forgot all about today's events. Is my phone over there? And my glasses?" The author reached for the tray where her glasses, a plastic pitcher, and her phone sat.

Jules set the basket down on the table and handed the author her phone. "The library took care of rearranging today's events. Get well. Don't worry about the talks. They'll be so excited to have you back when you feel better."

"I know. But I miss seeing my fans. This has been such a fun festival. If you'll excuse me, I've got to call my assistant and get her to reschedule some things and post on social media for me. I want everyone to know not to worry, and I'm hoping I'll feel better in a day or so. I want to attend the last couple of events. Thanks for stopping by," the author waved with one hand as she adjusted her glasses.

"Bye," Jules said quietly, slipping into the hall where she almost ran into Sheriff Hobbs.

"Morning, Jules. What are you doing out and about so early?" He raised one eyebrow and then glanced toward Allegra's door. "I hope you're not snooping around. Did Rox send you over here?"

Jules tried not to fidget. "No, I wanted to check on Allegra and bring her a gift basket. Just a quick visit." She finger waved over her shoulder and made her escape to the elevator before he could ask questions or chastise her for poking around in his investigation.

Chapter Twenty-Two

Thursday

A car door slammed outside, and Jules looked up from behind the laptop at the store's front counter. Tiny taps sounded across the wooden porch. She closed her inventory spreadsheet. The bells on the door triggered a barking jag from Bijou from behind the Dutch door. "Shh! Puppy. Everything's okay."

A tiny silver head popped in the doorway, and the rest of the body with a shopping bag shuffled through. "Good morning. Could I get someone to take me to my accommodations?" Allegra asked in a soft voice.

"Ms. Rhodes, did they release you from the hospital?" Jules hurried around the counter to face the author, dressed in black boots and a vintage red faux fur coat with a matching hat.

She made a prune face and a tsk tsk sound. "I'm perfectly all right. That doctor looked like he had recently graduated from middle school. He was so overdramatic about everything. I'll be fine. I'd like to finish out this week and get home for some rest. I feel fit as a fiddle this morning. I can't wait to see everyone."

"What a lovely coat and hat…"

Before Jules could finish, Allegra said, "Carrie was kind enough to bring over a change of clothes and some necessities. Glad to be back. It's nice and calm here. Not like that hospital. When I couldn't take being awakened every twenty minutes, I checked myself out and Ubered over here."

"From Charlottesville?"

The woman nodded slightly, like it was an absurd question from a five-year-old. "Could I get someone to take me to my camper? I need to lie down before today's festivities."

"Of course. Let me get my coat," Jules said.

Sliding into her coat without buttoning it, Jules returned to the front. "Do you have anything I need to carry?"

Allegra held up her purse and shopping bag. "No, thank you. I seemed to be traveling light this time. My agent said that I didn't have shoes or winter wear on when I was found. I still have no recollection of that evening. I remember dinner and returning to my accommodations. After that, it's all a blur."

"Are you feeling okay?" Jules wondered how bad her head wound was. Should she really be returning to her normal activities so soon?

"I'll be fine. Nothing that some hot tea and a nap won't cure. It was a little bump on the head."

"I'm glad you're back on your feet. If you'll wait here, I'll bring the golf cart around to get you," Jules said.

"I'll wait on the porch. The view is so lovely here," Allegra said.

After Allegra settled in the passenger seat of the golf cart, Jules drove with care across the field to the vintage trailers.

Barely waiting for the cart to stop, Allegra hopped out and picked up her belongings. "Thank you so much. I need to call Carrie to make sure she's picking me up this afternoon. And I guess I should let that nice bookstore owner know, too. I need to call Lynette as well. She might want to put out a statement that I've returned from the dead. Too many things to do this morning."

"Please call me if I can help you with anything," Jules said as the woman fumbled through her purse and her pockets. "Oh, there it is." Pulling out the key, she unlocked the aluminum door. "I know Carrie gave it back to me. I keep hotel keys in my wallet so I can find them easily. I can't tell you how many I've lost over the years. Thank you for the ride. I'll see you later." Jules glanced around her and let out a long breath through her nose when she saw the clean accommodations. Mel and Crystal took care of everything. The older woman waved and disappeared inside the trailer.

Jules hoped Allegra was right about her injuries. Putting the cart and gear, she sped off toward the office. The attack on Allegra kept nagging at the back of Jules's thoughts. Someone killed Cinnamon, and it could be the same person who attacked Allegra. Two attackers running around Fern Valley would be too much of a coincidence. The thought sent a chill down her spine. Who was targeting her guests?

Jules parked the cart under the carport and sat in the driver's seat for several moments. She closed her eyes and rested her chin on the steering wheel. There had to be a link between Cinnamon and Allegra. What was going on in their world to cause someone to attack and kill? And why do it now during our book festival? Was it just convenient that the authors were here in one place?

Pulling out her phone, she tapped a text to the sheriff and then one to Elaine and Elizabeth, letting them know Allegra had returned.

What? After those injuries? The sheriff replied.

She looked tired, but she seemed okay, Jules responded.

After no other response, Jules shook off the gloomy feeling and hustled up the stairs. Before she could get situated in her chair, her phone rang.

"Hello, Sheriff. How are you?"

"Fine. Allegra is back at the resort?" he asked, slurping something.

"Yep. She was tired of being in the hospital and checked herself out." After a long pause with no response from him, she continued, "She Ubered back here this morning, and I took her to her trailer. She said she planned to rest up before this afternoon's events."

"Did she act well enough to be out of the hospital?" he asked.

"I guess so. She seemed fine. Her agent brought her a coat and some clothes. When I talked to her, she was soft-spoken, but firm about her opinions. I haven't been around her much. She was chatty on the ride over to her trailer. She hopped out of the cart, and I watched her go in."

"I'll be by in a bit to check on things. She probably shouldn't be released from the hospital yet with a head injury and amnesia. And who knows what else, but she's an adult." He let out a slight puff of air. "I'm sending a deputy over to watch over things at your place. Let Jake and your contract security guys know that a deputy will be around," Sheriff Hobbs said.

"Will do. Any new leads?"

"Nope. What about you?"

"Nothing, really. Allegra did have the key to her trailer with her," Jules said,

"That means her attacker didn't take her purse and belongings. It didn't seem like a robbery." Sheriff Hobbs paused and took in a deep breath. "We're still trying to piece together what happened to her from what she could remember and your camera footage. Don't hesitate to call me if anything else comes up." He disconnected before she could reply.

If the attacker wasn't some random stranger, then the person could still be around the property. Hiding in plain sight? Was Allegra or anyone else in danger? *I'm glad the sheriff is sending over the deputy to keep an eye on things. What happens when the festival ends, and this person disappears?*

Jules tapped a text to Mark O'Rourke. **Hey, got anybody available through Sunday for an overnight detail at the resort?**

Her phone dinged before she could set it down. **Always. I'll call you later to get the details and schedule someone to start tonight.**

Settling into her desk chair, Jules tapped a quick text about the deputy and Mark's overnight security to Jake and Lester. Trying to shake off the doldrums, she scanned her notes. Lots of disparate facts and no obvious connections. Her phone interrupted her frustrated search.

A series of rapid-fire texts from Elaine filled her screen before she had a chance to respond to the first one.

Really??? She's back?

I'm glad, I guess. Is she okay?

I wonder if she'll feel like finishing out the festival.

Maybe she can be here today. See you later.

She seems to be fine, Jules tapped in her phone, followed by a string of smiley emojis.

Jules rubbed her eyes and made a beeline for the coffee maker. Locating a doughnut shop blend, she waited for the machine to brew. Thoughts about the events of the last two weeks swirled around in her head. Cinnamon and Allegra seemed like the nicest authors in the bunch. What secret did they hide that could cause someone to attack them?

When the machine spewed out the final drips of coffee and a puff of steam, she took the mug to her desk and rummaged through the drawer for a large piece of paper. Remembering the roll of craft paper in the closet, she tore off a sheet about four feet long and returned to the worktable.

With a black marker and her notes, Jules listed all the players and the facts she had accumulated. Then, she used a red marker to draw connections between the events and the people. One murder. One attack. Lots of arguments and fussing.

Jules spent the next hour looking at every note she collected and all the disagreements and complaints she could remember. Gigi and Phoenix seemed to be the winners when it came to expressing their dislike for things. Her drawing looked like a spider's web with all the connecting lines. The only person without much attached to her name was the publicist Lynette D'Angelo. *A red flag, or did she fly under the radar?* The lack of information on the publicist bothered Jules. Firing off a quick text to Elaine. **Morning again. Is Lynette D'Angelo at today's event?**

Tapping the end of her pen to her lips, Jules tried to remember any details about the publicist. Besides being medium height with dark corkscrew curls and working for the festival's headliners, nothing stood out for Jules.

Elaine's text interrupted her thoughts. **Nope. Haven't seen her today.**

After checking the number of Lynette's camper, Jules grabbed her coat and keys and hustled out the back door to the 1955 Terry model, themed in honor of James Dean and *Rebel without a Cause*.

Jules walked the path from the office to the village of trailers. Not seeing anyone around, she ducked down the closest cut-through between the vintage trailers and headed toward Lynnette's accommodations.

When she rounded the corner, Jules spotted Lynnette in the grassy area between the rows. "Lynnette. Hey, Lynnette. Do you have a minute?"

"Oh, hi," the publicist said. "I was getting in some steps this morning. I love the crisp mountain air. I took a long walk all around the property. Just beautiful!"

"I'm glad you're enjoying the resort. I'm Jules Keene, the owner. I talked to Allegra and wanted to run some communications things by you."

"No problem," the other woman paused and waited for Jules to continue.

"I've been referring all media inquiries to the sheriff's office, and I then I remembered that I hadn't touched base with you to see if you needed me to do anything differently."

"What you're doing is fine. I'm sure you've been bombarded with questions from all kinds of outlets. Allegra's author sites have had thousands of well-wishers. Now that she's on the mend, I'll do some posts and maybe some videos of her to reassure her fans. She's planning to get back to her scheduled events today."

"I'm so glad she's out of the hospital," Jules said.

"Yep. She's back to being her spunky self. She is such a great client. I never have any complaints from her. She is always so appreciative of what my team does." Lynnette pulled out her phone from her pocket and paused to respond to an alert.

Jules shifted her weight from one foot to the other while she waited.

At about the time Jules was ready to wave goodbye, Lynnette continued, "Sorry about that. I am tied to this thing twenty-four-seven. It's always something."

Jules smiled when the woman looked up from her screen. "I can only imagine. My sites for the resort take a lot of time. I hate to think what it's like to keep up with so many authors and all their activities."

Lynnette chuckled. "Oh, I have help. And I schedule most things. It seems to be a whole lot of little fires and sometimes big fires that need attention constantly."

"Any idea who would target Cinnamon Moon or Allegra Rhodes?" Jules asked.

Lynnette shook her head, and her curls bounced around in all directions. "No. Of all my clients, they made the fewest waves. They were beloved by everyone. Noooooo one ever said anything bad about either of them.

I was so shocked at the murder and the attack." Her phone alerted again. "I've heard rumblings, but nothing concrete to tell the police. Some of the authors are super jealous of Allegra and Cinnamon's success. One even showed her crazy by accusing Cinnamon of stealing her ideas for a series. And a bunch of them are quick to complain if they feel they aren't getting the same amount of attention as the stars."

Jules stared at the publicist, hoping she'd continue.

"It's Echo Aames, but you didn't hear it from me," Lynnette whispered. She diverted her eyes to her phone, and Jules said, "That makes a lot of sense. Some of these folks are a little temperamental."

"Ha! Try downright nuts," Lynette said.

Jules let a slight smile creep across her lips. "Let me know if my team can help you in any way. I know you're busy. I'll let you get back to work."

"See ya," Lynnette said, focusing on her phone.

Jules strolled through the campers on her way back. Jealousy and rage could be motivators to attack these two beloved authors. There are a couple of folks around here that fit that bill.

Lots of facts and no neon arrows pointing to a guilty party. Jules let out a sigh and texted Pixel when she was back at her desk.

Hey there. Do you have time this week for lunch? My treat.

Seconds later, her college friend replied, **We're on the same wavelength as usual. It's been too long. How about this afternoon? 1:30 work for you?**

Perfect, Jules tapped into her phone. **Where?**

How about that bistro near you?

The Good Thyme Bistro. See you at 1:30.

Maybe Pixel will have something interesting to share. Jules folded her diagram and slipped it into her purse.

Chapter Twenty-Three

Thursday Afternoon

Checking her watch, Jules locked the office and texted Jake that she was heading to town after Bijou's walk. The Jack Russell Terrier had other ideas. Their excursion turned into an extended walk that included a hike around the meadow and the amphitheater.

After getting Bijou settled at home, Jules said to the terrier, "See you in a bit. I'm having lunch with Pixel. Love you." The little terrier made a nest on the lap blanket and curled up on the couch.

The quick ride into town came to a jarring halt when she hit traffic on the outskirts. The cars creeped and beeped for about a half-mile. Not spotting any empty side streets to duck down to avoid the jam, she texted Pixel that she might be a little late. She could count on one hand the number of traffic jams she had seen in Fern Valley. Between Bijou and the traffic, everything today seemed to take longer than normal.

Her phone's alert distracted her from the traffic. **Found a parking spot, but the Bistro is packed. Wanna try Pop's?** Pixel texted.

Sounds like a plan, Jules responded. When there was a break in oncoming traffic, she signaled and whipped the Jeep around.

Thankfully, traffic heading in the other direction was normal, and she found a parking place behind the silver diner.

Jules pushed open the heavy door with the Art Deco porthole window and hurried inside toward Pixel.

"No, wait at this place," Pixel said, hugging her friend.

"I have no idea what's going on in town," Jules said, following Pixel and the host, who looked like a character out of *Grease* with his slicked-back pompadour and leather jacket. He pointed to a small booth in the back in the Monkees's section of the restaurant. A huge poster of Mike, Davy, Peter, and Mickey smiled down over Pixel's head. Davy Jones was still Jules's favorite of the comedic band.

"Here we are, ladies. Your server will be right with you." The host handed each of them a menu.

"This place is more fun than the bistro." Pixel thumbed through the colorful menu. "I talked to some of the folks while I was trying to get our name on the lengthy waiting list at the bistro. Seems word got out that Echo Abbott and Windsor Abernathy were holding court there and were giving away tons of freebies. The management turned all the tables into a big rectangle for a spur-of-the-moment group lunch. And nobody was in a hurry to leave. I also got wind of some online rumors of a cash giveaway and a chance to be part of the filming of today's event, which seems to be some sort of documentary. Who knows if they're true, but it might explain all the traffic."

"And the crowd at the bistro," Jules said, checking her phone. "Our big event today for the festival is the dinner at the high school. And I saw the publicist at the resort. She didn't mention any special media events. You would think she'd be involved if it was some kind of filming."

"I think the authors decided to do their own impromptu thing, and word and rumors spread quickly. They both have vast social media followings. Never underestimate the reach of one viral post," Pixel said. "Plus, it's a lot like that old telephone game. The message got changed and expanded as it passed from person to person."

Before Jules could comment, Marsha bustled over and pulled a pen out of her pink bouffant. "Hey, gals. What can I get for you all today?"

"I'll have the veggie wrap and water with a lime," Pixel said.

"With the avocados and jalapenos?" the waitress asked.

"Yep," Pixel nodded vigorously. "The more, the better."

"And how about you, Jules?"

"Let's see. I'll do the sourdough grilled cheese with fries and an unsweetened tea. Thanks."

"Be back in a jiff. And y'all save room for dessert. Alphonzo made a batch of his famous peach pies."

"Yum," Pixel said. "We may have to celebrate."

When Marsha headed for the kitchen, Pixel pulled out her phone. "Let's see. Where's the new stuff I haven't told you about? Phoenix Abbott writes under multiple pen names in different genres. I told you about the authors complaining that she cheated them with her promo services that didn't deliver. Oh, this is new. I found someone using one of her pseudonyms on the dark web, railing against publishers, agents, and other authors. It's full of lots of vitriol. I couldn't verify that it was from her account, but the language in that chat room was similar to some posts that I could attribute to her. She's not a fan of Echo, Cinnamon, or Windsor. The written attacks were pretty ugly."

"Hmmm. Burning bridges. Not the best way to win friends. That could be a motive." Jules said, jotting notes in a small notebook.

"Oh, she set fire to a bunch of stuff on the dark web and the public internet. She didn't seem too concerned about what she posted or who she offended. A dumpster fire. Let's say she has a reputation, and it's doubtful that she'll ever get a traditional book contract," Pixel said.

"From the talks I attended, she was totally on the indie bandwagon. She praised the freedom she had to make all her own decisions. Phoenix had a couple of tiffs with some of the established authors during the festival. She and Gigi felt like they were left out of opportunities. They didn't have the clout like the established writers. Phoenix lashed out at anyone who was doing better than she was."

"Maybe it's work ethic. Just saying. A lot of comments on Phoenix's posts center on her typos, bad grammar, and cartoony book covers. Some of the gals that Phoenix complains about really produce and have the income to back it up. Plus, with all the changes in the industry, many of the traditionally published authors have old series that they've re-released. Some have even released stuff as an indie author. Most authors these days have all kinds of book contracts. It's not like the vanity presses of the past. And there are gobs of successful writers who go that route." Pixel paused and watched a toddler and her mother walk past the table.

"Let's see. I found a little bit on Cinnamon Moon. I dug around and found some info on an online dust-up with another writer, one of her critique partners, who claimed to have given her the idea for Cinnamon's series, the Romance Wrangler. The same idea coming to a TV screen near us soon." Pixel paused and looked up at Jules. "Drumroll, please. And that author was none other than Tracey Davis, also known as Phoenix Abbott."

"Very interesting. Think there is any truth to it?" Pixel shrugged, and Jules continued, "All of these authors have past relationships, good or bad. Phoenix seems to be fighting multiple online wars. And when I talked to the publicist, she said that Echo made a claim that Cinnamon stole her ideas."

"When you have something popular, the scammers and ne'er do wells come out of the woodwork," Pixel said. "I'll see if I can find out more about the plagiarism claims from Phoenix and Echo."

"One of the claims is a strong accusation that involves a big chunk of money. Optioning involves big money, right?" Jules asked as Marsha approached with their drinks.

"Here you go, gals. Your lunches will be out lickety-split. Sorry to eavesdrop, but are you talking about Cinnamon Moon? I have read all of her books, some more than once. She can do the steam." Marsha fanned herself with her hand. "Whoooo doggie. Love me some of her Western series. And I can't wait until that movie gets made." A somber expression spread across Marsha's face. "She will be missed." She sniffed and brushed away a tear that leaked from the corner of her eye. "Be back soon with your meals." She turned in her saddle oxfords and disappeared in the back.

"Romance writers have a dedicated fan base of avid readers. Where were we? Oh, yeah, optioning. Movie and TV production companies often offer options or contracts to writers for their stories. Sometimes, they want to recreate it as is. Other times, they want to buy the characters for a different storyline. And sometimes, they'll even put it under contract with no intent to ever produce it," Pixel said.

"Huh?" Jules asked.

"It's part of a strategy to keep something that competes with a project that they're already doing from being released. Keeping the competition in check. Anyway, the author usually gets money from the production company to consider the project. Then, if the time elapses, there's no movie, but the author did get something for her effort."

"Interesting…" Jules said. Before she could continue, Marsha returned with an armload of plates.

"Here you go. Ketchup and mustard are on the table. Do you all need anything else?" Marsha asked.

"Looks good. Thanks," Pixel replied.

"Y'all save some room for that pie, and I'll be back to check on you in a bit." Marsha's pink bouffant jiggled like Jello as she moved to another table.

"What else? What else?" Pixel said, scrolling through screens on her phone. "Oh, it seems Tammy Jones, also known as Echo Aames, was also in the same critique group with Cinnamon and Phoenix. Phoenix also ranted about Echo. She claimed that Echo took some of her ideas and went on to parlay them into book contracts. Wow. They're throwing accusations around about everybody."

"Any proof?" Jules's eyes widened at another possible motive.

"Just her rants and posts. I couldn't find any lawsuits or real proof. Pixel raised an eyebrow. "And last but not least, Windsor Abernathy collects antiques and unique things from the eras that she writes about."

"She showed us some of her Victorian collectibles. She's extremely proud of her treasures. There was an incident at one of the events where some of her things were stolen. She was beside herself. Her items are fascinating like the poison ring with a secret compartment for a murderous stash. I don't know if I could walk around knowing that I had a fatal dose of poison right at my fingertips."

Pixel smiled. "Hopefully, none of the poison spilled out by accident. She does like to collect odd things. I found an article from a month ago where the authorities were looking at her residence. According to the story, the police received an anonymous tip about dangerous substances in a residential neighborhood. It seems she had amassed quite a collection of old medicine bottles, flypaper, and Victorian wallpaper. Oh, and a collection of antique taxidermy. And what do these have in common? I know you're about to ask." Pixel's eyes twinkled with excitement.

"Well?" Jules asked, popping a French fry in her mouth.

"I'm building anticipation." Pixel giggled. "They all contain 'inheritance powder' or, as it's commonly known, arsenic. You can still find these things on eBay and in antique shops. And it's perfectly legal to buy them. The green wallpaper was popular during the Victorian era. They didn't realize it was deadly until folks came down with arsenic poisoning from the constant exposure. Anyway, it seems Windsor went on a deadly buying spree, and someone online tipped off the authorities. They confiscated her stuff but returned it later."

"Eeeks. Do you think she was trying to collect arsenic to use?" Jules asked. Murderous thoughts bounced around her brain.

"I couldn't find anything more nefarious than purchasing the deadly collectibles. She has display cases all over her house. She has a thing for old stuff. But it's still an interesting tidbit. The online articles portrayed her as an eccentric writer. She's done several video interviews where she gave tours of her odd collection. Her house looked like a museum. I'll email you the links. It sounded like she was buying props to use at her book talks. She happened to buy a lot of things full of arsenic at about the same time. It triggered someone somewhere to report her."

"Too bad poison hasn't been an issue here. We'd have a suspect. Our attacks have been with some unknown object, and we had a stabbing with a knitting needle. And a frail woman left unconscious out in the cold. And she was knocked in the head with something."

"No obvious patterns. Both got hit in the back of the head, right? Maybe that's your pattern."

Jules nodded. "I haven't seen any knitters hanging around the resort. It's too bad I didn't get a picture of the one they found with Cinnamon. I heard it was fancy."

"Another creepy weapon. I'm still fascinated by all the things that contain arsenic. That and the poison ring. Lots of story plots there."

"I'm surprised that anyone can go and buy these things. You'd think they'd be regulated or controlled somehow," Jules said.

"Who knows? How many crates of old bottles have you seen at antique stores and junk sales?" Pixel wrinkled her nose and pushed her plate to the middle of the table. "It does make you think. It would be a pretty innocuous way for somebody to collect poison without raising too many eyebrows if they did it in small, unrelated batches. Enough about poisons. What's going on in your world besides murder and mayhem?"

Jules smiled. "They've been the dominant themes. I told you about Jake's tree house. That's where we found Allegra Rhodes. Speaking of her, she checked herself out of the hospital and turned up back at the resort this morning." Jules swiped a dab of ketchup on her plate with a fry. Hey, are you still seeing that gamer you mentioned the last time we chatted?"

A slight smile crossed Pixel's face. "It's been fun. I haven't had much free time with my new FBI gig. His name is Carlos, and we chat during games once or twice a week. If we can ever clear a spot in our schedules, we hope to meet in person." Her voice trailed off.

"What's the matter?

Pixel shrugged. "Not sure how he'll be in person. Sometimes, people are more exciting than their online personas. His avatar looks like a cross between Mad Max and Rambo. Sexy and exciting. Unfortunately, real life doesn't always match the fantasy. We'll see." Jules wondered what Pixel's avatar looked like.

Marsha whizzed by the table and stopped abruptly, reaching for the dirty plates. "Y'all want dessert?"

"As tempting as it sounds, I think I'll pass," Pixel said.

"Me too. I'm stuffed." Jules reached for the check, and Marsha pulled out a vinyl folder from her apron pocket. "I'll take that when you're ready."

Jules handed Marsha her card. When the waitress headed for the register, she continued, "I appreciate all the digging you did for me, especially since you're swamped with your new gig. And don't give up on your gamer friend.

CHAPTER TWENTY-THREE

He might surprise you."

Pixel rose and hugged Jules. Outside, they headed in different directions. Jules slid into her Jeep and blasted the heat to knock off the early afternoon chill. When the interior felt toasty, she found a jazz station and enjoyed the ride down the country roads to the resort. Spring was around the corner, and the new leaves and then the first flowers would pop out, adding so much color to the mountain vistas. Spring was the harbinger of summer, and Jules loved the outdoors and all its adventures in the warm weather.

Shaking herself out of her daydream, Jules focused on the information Pixel provided about possible new motives. The guests from the book festival would be checking out in a few days. *I've got to turn something up quickly. Could the knitting needle be part of someone's collection?*

Chapter Twenty-Four

Thursday

Jules spent the afternoon wrapping up tasks that had fallen to the bottom of her to-do list. After checking over the books, balancing the bank accounts, and cleaning her desk, she finally packed up and put the phone on auto-attendant. Quickening her pace, she set the alarm and scooted out the back door. She had enough time to take Bijou for a walk and find something to wear to tonight's author dinner.

After feeding Bijou and trying on two outfits, she settled on a purple tunic sweater, a pair of black leggings, and her tall black boots. Jules's thoughts wandered while she redid her makeup. *I'm on a mission to find out who's attacking authors on my property. Why pick two of the nicest women? Could it possibly be someone not involved with the festival? There has to be some connection that I'm overlooking.*

Jules had hit a wall. In the past, she had had a knack for ferreting out secrets and helping the sheriff. *Has my luck run out?* Shaking off the melancholic feeling, Jules slipped into her coat, kissed Bijou, and headed out the door. *What am I missing?*

A large crowd of women milled around on the sidewalk in front of the high school. Not wanting to stand outside any longer than she had to, Jules enjoyed the warmth of the Jeep and flipped through emails until the doors opened and the guests streamed inside.

Hurrying to catch up, she mixed in at the back of the line at the registration table.

The tall blond in front of Jules turned to her friend and said, "I still can't believe what happened to Cinnamon Moon. This place will forever be known as the location where she was murdered."

Her friend nodded her head vigorously. "And if that's not enough, it's also where sweet Allegra Rhodes was attacked."

The first woman shook her head and made a tsking sound.

A pang of dread zinged through Jules, and she hoped the anxiety didn't show on her face. She leaned slightly forward to hear what else the pair of women in front of her had to say.

The second woman added, "I am so relieved that Allegra is on the mend. My heart couldn't take two tragedies. I mean kidnappers and murderers running around my lands." Her hand flew to her mouth, and her eyes widened. "It's not like we're in New York or Chicago. I thought tiny, little towns were safer. You know, places where everybody knows everyone, and no one locks their doors. You'd never think a murder could happen around here."

Jules stepped closer for better eavesdropping. She bit her tongue when she wanted to defend Fern Valley. Before the pair could continue their conversation, Kim Lacy welcomed them to the dinner.

The women picked up their packets and wandered to the library, and Kim turned to Jules. "Hey, it's nice to see you."

"You too. Y'all need any help?"

"Nope. Almost everyone has checked in. Here are your drink tickets and a ticket for tonight's raffle. Cocktails are in the library, and they'll announce dinner in a bit. Your table number is on your name tag. Have fun."

"Thanks." Jules scanned the information Kim handed her. At the end of the table, Elaine fanned herself with a program.

"Everything looks nice. Need anything?" Jules asked.

"I think we're okay. Everyone will be enjoying cocktails and mingling soon, and then it's off to the dinner and our keynote speaker. I am so relieved that Allegra could join us," Elaine said. "We've had enough chaos around here."

"How's she doing?" Jules asked.

"She seems fine. I told Darlene and Kim to keep an eye on her. Her agent, Carrie, is with her, so she'll be okay. Allegra's making an appearance. She doesn't have to do a lot of speaking. I'm hoping it goes off without a hitch." Elaine looked over her shoulder and then leaned toward Jules and whispered, "There's some chatter about the murder. It seems to be the topic du jour. And Sheriff Matt has had no updates for us. Not even a press release. I hope we don't get a bad rap for this."

"We've endured disasters before. I thought for sure that the other murders would put an end to the filming of *Fatal Impressions* last fall, but it actually had the opposite effect, making its popularity skyrocket. Despite the tragedies, the folks staying at the resort are enjoying all the activities," Jules said, hoping to deflect some of the spotlight off of the sheriff's office.

"We'll see what comes back on the survey and comment cards. You can never tell. I was in town yesterday, and I overheard J. P. Gross. He was jawing with Boogie Jones and Ralph Teagle outside the post office." She lowered her voice again to slightly above a whisper. "They're plotting to take over the business council at the next election. They want to stack the council with like-minded thinkers and stop all activities that have led to the crimewave around town."

Jules felt her cheeks flush. She opened her mouth and then clamped her jaw shut. No need to add fuel to the fire. *I can't take this personally. I've tried my best to champion ideas that benefited all the business owners.*

"Don't worry about it," Elaine said. "You're doing a great job as our council president. They're blowhards and complainers, but we need to keep an eye on them to ensure they don't end all the great work we've been doing. We need to stay vigilant. And the sheriff needs to get on the stick and make some arrests, so we can get on with our business."

Jules pasted on a weak smile. "I'm sure the sheriff is plowing through all the leads. He said he had a state trooper helping with the investigation. I plan to check out the events in the library. Want to join me?"

"I'll be down in a minute. I want to pop in on Elizabeth and her team in the dining room to see if everything is following the plan. Seating is in about twenty minutes. Go mingle. Have fun."

Jules hoped she didn't roll her eyes. She had to shake off the dreary feeling that the conversation gave her. *Girl, get a move on. We have weathered storms before and come out okay. Now, go in there and find something that will help point to the culprit in these attacks.*

She took a deep breath and felt some of the anxiety slip away. J. P. Gross and his pals look for every opportunity to undermine the council's hard work. She knew down deep that she was helping the town by bringing in tourist dollars, no matter what the other faction claimed. Fern Valley was in a much better place than some nearby rural towns.

Opening the door, she stepped into the school library, which had been transformed with posters and red, white, and pink decorations. It looked like a cocktail lounge with high-top tables, with book-themed centerpieces and posters of exotic places on every wall. The local travel agency sponsored the cocktail hour and door prizes with its "Escape to Romance" theme. Guests chatted and sampled the hors d'oeuvre platters.

Two bartenders, who looked like they could be romance cover models, mixed drinks with some dance moves like a scene out of *Cocktail. If they keep up that hip action, Elaine will never get this crowd to move on to the dinner course.*

Jules stood in line at the bar and was quickly absorbed into the conversation of the group of women ahead of her. "This is so much fun," the one with the short curly hair said. "By the way, I'm Carol, and this is my sister Laurie and our friend Jackie," she said, pointing to the women on either side of her.

"Hi, I'm Jules."

"What a nice festival. I hope they do it again next year. We drove over from Waynesboro. And I'm glad we did," Jackie said.

"We're so excited to have so many authors and fans visit our town," Jules said. "I've enjoyed meeting everyone."

"I love it. We've tried all the restaurants, and we're coming back in the spring to check out the art galleries," Jackie said.

"And don't forget the wine tours," Laurie added, her large diamond catching the light as she waved her hand around.

"We'll have to do those twice," Jackie added.

"So, who's your favorite author?" Jules asked as the line inched closer to the bar.

"All of them," Laurie and Carol said at the same time.

Jackie rolled her eyes and drained the last drops of her current drink. "They read constantly. I stick to the ones with historical themes. Windsor Abernathy is by far my favorite of the authors here. She knows so much and has all these little cool tidbits to share. I love her. And she always has such neat little knick-knacks to talk about. It's too bad that some of her antiques were stolen. What a shame. It could have been an inside job."

Her sister raised both eyebrows. "Who knows? I'm here because of Cinnamon Moon's westerns. What fun. I will truly miss her."

"What can I get for you, ladies?" asked the blond bartender with the unbuttoned shirt.

The three women giggled and made eyes at the man behind the counter. "Hi, Ace. We're back for your passion punch."

"Coming right up. And for you?" he asked, looking at Jules with his piercing baby-blue eyes.

"Ginger ale is fine," she said.

He flashed a toothy smile and poured a can of the fizzy drink. Ace winked when he handed her a flute of the soft drink. Then he lined up three martini glasses on the counter and proceeded to do a *Cocktail* impression of Tom Cruise that ended with him pouring pink punch over his shoulder into the glasses.

Sliding her drink ticket on the bar top, Jules said, "Thank you. And ladies, you all enjoy your evening."

"Oh, we will, as soon as we convince Ace here to join us for dinner," Jackie said loud enough to turn heads around the trio.

After finishing her soft drink, Jules trekked down the long corridor to the cafeteria. Before she reached the information table, Kim Lacy yelled, "Whoo hooo, Jules. How's it going?"

"Great. How are things at this end?"

"Just peachy. Folks are trickling in and finding their places. You're at table B14 over on the right. We're in for another fun night of romance talk." She winked, and it was hard for Jules to tell if she was excited or sarcastic.

"Thanks. See you inside." Jules wended her way through a sea of round tables to her seat. Four other women had already spread out around her designated table. Pulling out an empty chair, she said, "Good evening. I'm Jules Keene."

"Welcome," a woman in orange with a pixie cut said. "I'm Alex Ramírez, and this is my sister Kate." The woman in yellow nodded.

"Hi, I'm Terri Singleton, and this is my sister Alma Hendricks. We're staying at your resort and loving our little trailer."

"I'm so glad," Jules said. "Y'all will have to come back in the summer or the fall. We're ground zero for the autumn color explosion."

"Oh, we'll definitely be back. Our husbands love to fish, and we can tour all the cute stores and wineries while they're out. I want to come back this summer, too," Alma said, draping her napkin across her lap. "I heard about picnics up at the waterfall."

"So, who is everyone here to see?" Kate sipped her water.

"All of them," Alma said. "We are having so much fun talking to all the authors. This has been great. I love that we've had so many opportunities to chat with them."

"It was too bad about Cinnamon Moon," Alex said. "I'm glad I was able to get her autograph before she was killed. Such a tragedy."

"I heard it was a crazed fan," Alma said, lowering her voice. "Someone who's stalking the authors. Allegra Rhodes barely escaped with her life. I hope nothing else bad happens and that the authorities have stepped up security. I heard some of the authors were getting bodyguards."

"It's kinda exciting," Terri added. "It's like being in the middle of one of those crime shows. I'm taking pictures of everything in case I happen to snap a shot of the killer and don't know it."

Alex rolled her eyes. "I'm sure the police are investigating thoroughly."

"Maybe," Terri said. "But you never know when leads come from ordinary citizens. Alma and I are being super vigilant. We always try to be aware of our surroundings."

"I read a bunch of fan pages online and listen to podcasts. I heard that Phoenix Abbott is under suspicion. She doesn't fit in with the others. I heard she's a loner who has an axe to grind with the popular authors. And they said she is angry at everyone and not nice to fans." Alex raised a perfectly manicured eyebrow. "Just saying what I heard. There may be some truth to those gossipy blogs. She wasn't all that friendly when I tried to talk to her in the bathroom." Alex lowered her voice and glanced over her shoulder. "I also heard that Echo Aames has been ranting a lot about how Cinnamon is a thief. She blurted it out when a reporter asked her about Cinnamon's death. How inappropriate. She made the whole thing about herself. Maybe I watch too much TV, but I wouldn't have answered the question that way. It could raise suspicions."

Before the conversation could continue, Elizabeth Rhoney tapped a glass with a knife. "Ladies and Gentlemen, please take your seats. We'd like to thank the folks at Good Time Bistro for catering tonight's gala. Dinner will be served momentarily, and then our program will begin. I am pleased to have Windsor Abernathy as our guest of honor this evening. I'll be interviewing her about her books and her heroines. But before we feed you, the Fern Valley Business Council would like to welcome Allegra Rhodes back. It is so good to have her here with us this evening. Ms. Rhodes, would you like to address your fans?"

Allegra nodded and stood while Elizabeth made her way around tables to hand the author the microphone.

"Thank you," Allegra said. "It is so great to be back with you all after my little scare. This has been such a fun festival. I'm trying to put a bug in Elizabeth's ear that she and her team need to host another one next year. What do you all think?"

A roar went up from the audience, and the applause and the whistles turned into a standing ovation for Allegra.

"Thank you. You are too kind. Your sweet thoughts and well wishes helped me get back on my feet. I'm so glad to be here tonight. I can't wait to talk with you all." Allegra waved to the room with both hands.

"We're so glad to see you, too," Elizabeth said, patting the author's shoulder. "So everyone, enjoy your dinner and dessert and get comfy for some great discussions."

Servers dressed in all black balanced large trays and fanned out to the tables. In the blink of an eye, the first course appeared. The ladies at Jules's table chattered on about murder, romance novels, and their favorite TV shows through the courses that included a wedge salad, Italian wedding soup, chicken cordon bleu and mixed veggies, and a decadent chocolate raspberry torte.

The table conversations were lively, but Jules didn't glean anything else about Cinnamon's murder or any possible suspects. The lack of any new nuggets was disappointing. Distracted from the glumness of making no progress in her information gathering, Jules concentrated on Windsor's interview, which turned into a show-and-tell of her deadly toys. The author knew her history and the uses for all kinds of vintage knickknacks. Jules would love to get a peek into her house, which must be part antique store, part museum.

After the final round of applause for Windsor died down, Jules said her goodbyes to her tablemates as her phone trilled from her purse.

"Hey, Jake. What's up?" A little flutter of excitement rocketed through her.

"Hey, Boss. I found something on my rounds tonight. You may want to check this out. I think we need to call the sheriff."

"Not again! I'm at the high school. Where are you?" Jules asked, making her way to the exit.

"Over by the trailers. Near the Elvis one. It's probably better to show you than tell you."

Jules's earlier tingle of excitement turned into dread. Dinner felt like a lead balloon in the pit of her stomach. "Be there as soon as I can."

Chapter Twenty-Five

Thursday Evening

Jules broke the sound barrier on her way from the high school to the resort. She flew into her driveway and then jogged across the field to the trailers, hoping she remembered to close the Wrangler's door.

Catching her breath on the row where the Elvis-themed trailer sat. Jules noticed a flick of movement out of the corner of her eye. Her body tensed when someone touched her shoulder. Letting out a yelp, Jules turned.

"It's me. Sorry. I thought you heard me," Jake said.

Expelling a breath that sounded like a slow leak, Jules hugged him. "Nope. Just a tad jumpy these days. I was focused on getting over here. What did you find?"

"Over here. I was doing my rounds, and I saw a quick flash of light." He pointed to the trailer across the row.

"Like a flashbulb?"

"Not really. It looked like something glinting when the light hit it. I wasn't quite sure what I saw. On closer inspection, it was this. Something metal in the grass. It turned out to be a dagger," he said, lowering his voice.

Under the camper, beside what looked like a sleeping bag, lay a six-inch dagger and several large rocks. The ornate handle made Jules's thoughts flash immediately to Windsor. She pulled out her phone and clicked Sheriff Hobbs's contact. Why do Windsor's stolen items keep showing up around the resort?

"Jules, what's up?" the sheriff asked.

"Sorry to bother you when you're off."

"I'm still at the office drinking cold coffee and eating stale doughnuts. What can I do for you?" he asked.

"Jake was doing his rounds this evening and found something under one of the campers. It looks like a sleeping bag, but there's an ornate dagger beside it. And some pretty good-sized rocks. I think the dagger may belong to Windsor Abernathy."

"A dagger, huh? And rocks. Jules, your calls are always interesting. If you haven't yet, don't touch it. I'll be over as soon as I can."

"Did you touch it?" she asked Jake.

When he shook his head, she said, "We haven't touched it. We'll be between the second and third row of campers if you park in the main lot."

"Got it." Sheriff Hobbs ended the call.

"Now, we wait. I guess," she said.

Jake pulled her close in an embrace. She was enjoying the warmth of his hug when someone hurried around the corner of the trailer and almost slammed into them.

Shining his flashlight toward the visitor, the female stopped short and covered her face with her arm. "Ow. That's bright."

"Sorry," Jake said, pointing the beam toward the woman's feet.

"I thought I'd take a little walk this evening," Tiffany Blake said with a slight giggle. "I needed some fresh air and a break from, you know, stuff."

Jules nodded her head, and Tiffany continued, "Windsor's been texting me a list of demands all night. And I needed a couple of minutes of peace. The crisp mountain air is lovely. Cool enough to clear my head. It's nice to have some time to myself." The personal assistant twisted a tissue in her hands.

"It is. It was nice to see you. Can we help you with anything?" Jules asked, hoping to find out if Tiffany's nervousness was from stress or something else.

"Uh, no. It's just been crazy busy," Tiffany said. "Windsor always has ten or fifteen things that need doing immediately. And Phoenix has been pestering me to arrange a lunch with her and Windsor. She won't take a hint and drop it." Her voice trailed off. "All the yelling and fighting is disturbing."

"Fighting?" Jules asked as Jake shifted his weight from leg to leg.

"Yeah. It's been a lot lately. I'm kinda used to Windsor's outbursts. But Phoenix had a shouting match in the bathroom at the school with Gigi, and they tried to drag me into it. And then Echo started yelling at Allegra Rhodes about some slight she said she made toward her. She was downright ugly in front of some fans."

Jules made a tsking sound. "And after what Allegra's been through lately."

"No. I mean, the fighting was before that," Tiffany said dismissively. Her phone alerted, and she let out a heavy sigh. "Her Highness is calling. I guess I'll mosey my way back to our accommodations. See ya." She turned and headed back the way she came, away from the tiny house where she was staying.

When she was sure the younger woman was out of range, Jules whispered, "If she'd only known what you found tonight. She was the last person seen with the items that were stolen from Windsor. Awfully chatty tonight. And she's not heading back to her accommodations unless she's taking the scenic route. Her relationship with her boss is strained. At times, she seems terrified of upsetting the writer, and then, in the next moment, she's ready to quit and find a better job. And what she said about Phoenix, Gigi, and Echo was interesting, too."

"They're definitely interesting folks," Jake said. Then he turned his head toward the parking lot. "And she answered questions we didn't ask. She acted overly nervous. Any idea why the dagger would be under that trailer? I'm surprised nobody noticed it there before?"

"This was Cinnamon's trailer." Jules pointed to the camper behind her. "And Allegra's is over there. Why would someone dump this stuff out here now? And it's not even well hidden. The police went over this area when they were investigating."

Jake nodded, lost in thought. "The forensic team was thorough. They couldn't have missed this stuff."

"Sheriff Hobbs must have crime scene photos." Jules leaned over and pointed her flashlight app under the camper. "I don't think that's a sleeping bag. It's puffy, and it looks rumpled. I wish the sheriff would hurry. I'm curious about all this stuff. You think we have squatters?"

Jake shook his head. "Nah. I think we or the night security would have noticed. Those river rocks look like they've been stacked there for some reason. Who takes the time to dump stuff and then stack rocks neatly in such a small space under a camper?"

Jules shrugged. "The rocks kinda look like one of those cairns that hikers leave on trails to show others they are on the correct path, or sometimes they're a memorial to something," Jake said.

Jules dropped to her knees and scooted under the trailer for a better look. She focused the light on the rocks, and a charge of excitement zinged down her spine and landed in her stomach. Why would a trail marker be here? Is someone sending some kind of message? "From here, it looks like that one has some kind of stain on it. That's interesting. I wonder if it was used…" *Nah, I'm not even going to say anything about it being the murder weapon.* Jules's voice trailed off as she slithered out from under the camper.

Jules hoped their conversation and the flashlights didn't bother any of her guests. She glanced over her shoulder; not many of the trailers had lights on. They hadn't drawn attention from anyone, so maybe they hadn't been as loud as she imagined.

Crunching footsteps cause their heads to turn.

"Hey, Jules. Hey, Jake. What did you all find this time?" Sheriff Hobbs asked as he approached. His baritone voice echoed in the night air.

"Something caught my eye during rounds," Jake said. He flashed his light under the trailer. The light glinted off the dagger.

The sheriff set a dark nylon bag and a digital camera in the grass and pulled out a pair of gloves from his utility belt. Leaning on one knee, he swept his light back and forth under the camper. "Looks like quite a collection under there."

After snapping a couple of pictures from all angles, he pulled out a dark, puffy coat and set it on the ground. Reaching further under the camper, he retrieved a pair of boots and a dark nylon stocking. Crawling back out from under the trailer, he pulled out the dagger and set it next to the pile of clothing.

He photographed everything spread out on the ground and then carefully bagged them.

"I can't imagine that y'all didn't spot this stuff before," she said.

The sheriff straightened up. "They weren't there when we searched the first time. We went over every inch of this space."

"Those rocks look interesting," Jules added. "I thought I saw a stain on the squarish one."

"It kinda looks like a trail marker. But it's out of place here." The sheriff crawled under the camper again and took photos. Before backing out from the crawl space under the camper, he carefully moved the rocks to the grassy area.

The sheriff bagged the rock with the stain. "This looks like blood, but it could be mud or red clay. We'll get it checked out." Then he bagged the rest of the rocks and set them beside the other items he collected. "This is the first time I've ever sent a bag of rocks to the lab. I can hear the jokes now."

After a search around all sides of the nearby campers, Jules and Jake watched the sheriff's flashlight beam dance under the trailers and across the grass. "I don't see anything else. My guess is that the clothes belong to Allegra Rhodes," Sheriff Hobbs said when he returned to where the pair was standing.

"The dagger looks like one on Windsor Abernathy's site," Jules added. "Her assistant walked through here a little bit before you arrived. She said she was out for an evening stroll."

"Did she now? I may stop by and talk with her and the author before I leave. They still in the same tiny house?'"

Jules nodded.

"Good find, Jake. Maybe we can get some DNA off these that will help." He picked up his things and the evidence bags.

"Do you need some help with that?" Jake asked.

"Sure." Sheriff Hobbs handed him the nylon bag and Jules his camera. The pair followed him to his cruiser. After the sheriff had situated all the evidence in the back, he shut the trunk firmly and walked toward the tiny houses. "Thanks."

"You want to hike over there and eavesdrop?" Jake whispered in her ear.

"Yes, but I don't want to be too obvious. We have to make it look like we have a reason to be over there."

"I have an idea. My lumber order came in this afternoon. This way." Jake motioned for her to follow him.

Jules tromped behind Jake and trailed the patches of light from his flashlight. No sense twisting an ankle on the uneven ground.

He trekked around the perimeter of the tiny house village and stopped near the construction site. The wind rustled through the bare trees. They crept closer to a pallet full of lumber and hunched over. The pile of wood blocked them from view, and the trees hid them from anyone approaching from the other side.

Jules leaned forward, trying to hear the sheriff's conversation with Tiffany, but the breeze and night noises drowned out some of the conversation. The young woman stood on the top step under the porch light of the Baum house. Shadows danced around her as she waved her arms in response to the sheriff's questions. Disappointed that she couldn't hear both sides of the discussion, Jules's imagination wandered as the pair continued their talk. Then Tiffany rose and bowed her head. The sheriff climbed the steps to the small porch and rapped on the door.

Windsor opened the door a crack. Opening it further, she motioned for the sheriff to step inside, leaving her personal assistant alone on the porch. Looking around, Tiffany pulled out her cell phone and leaned against the railing.

"Come on. I don't think we're going to learn anything new here. My toes are frozen, and I need coffee. I may even have some apple pie in the fridge. If not, I know I have a stash of frozen Girl Scout Cookies in the freezer," Jules said.

"Dessert's always important," Jake said, taking her hand and shining the light ahead of them.

As they walked to her cabin, Jules's thoughts ping-ponged around her head. Jake had found Allegra's missing coat, shoes, Windsor's dagger, and probably the weapon used to knock Allegra in the head. But why would someone dump them where they would easily be found after the police did their search. That seems like an awful lot of trouble unless it was meant for some kind of a marker. Why not discard the stuff in a dumpster or in the woods instead of providing the police a chance to uncover DNA evidence? Or, since it was under Cinnamon's trailer, was it supposed to serve as a message?

Thoughts of evidence and weapons collided in Jules's head with Tiffany's unusual evening stroll. She always seems like she's on the edge. Could the assistant be lashing out at the other authors? That didn't make all that much sense either. Was she trying to frame Windsor? And Tiffany didn't look tall or strong enough to drag Allegra up the ladder. Jules sighed. Lots of bits of information and no a-ha moments. She needed to find out who had a flowing cape.

Capes, daggers, knitting needles, poison rings, and cairns. This sounded too much like a romance novel without the fairy tale ending.

Chapter Twenty-Six

Friday

After staring at her bedroom ceiling for what felt like hours, Jules got up, made some tea, and settled in at her kitchen table. She pored over her diagram of all the players and the connections until her eyes burned. Today and tomorrow were the last hurrah for the festival, and that would make it that much harder for the sheriff to solve the attacks when everyone left Fern Valley. It would also be her only chance to have all the players at the resort.

Opening a new file, Jules made a list of all the happenings that might be related to Cinnamon's murder and Allegra's attack. Then, she reordered them according to the timeline.

"Okay, besides the murder and attack, we have Windsor's stolen items, the knitting needle, the tatting shuttle, and the dagger. I need caffeine, Bijou," she said to the dog, who was snoring under the table.

Jules added the list to her diagram on the craft paper. "Okay, now here are some motives. Phoenix and Gigi feel marginalized and resentful, and Tiffany is not thrilled with her job and the way she's been treated. Then there's the list of rumors that Phoenix cheats her clients, Cinnamon supposedly stole someone's idea, Gigi and Echo are always disagreeable, Allegra had an affair, and Windsor collects vintage poisons and deadly doodads." Jules let out a long puff of air and rested her head on her crossed arms. That sounded like plenty of reasons for unhappiness, but were there any that would spawn two attacks and a murder?

"What is the connection between the murder and the attack? Think, girl. It's got to be right here. There are pieces missing from this puzzle." Jules stared harder at the diagram, hoping for a clue.

When nothing jumped out, she padded down the hall for a hot shower.

Bijou pushed the bathroom door open and toddled in when Jules finished drying her hair. "Hey, puppy. I had an idea. I always do my best thinking in the shower or while driving. What if I really push today and tomorrow. Maybe, I can make the killer uncomfortable enough to reveal something. It's worth a try. I bet he or she is sitting back, thinking about slipping away without getting caught. It's a matter of time until he or she returns home and gets on with a normal life. It's time to see what shakes loose. You in?"

Bijou turned her head and sat on the fluffy bathmat.

"Okay, hear me out. I'm thinking the attacker is one person. And I think it's a she. One, since all the authors are female, and the majority of the fans are. Also, I think it's someone the authors know enough to either talk with or let in their room. At both attack sites, there was no sign of someone dragging a body to where we found them. I think the killer approached both Cinnamon and Allegra, and they walked to the barn and the tree house with them, willingly or not. Allegra is petite, but someone would still need to be strong enough to heft her up a ladder and onto that platform."

Bored with the conversation so far, Bijou lay down and closed her eyes.

"The attacker hit both women in the back of the head with something heavy. Probably a rock. That could do some damage. Maybe the sheriff's team can get some DNA from it. I'm not sure of the significance of the knitting needle. Did I miss some inside joke? And what was the pile of rocks supposed to symbolize? Why leave a trail marker under one of my campers?" Jules pulled her hair into a high ponytail and headed back to the dining room.

Searches for knitting and knitting needles turned up thousands of posts and videos on the craft and tools. Switching tactics, she Googled each author's name with knitting. "Now, that's better," she said out loud.

Cinnamon had a knitting theme in her early western series. She did posts on techniques and early American crafts. Allegra had a crafting series early in her career, and Echo had a series with a similar theme that she had self-published. Jules opened her browser and perused sites of authors' book covers. She let out a slight gasp when she spotted an old one of Phoenix's with a cairn as the focus. Saving a copy, she dashed off a quick email to the sheriff.

"Okay, at least that's a start for today. I found some themes and piles of rocks. But who had the most to gain from the murder and attempted murder?"

She checked her phone for the festival's schedule. Writing panels and workshops with the authors were at the high school until four, followed by tonight's costume party. Jules packed her things for work and pulled a yogurt from the fridge. Her rustling in the kitchen brought Bijou scampering for any chance at a snack.

"Come on, kiddo. Let's go check on the office and get this day started."

Jules barely had time to shut the cabin's front door before Bijou pulled on her leash to explore. She sniffed around the dormant flower beds around the perimeter of Jules's cabin.

Jules's phone alerted and distracted her from Bijou's dillydallying. The little dog was on a sniff mission and was in no hurry to go back inside.

Jake texted, **It's supposed to be sunny today. Working on the tree house. Should have the lower room and deck done today. Wanna do dinner?**

Jules tapped a quick reply into her phone. **Sounds like fun. How about dinner in town and then we can pop into the author party and snoop?**

If there's pizza first. He followed his text with a string of smiley and pizza emojis.

Deal. Let me know when you're ready, she typed into her phone.

I should be ready by 5, he replied.

"Come on, Bijou. We can't stay outside all day. It's chilly out here." Bijou looked at her like they really could and then reluctantly trotted toward the office.

After checking the resort's overnight messages and scheduling some posts for Instagram, Jules searched in her bag for her notes on the attack. Thoughts of murder swirled around in her head. *Something is tickling the back of my brain, but I can't quite put my finger on it.*

The bells on the front door jarred her from her thoughts.

"Good morning," Windsor said faintly as she stepped through the front door.

"Hello. May I help you?" Jules asked, closing the Dutch door behind her.

"Uh, I'm not sure what to do. I was hoping you could help me." The author stepped up to the counter and clutched the edge with both hands.

Stepping behind the counter, Jules paused and waited for the woman to continued.

"The police came back this morning, and they took my assistant Tiffany away. I don't know where they took her or what to do." She looked around over her shoulder and then rummaged through her purse when a shrill alert emanated from somewhere in the deep bag.

"Do you know if she was arrested?" Jules asked.

Ignoring her phone's ring, Windsor said, "I'm not sure. A tall deputy arrived this morning and left with her. She wasn't in handcuffs. But she looked terrified. I have no idea what to do or who to call."

"Maybe they had more questions for her." Jules pulled her phone out of her back pocket and tapped in a quick message to the sheriff. "She would be at the sheriff's office in town. I sent him a text to see if I can find out anything for you."

"Thank you," the author almost whispered. "I have to get after her all the time about not paying attention and losing her focus, but she's a criminal."

"Can I get you something while we wait to see if I get a response from the sheriff?" Jules asked.

"No. I don't need anything except to know what Tiffany has gotten herself involved with. I hope it's not serious. I have a list of things I need her to do this afternoon. This will throw a wrench in my day. And I trusted her. I can't have a betrayal."

Jules's phone alerted, and she swiped the screen.

Tell her that Tiffany will be back soon. We needed to ask her some

questions, Sheriff Hobbs texted.

She'll be relieved. Thanks, Jules tapped into her phone.

"The sheriff said that she's being questioned. The deputy will bring her back here soon."

A wave of relief swept over Windsor's face. "Oh that's wonderful. Tell him to bring her back as soon as possible. We have to be at the events by ten-thirty. And I don't want to have to drive myself. And if I do, she won't have a way to get to the event. Tell them that if it's after ten, then take her directly to the school. She has work to do. What an inconvenience." She turned and slipped out the door.

"I'll pass that along," Jules said to the shut door. She tapped a quick message to the sheriff about Windsor's concerns and then to one to Roxanne. **Sheriff took Tiffany in for questioning. See what you can find out. I got no details.**

Her aunt responded quickly with **I'm on it.**

Before she could return to her desk, her phone alerted again from the sheriff. **She better drive herself to the school. It'll take as long as it takes**.

Jules grinned and headed back to her desk.

"Okay, Bijou. It's now or never. I plan to crash the workshops and see if I can poke the bear a little. I'll drop you off at the cabin so you can guard the home front." The small dog raised one eyebrow and scampered to the door.

After getting Bijou settled and answering a string of resort calls, Jules cruised into the school's overflow parking lot. Slipping out of her coat, she locked the Jeep and trekked to the main entrance.

"Jules, what are you doing here this morning? You want to learn how to write a romance novel?" Elaine asked from behind the registration table.

"I thought I'd pop by and see if you all needed any help. From the parking lot, you've got another wonderful turnout."

"Yep. We even had a couple of walk-in registrations. Lots of wanna-be writers out there. Oh wait, Allegra calls them pre-published authors. Anyway, here's a program. The three panels are in the auditorium. I think they might be near the end of the first one by now. After the second panel, it's boxed lunches and hands-on workshops in the afternoon." Elaine glanced down at her watch. "A jam-packed day. Darlene and her team will be here after lunch to decorate the library and the cafeteria for tonight's festivities. Are you and Jake coming as your favorite book characters?"

"We plan to swing by. I don't think we'll be in costume," Jules said.

"Aww. That's half the fun. You and Jake should come up with a literary pair. You know, like F. Scott and Zelda, Nick and Nora. Wait a minute, are you investigating tonight? I knew you would be the one to figure out what happened to Cinnamon and Allegra. Fern Valley's own Nancy Drew," Elaine said, lowering her voice. "Nancy and Ned would be fun costumes for you all, too."

A wry smile crossed Jules's face. "I wouldn't call it investigating. I'm looking for information on the things that keep happening at my place. We can't let what's happened undo all the hard work the business council has put in."

Elaine waved. "Either way, it'll be fun. Don't tell anyone. I'm coming as Lady Macbeth."

Eleventh-grade English class flashed through Jules's head. "Sounds interesting." She neglected to point out the murder angle in Elaine's costume choice. "I want to check out the panels."

"The audience seems to be having fun. The authors who are not on stage are in the green room getting ready. There are snacks in there if you get hungry or need coffee," Elaine said.

"Thanks. Any hiccups this morning?"

"Nope. Everyone has been on her best behavior. Well, except Gigi. She's always got something to complain about. I've never seen someone that miserable. She's like a little black raincloud wherever she goes. I wish we had known that before we invited her." Elaine squeezed her lips together and made a face like she had licked a lemon. "I'm keeping a list of who not to invite in case we do this again."

Uh-oh. Someone made Elaine's naughty list. Jules cracked a smile.

"And I am so ready for us to work on our spring slate of activities. I love the warmer weather, all the blooms, and the birds and butterflies. There are so many possibilities for outdoor events. Put your thinking cap on. We've got to raise the roof," Elaine said, waving her arms toward the ceiling.

Jules entered the auditorium from the back and walked down the sloping aisle to a spot near the stage. Finding a place where she could lean against the wall, she focused on the audience as Elizabeth asked Windsor and Allegra questions about querying agents.

Not hearing anything new or spotting anything out of place, Jules slipped out the side door to the green room, where tables overflowed with baskets of snacks and ice buckets full of drinks. Echo chatted on the phone at a table in the corner while Gigi and Phoenix sipped drinks near the window.

"Morning, ladies," Jules said, easing between Gigi's table and the snacks to get a cup of coffee. "Who's up next? There's a healthy-sized crowd in there for Windsor and Allegra."

A dark look crossed Gigi's face, but she recovered and said, "I'm next with Phoenix on a panel about hybrid authors and their platforms. My focus will be on social media, newsletters, and email lists. Thankfully, I don't have that much experience with self-publishing. My team at my publisher does most of the marketing and heavy lifting for me. I am so fortunate to have such wonderful people who work so hard for me." She looked down at her sleeve and dusted some imaginary spot on her arm.

Phoenix, who looked like she was about to snap back, paused and stared daggers at her panel companion.

Echo set her phone on the table and said, "Don't be so cocky, Gigi. It's only a matter of time before you get dropped or you have to re-release an earlier series to keep it from going out of print. There's nothing wrong with taking control of your own work. Most authors have something in their catalog that is indie-published these days. So get off your high horse."

Gigi cut her eyes at Echo. "I guess I'm lucky. I don't have that problem. And, unfortunately, I'm not as old as some of you who have been around the block a time or two with multiple series and tragic stories of demon editors and publishers. I have a reputable publishing contract and a great editor. I count my lucky stars every day." Gigi rummaged under the table and avoided making eye contact with the others.

"Speak for yourself," Phoenix added. "I'm way younger than both of you. And the indie life works better for my generation, which doesn't want to let someone else control the creative process or the money. Plus, who has the time or the energy to wait years for a book to be published? There is something to say for being able to call all of the shots and put out your work when you want to."

"Keep telling yourself that. It also means you have to work ten times harder than the rest of us." Gigi glared at Phoenix, and then she ducked under the table again to continue her search.

Phoenix looked surprised, but she didn't respond. Echo stifled a sharp retort and returned to her phone.

"Where is my purse? Did you see anyone take it? I swear. This place is full of murderers and thieves," Gigi said, bumping her head on the tabletop. "Ouch."

"Are you talking about that ugly old bag?" Phoenix asked, pointing to something on the floor next to an empty chair. "It's so dated. It's not even cool retro. It looks like something my grandmother would carry to church. Do you have crumpled-up tissues and mints in the bottom covered with purse dust?" Echo let out a cackle and continued her call.

Gigi made a harrumphing noise and sneered at Phoenix. She snatched the purse and stomped across the room. She wobbled a bit and supported herself by grabbing the door jamb.

That will be an interesting panel. I hope Elizabeth can keep them focused and on topic, if not, it could easily turn into a shouting match or smack-down.

Echo gathered her things as the door flew open, and Darlene Denunzio popped her head in and scanned the room. "Phoenix, Gigi, y'all ready? We need to head backstage. Where's Gigi?"

"She stepped out in a huff," Phoenix said. "She's probably out back smoking or drowning her sorrows with whatever is in that flask. Or maybe she's taking her happy pills. She didn't look all that steady on her feet when she stormed out. You might want to keep an eye on her."

A moment of panic crossed Darlene's face. "Oh, I need to go see if I can find her and make sure she's okay. Phoenix, can you head backstage? We'll be there in a sec."

"Not a problem. I can handle it if she chickens out or is incapacitated." Phoenix fluffed her Raggedy Ann-colored hair and flounced out the door with a grin that looked like the cat who ate the canary.

"That should be a hoot. I'm glad I don't have to deal with all that drama. Some people are so unprofessional. I'm glad they put me on panels with serious writers," Echo muttered.

"You've been in the business a while to know the ropes and how to navigate the system," Jules said. "I saw that you have over eight different series."

"Yep. I've done my time and put in the work. Not like some of these who think they should jump to the head of the line." She looked at her mostly manicured nails, several were broken. When she noticed Jules watching, she balled her hands into fists. "I've also been around enough to know the scams and the cheats. These greenhorns are easy pickin's, and they don't have the hutzpah to do what it takes to be successful. If you'll excuse me, I need to check in with my assistant. Gotta get my schedule organized for the next set of festivals. I must keep the book events and the work rolling along. Today, one must constantly be marketing. Out of sight, out of mind is a death knell for authors."

"I hope you have a great panel." Jules waved as she headed for the hallway. Echo followed a few steps behind her. Jules turned as Echo flipped her bag's strap over her shoulder and disappeared down a back hall.

Gigi, Tiffany, and Phoenix all have axes to grind. But Tiffany doesn't seem big enough to haul Allegra up to the second level of the tree house. *I need to figure out a way to get these authors to spill what they know.*

Darlene whizzed by in the hall and stopped in the doorway. "You haven't seen Gigi, have you?"

"No, not since she stepped out."

"I've checked the bathroom and down this hallway, and no sign of her."

"I'll help you look. Maybe she walked around the back of the school for some air," Jules said.

"Thanks, you're a doll. One more lap, and then I'll have to let Elaine know I lost one of her authors. That won't go over well." The taller woman hustled toward the backstage doors.

Jules stepped outside, wishing she hadn't left her coat in the car. Pulling her cardigan closer around her, she hurried to the left, near the maintenance area and the tennis courts.

"Gigi, Gigi," Jules called. *Where did she go? She knew she was up next. Was she so upset that she'd miss her panel? I hope she's not sick.*

Jules picked up the pace and hustled toward the metal tanks near the school's maintenance office. "Gigi, Gigi," she yelled louder.

Chapter Twenty-Seven

Friday

Jules heard a noise that sounded like a groan. She paused. Nothing but the wind. Then she heard it again. A moan and then another. Jogging toward what looked like a rusty oil tank, she looked around for the source of the noise.

"Help, I fell," she heard faintly from behind the tank. "Help."

"Where are you?" Jules yelled. "Gigi! Gigi!"

The woman let out a string of profanities. "I'm over here. I broke the heel of my shoe, and I can't find my purse. I have to go on stage, and now I'm a hot mess."

Jules poked her head behind the tank to find Gigi sprawled out, with her skirt hiked up over one knee and her stockings torn. The contents of her purse lay scattered on the cracked cement behind her.

"What happened to you? Are you okay?" Jules asked, rushing over to the author.

"I'm fine. Nothing that some makeup and a stiff drink can't fix," the woman slurred.

"How did you get back here?" Jules asked, looking at the metal drums, pallets, and stacked crates.

"That stupid door wouldn't open. It locked me out. I banged on it and screamed, and no one came to let me in. And now my head and throat hurt." Gigi pushed up to a semi-seated position, leaning on one elbow. "And then I had a brilliant idea. I saw that cracked window up there," she said, pointing a finger with a broken nail at a spot over the tank. I thought I could crawl up there, but I must have fallen. Dern. I broke the heel of my shoe. And they were so expensive," she wailed. "This is not my day. Life is so unfair. Crap like this always happens to me. Oh, there's my purse. I need to hurry and get back inside."

"What are you doing out here? The door to the auditorium is way over there?" Jules asked.

"I dunno," she slurred again. Her head bobbled. Jules was afraid she was about to pass out.

"Here, stay still. I'll call an ambulance. You're bleeding, and your eyes are dilated. I think you need to be still for a little while. Your arms and knees are all skinned. Sit still for a minute."

"I'm jussssssh fine," she said, trying to rise. She swayed and plopped back down on the cement.

"Stay put. I'll get some help," Jules said.

"My head hurts, and I think I'm about to throw up." The author swayed from the waist like she had an invisible hula hoop. Then she slid down prone on the cement.

"No, no. Sit up for me. Don't fall asleep. I need to get someone here to check you out. Did you hit your head when you fell?" Jules tried to prop the woman up with one arm and dial 9-1-1 with the other.

"I don't think so, but I don't feel so great. Hurry up and get me something to drink. Maybe it's nerves." Gigi's voice faded by the end of her sentence. "Cheese and crackers! I'm not sure I can go on stage like this. I am a total mess. And my hands and knees are bleeding," she said, looking at her skirt and stockings. "That chubby woman will yell at me for messing up her program. She needs to get over herself. I don't think she knows how famous I am. Shhhh. Don't tell anyone." Gigi held up one finger to her lips and made a shushing sound.

When the call to the emergency dispatcher connected, Jules said, "Hi, this is Jules Keene. I'm out behind the high school near the maintenance office with one of the authors from today's program. She's fallen and hurt herself, and…"

"I have not. I am perfectly fine," Gigi bellowed, waving her arms around again.

"What was that?" the dispatcher asked.

"I think she's taken something. The author, Gigi Jones, is not coherent, and she hurt herself. She seems to have fallen. I don't know if she hit her head or not. Her eyes don't look normal, and she's not making a lot of sense."

"I said I'm perfectly fine," Gigi yelled. "Never felt better. Quit saying things about me or telling whoever you've been talking to about my business."

"And you're outside at the high school?" the dispatcher asked.

"Yes, in the maintenance area. There's a patio with tanks and pallets. It's over near the tennis courts." Jules tried to push Gigi back to a seated position with her free hand when the author tried to stand up.

"She's awake?" the dispatcher asked.

"She's awake and talking, but she's slurring her speech and not steady on her feet. She complains of a headache and nausea."

"Keep her talking. The ambulance is on its way. You should see them any minute now."

Jules paused. "I think I hear them."

Moments later, the ambulance driver slammed on the brakes and parked on the asphalt. Two EMTs rushed over and surrounded Gigi. Jules repeated what she knew and stepped out of the way.

Time seemed to stretch out and then drag on. At least Gigi was awake and talking to the emergency responders. Actually, she found a second wind and hadn't stopped talking since they arrived.

Pulling out her phone, Jules typed a quick text to Elaine, Elizabeth, and Darlene that she had found Gigi out near the maintenance area.

Thank goodness, Elaine fired back. **Be there in a sec.**

Then she typed one to the sheriff and erased it. She spent some time rewording her note, so it didn't sound hysterical. **Had to call the ambulance for Gigi Jones. She fell at the HS. Something isn't right.** Jules pressed send as the medics checked Gigi's vitals. Something tickled the back of Jules's memory, but she couldn't quite put her finger on it with all the distractions around her.

Before she could pinpoint what was bothering her about Gigi, Sheriff Hobbs replied, **Be there in a minute. Where are you?**

Out back near the tennis courts. The ambulance is still here.

The little bubble appeared that he was typing. Seconds dragged on until, **Stay put. I'm on my way**, popped up on her screen.

"What happened?" a breathless Elaine sputtered as she toddled over.

"I'm not quite sure. Darlene couldn't find Gigi, and someone said that she had gone outside. I walked around until I heard a noise and found her sprawled out behind that tank. She said she was looking for a way back in. She had fallen, trying to climb up to that open window. And she wasn't all that coherent. The sheriff's on his way over."

Elaine's eyes widened. "What possessed her to climb way up there? She could have walked around to the open door over there. What else is going to happen around here? I'm running out of authors to be substitutes. Thank goodness, the festival ends tomorrow." Peeking around Jules to see what was happening, she whispered, "Is she okay?"

"She's awake and talking. A lot. But it's more like babbling."

"I hope she wasn't attacked," Elaine said. "That's not something we need right now."

Before Jules could comment, Gigi's arms flailed, and she yelled, "I'm fine. Stop asking me all these stupid questions. I jussssth had a little accident. I'll be fine."

"Ma'am, you need to calm down. We need to transport you to the hospital for further tests," one of the EMTs said.

"I am calm. You'd be put out, too, if two guys were keeping you from your fans. I need to get inside. That chubby woman over there is already mad at me. She's soooo cranky."

Elaine's face flushed slightly, but she ignored Gigi's outburst. "What is wrong with her?"

Before Jules could reply, Gigi tried to stand up again, swaying like a tree in a hurricane.

"Ma'am, please sit down and stay still. You've sustained some injuries, and you may have a concussion," the EMT said.

"Thazzz ridiculous," Gigi yelled. "Just help me up, so I can do my presentation. My fannzz are waiting."

"Ma'am, we need to transport you to the hospital. Don't worry about your presentation. You can take care of that later when you're feeling better," the dark-haired EMT said.

"Now that you mention it, I am a little light-headed. You're cute. Okay, I'll go with you. But not her." Gigi pointed to Elaine. "She needs to stay here and boss everyone around. I'll go with these two cute doctors."

The other EMT rolled a gurney toward her. After getting Gigi strapped in and inside the ambulance, a car door slammed. All heads turned to watch Sheriff Hobbs approach. Nodding at Jules and Elaine, he spoke briefly to the ambulance driver.

"Morning, ladies. It sounds like you had more excitement than you bargained for," the sheriff said as the ambulance headed for the main road.

"You can say that again." Elaine wrung her hands. "This whole festival has been one thing after another. Luckily, Phoenix Abbott can do the panel herself. The audience has no clue that all this even happened."

"What did happen?" Sheriff Hobbs asked, pulling a small notebook from his shirt pocket.

"Jules, where is your coat?" Elaine exclaimed.

"I didn't plan to be outside for so long." She rubbed her arms. "I stepped out to see if I could help Darlene find Gigi."

"Let's take this inside. We can talk as well in there, and I'm sure the sheriff will want to investigate who was with Gigi before her adventure outside."

The trio retraced Jules's steps to the exit near the auditorium. Finding the band room empty, they ducked inside, and Jules repeated her story. Elaine chimed in periodically with random comments.

"Who was with her before she went outside?" Sheriff Hobbs asked.

"Phoenix, Echo, and me. In the green room," Jules replied. "They were kinda sniping at each other as Phoenix and Gigi had coffee. Later, I helped Darlene look around the building when she couldn't find Gigi. Somebody said that she stepped outside, so I walked around by the tennis courts."

"Anything else?" he asked.

Jules shook her head.

"I was busy with the program. Jules had front-row seats for the Gigi show," Elaine added.

"If you all think of anything else, let me know." The sheriff strode into the hallway.

"I need to check on things. Why don't you get some coffee? I know you're frozen." Elaine led the way to the green room.

Echo sat alone at a table, tapping away on a laptop. The author looked up as Jules entered. Then, her expression darkened slightly when the sheriff filled the door frame.

Jules moved toward the coffee carafe as Elaine stepped out into the hall, where she could still hear the conversation.

"Good morning, Ms...." Sheriff Hobbs said.

"It's Tammy James, but I write under Echo Aames."

"Thank you, Ms. Aames. Could you tell me about your encounter with Gigi Jones this morning?"

The author paused. "Every conversation with her turns into a shouting match or an ambush. She was rude today, but she's always brusque. Why, what happened?"

Ignoring her, he continued with his questions. "Did she complain about being ill or eat or drink while she was with you?"

Echo pursed her lips. "I have no idea. What she says or does is little consequence to me. I was hardly paying attention when she was in here yammering. I have a deadline that is taking up most of my time. Now that I think about it. She did have something to drink. It might have been bottled water or coffee. I can't remember."

Jules set her mug down on the counter.

"How would you describe Ms. Jones's behavior?" he continued.

"Annoying. Like one of those mosquitos that buzzes around your ear. She is always talking. If she's not bragging about something, she's complaining. Truthfully, I tune her out whenever she's around. She's argumentative if you try to have an adult conversation with her." She looked around the room, and her gaze landed on Elaine, who stood in the doorway. "She may have had a pastry too while she was in here. She was blabbering on about being jumpy and nervous."

"Nervous about what?" he asked.

"I dunno. I guess about speaking in front of a group. She seems to be the anxious sort. She chatters incessantly and paces. She was wound up about something. Oh, wait. She and Phoenix had words earlier about her purse being missing," Echo said.

"What was wrong with her purse?"

"Nothing. She couldn't find it, and she accused someone here of taking it. It was over on the couch. I tuned both of them out when it didn't affect me," the author said.

"Did you see her take anything like medicine?" he asked.

Echo shrugged. "Like I said. I wasn't paying that much attention. I have no idea what got her into such a tizzy this morning. Authors do talks like this all the time. Not sure what would cause her to be so jittery."

The sheriff jotted something in his notebook and walked over to the snack table. He glanced in the trash can.

"Thank you for your time," he said to Echo. "Please let me know if you think of anything else." He dropped a business card on the end of the table close to her.

"Gigi and Allegra had a spat earlier, but she seemed to have an argument with just about everyone. I heard Gigi fussing at the woman at the registration table, too. Sorry that I'm not all that helpful." Echo shrugged again and focused her attention on her messenger bag.

Sheriff Hobbs nodded and walked past Jules. Elaine rushed to his side and launched into a conversation that faded like their footsteps down the hall.

Echo never looked up, so Jules scanned through her own emails.

Darlene Denunzio popped her head in the doorway. "About ready, Ms. Aames. It's almost time for your presentation."

The author slipped her phone into her bag. "Thank you. Is there water on the table in there or do I need to take one?"

"It's all set for you. May I carry anything for you?" Darlene asked.

"I'm fine. I'll take everything with me since this door is left unlocked." Echo bustled out behind Darlene, leaving Jules alone with her thoughts.

Echo never asked what happened to Gigi or why the sheriff was there asking questions.

Chapter Twenty-Eight

Friday

Jules, lost in thought about Echo's nonchalant attitude, didn't hear Tiffany slip in the green room.

"Good morning," the personal assistant said, heading to the coffee station. Her voice echoed through the empty room and made Jules jump.

"How are things going?" Jules turned toward the younger woman.

"Oh, fine. I'm getting Windsor's java juice ready. She's particular about her coffee. We've got lunch and then several workshops this afternoon. It's nice to see a big crowd today." Tiffany hummed to herself as she poured her coffee.

"Have you seen Gigi?" Jules asked.

"I don't think so. I stay busy keeping Windsor on schedule. She's still annoyed that I got a late start today. I don't have much free time to chat with the other authors."

Jules placed a hand on the assistant's arm, and Tiffany recoiled.

"Sorry," Jules said. "I wanted to ask you about this morning. Are you okay?"

"I'm fine," Tiffany said, stirring the coffee with a little more energy than necessary."

"Windsor came by the office. She was worried about you," Jules said.

A puzzled look crossed Tiffany's face for a moment as she continued to stir a tempest in the coffee cup. "She was probably wondering who would do all the work and chauffer her around while I was tied up at the police station. When I got here, I never heard the end of her complaints about having to drive herself all the way from the trailer to the school. It's what a ten-minute drive at most. Sheesh."

"Everything went okay with the police?" Jules asked.

"Of course. Why wouldn't it? They wanted to ask me some questions and show me some pictures. I didn't do anything wrong."

"Pictures?"

"Yes. Of someone in a cloak and of some random junk like rocks, clothing, knitting needles, and a dagger. The dagger was the only thing I could identify. The knitting needle was fancy, but it wasn't Windsor's. It didn't seem like I was all that helpful. It was probably a waste of time, but actually, it was a nice break for me. And I got to talk to those cute deputies again."

Tiffany's cheeks colored slightly, and she snapped the lid on the to-go mug. She tossed the wooden stir stick in the trash. "Ciao. Gotta get a move on. You-know-who is waiting for me with a list as long as her arm of things for me to do for her."

Seconds after Tiffany disappeared down the hall, Phoenix breezed in. "I'm glad that's over. That was intense," Phoenix plopped down in a nearby plastic chair. "But there were lots of good questions and high energy. I hope that translates into book sales." The author pulled out her phone and scrolled through a series of pages.

After a long pause that made Jules fidget, Phoenix broke the silence with, "Any idea what happened to Gigi? She was supposed to have been my partner in crime this morning. Elaine burst in backstage like two seconds before the session and said that she was incapacitated and that I would have to be the star of the show." The millennial yawned and glanced at her phone again.

"She fell outside," Jules said. "The ambulance took her to the hospital to look at her injuries."

Phoenix's mouth formed a small "o," and her eyes widened. "I had no idea. I thought she had left or something. She wasn't too keen on doing a panel with me. I figured she got cheesed off at something and hightailed it out of here."

"How did you know how she felt about the panel?" Jules asked.

"She told me and everyone standing in the hall yesterday." A nervous laugh escaped her mouth. "Don't worry about it. It happens all the time." Phoenix waved her hand and stuck out her tongue. "I'm used to it. There are some book snobs that are always trying to put down others to make themselves feel better. She's not exactly the bomb herself. I'm not too worried about it."

"I'm sorry," Jules said. "Not everyone feels that way."

"I know that. I'm tired of being on the outside looking in all the time. Some of them in the big girls' club aren't as willing to reach out and help newbies. Enough about her. I did fine without her, and I'm hoping the audience didn't miss her. If you'll excuse me. I need to freshen up before lunch and the next round."

Phoenix exited as quickly as she arrived, leaving Jules alone with her thoughts. *The sheriff isn't at a loss for suspects with this bunch. I hope he has better luck than I have. I keep waffling on my suspect list.*

Jules let out a long puff of air and tried not to feel so defeated. Was Gigi's incident related to the others or self-inflicted? *No one but Gigi seemed to be affected.* Too many facts. *I need a way to piece them all together.*

Jules wandered down the hall and waved to Darlene and Kim, who were staffing the table outside of the cafeteria.

"Hey, Jules," Kim said. "Are you staying for lunch?"

"Sounds like fun, but I have to check on things at the resort," Jules said.

"I hope you're coming back for tonight's shindig," Darlene said.

"Jake and I are looking forward to it."

"Can't wait to see your costumes," Darlene said as Jules hurried out to her car. The costumes were the last thing on her mind right now. Mustering her courage as soon as the Jeep's heater warmed up, she clicked the sheriff's contact and waited for the phone to connect.

"Hey, Jules. What's up?"

"Good morning. I was checking on Gigi. Any word on her condition? I was wondering if it's more than an accident."

"Nothing new yet. They're running some tests. We'll see what comes back. They said she didn't have a concussion. I'm waiting for the tox screens to decide the next steps."

"She was slurring and stumbling. Something was going on with her."

"And she had no idea if she had taken anything. Maybe her memory will improve after she gets some fluids in her," he said.

"I didn't see her take anything while we were in the green room. But I wasn't watching her every second. She was drinking out of a coffee cup."

"We'll see what she remembers when she sobers up. There was nothing in her purse that gave us a clue to what she'd ingested. You still at the school?"

"I'm heading out for the resort. Jake and I will be back tonight for the party," Jules said.

"Rox tried to talk me into that, but it looks like she'll have to go stag. I'm gonna be tied up here for a while. Hey, I gotta take this call."

"Bye," she said to a silent phone. *I wonder what Roxanne's plans were for their costumes.*

Lost in thought, Jules drove on autopilot to the resort and parked in her driveway. She slipped on her coat and jogged to the office to pick up the resort's key to the Barbie trailer and a housekeeping caddy. Without letting the reasonable side of her brain talk her out of snooping, she hustled to the campers. No one in sight.

Banging on the door to Gigi's camper, she yelled, "Housekeeping," and paused. After two knocks to reassure herself that she'd announced herself, Jules paused to put on a pair of gloves and then insert the key. She pulled on the aluminum door and stepped into the dark trailer.

In the back bedroom, clothes covered the unmade bed, and a half-empty suitcase sat open in the tiny guest chair. Other than the explosion of clothes, nothing else looked out of place. Jules spent several minutes poking around the suitcase and the bathroom. Her search turned up a half-full bottle of vodka. No pills or prescriptions. Not finding anything in the kitchen or den that looked like a clue, she paused to brush a stray curl off her forehead.

Trying to calm the jitters, Jules retraced her steps and locked the door. She backed down the steps and squealed when someone put a hand on her shoulder.

"Be careful and don't slip," Lester said.

CHAPTER TWENTY-EIGHT

"Hey, Lester. You startled me."

"Just trying to help. You looked like you were teetering there on that step."

"Thanks," she waved as she willed her heart rate to return to normal.

"Gotta get back to the weeding around the trailers. I'm trying to get it done before your guests come back. Don't want to bother anyone with the leaf blower or the whacker."

"You take good care of us." She waved again.

Nothing suspicious in Gigi's trailer. So, either she was drugged by someone else, or she was nipping her vodka ahead of today's presentation. Could this be another coincidence, unrelated to Cinnamon and Allegra? Or did the mysterious attacker strike again? Spiking a drink is different than bashing someone in the head. Did the killer change things up?

Chapter Twenty-Nine

Friday Evening

"Thanks for going with me to the thing tonight," Jules said as Jake shut the driver's door of his red Mustang. You still feel like pizza? If so, Pop's or Pie in the Sky?"

"I'm always up for pizza. I haven't been to Pie in the Sky in a while. What time do we have to be at the school?"

"Seven," she replied.

"We have plenty of time." He floored the accelerator, and the Mustang roared down the maintenance road. They made it to the outskirts of Fern Valley before Jules got comfortable in the passenger seat.

Jake slowed down long enough to signal and turn into the small strip mall, home to the pizza joint, an art supply store, and a gallery. "Here we are. Lickety-split."

Jake held the glass door to the restaurant for her, and the pair looked around for a hostess. About half of the fifteen booths and counter seating were occupied. Not spotting anyone in charge of seating, they claimed a booth by the wall.

A waitress with teal hair and several facial piercings swooped in with menus. "Good evening. Do y'all know what you want, or do you need a minute to figure it out?"

"Do you want to share a big pizza, or do you want your own personal one?" Jules asked.

Before he could answer, the waitress added, "We have a Friday night special with two personal pizzas with unlimited toppings, two salads, breadsticks, and two drinks for twenty-five bucks."

"That sounds good," Jake said.

"I'll have cheese and sausage on mine with an unsweetened iced tea," Jules said.

"What dressing on your salad?"

"Italian."

After Jake had ordered a pizza with all but six of the toppings on the list, the waitress headed for the kitchen.

"I'm impressed," Jules said as he leaned forward and took both of her hands. "You'll need a fork for that one. That's a ten-pound mini-pizza."

"Hey, she had me at unlimited toppings," he said with a smile. "What's captured your attention today?"

"I went over to the high school to see if I could ferret out any information. This investigation is not as easy as some of the earlier ones. I'm hitting a brick wall. The only excitement today was one of the authors was under the influence of something, and she fell when she was trying to get back into the school through an open window."

"The doors didn't work?"

"She locked herself out, and I guess in her state, she thought the open window was her best bet. They ended up taking her to the hospital. She fell and was a royal mess when I found her. The sheriff is waiting for her tox screens to come back. This incident didn't seem like the other two attacks. With all this weirdness around here, it's hard to tell what's related and what's not."

"So that's why you wanted to go tonight. To poke around for clues." Jake cocked one eyebrow.

"That obvious?" she said.

His mischievous grin reminded her of the teenaged Jake. "I know you. You'll use every opportunity that you can find."

"Keep your eyes and ears open. Since they're not all that many guys there, you may have an advantage chatting up the attendees."

"I'll turn on the charm. I can be irresistible," he said with a wink.

She smiled and changed the subject. "I know. And speaking of your talent, how's the tree house coming?"

"I finished the platform. The master bedroom and a sitting room will be on the elevated part. That's next on the construction schedule. Then I'll finish the modules that are at ground level and build a wrap-around deck for a three-sixty view of the mountains."

"I can't wait to see it. It will be hard to share this one. It would be the perfect getaway or office. I still haven't come up with a theme for it. Hmmm. Literary tree houses—"

"I know you'll find the right one," he said.

Jules picked up her phone and searched for images on Google. "Can it have a red door?"

"Sure. Why not?" a puzzled look crossed his face.

She handed him her phone. "I was thinking of an A. A. Milne theme. Winnie Pooh and the gang had a tree house. Milne also wrote *The Red House Mystery*. I can do something with that."

"Perfect. Sounds like a theme." Jake said as the server dropped off their dinners.

"Let me know if you need anything else," she said before she returned to the kitchen.

Jules watched Jake attack his top-heavy pizza. After a couple of spills, he reached for his fork and dug in. The conversation paused as they enjoyed their dinner.

"Tonight's the costume party and mixer. I hope everyone has fun and it gives us a chance to mingle."

"You mean snoop," he said with a wink.

"That too. Not sure what we'll encounter tonight. A lot of odd stuff has been going on. Gigi and Phoenix are always complaining. Gigi was the one who they took to the hospital earlier today. She probably won't be at the event. Allegra was the one we found at the tree house. Echo and Windsor seem to be the even-keeled ones as far as this bunch of authors goes. But Windsor does have that collection of deadly antiques, and she's not nice to her personal assistant, Tiffany, who seems quiet, but with anger boiling below the surface."

"Sounds like a bunch of people with opportunities. I need a dance card to keep up with all the characters. I'll infiltrate and see what I can find. We'll divide and conquer," Jake said.

"Let me know if I need to rescue you from some of these wild women." Jules smiled and returned his wink.

The waitress stopped next to Jake. "Can I get you all anything else?"

"Just the check next time you're by this way," Jake said as she lay it face down on the edge of the table and slid it closer to him. She smiled coyly when he glanced her way.

Handing over his debit card, Jake continued to talk to Jules about the new build. "I think the tree house will be a popular addition once we get it in rotation. You'll have a waiting list of people who want to book it."

"I plan to do a marketing campaign around it. But you know no good deed goes unpunished. If it becomes too popular, you may have to build others."

"It's a fun project. I wouldn't mind doing another. We'll have to find the right location. I like the view that this one has."

"We've got plenty of trees on the property. That shouldn't be a problem." Jules slipped on her coat as the waitress returned with Jake's card. She picked up the discarded plates as the couple headed for the door.

The heat in the car barely warmed the interior before they pulled into the high school parking lot. Jake took Jules's hand and led the way to the cafeteria.

Elaine's team had transformed the lobby and cafeteria with balloon arches and lots of stars. It looked like prom night with the "Over the Moon" banner over the door. Guests in every kind of costume mingled in the lobby.

"Is this a Comic-Con?" Jake asked, watching as a Renaissance lady and an alien passed the pair nearby.

Jules laughed. "No, it's supposed to be favorite book characters. I figured we'd be observers. Hope you're not disappointed about not wearing costumes," Jules said with a sheepish grin.

"No worries. You and I can be library patrons. Not sure who the alien was. But it's all good."

"I was all focused on ways to get information. I didn't think much about costumes. Next time, we're coming dressed up. Couples' costumes." Jules's eyes widened at the possibilities. "Hey, I thought of something. Be on the lookout for anyone with a long, flowing cape with a hood."

Jake tapped her lightly on the arm. "Ten-four on the cape. We might see all kinds of stuff," he whispered.

"Sounds like a plan. Zero in on anything related to Cinnamon, Allegra, or Gigi. This bunch will start heading home after tomorrow's events. I'd love to be able to find something big before then. Oh, and send me a signal if you need me to come and rescue you," she said with a wink.

The pair approached the table, where Darlene and Kim handed out gift bags and name tags.

"Hey, you guys. Welcome," Kim said.

"And where are your costumes?" Darlene asked, giving the pair a quick once over.

"We're here in case you need any additional hands. And to check out the fun. The place looks nice," Jules said.

"We're dressed as library patrons," Jake said with a nod.

"Of course. Silly me. I can see that now," Darlene said. "Y'all have fun. You want a name tag?" She handed Jake and Jules "my name is" stickers and markers.

Jules printed their names on the tags and handed Jake his. He headed to the far wall near the small stage that blocked the view of the school cafeteria's food line. Jules made a beeline for Elizabeth and Elaine on the opposite side of the stage.

"No costume I see," Elaine tsked and raised one eyebrow.

Jules smiled. "Jake said we were library patrons. We stopped in to see if you all needed anything."

"I think we're fine," Elizabeth said. "Everybody seems to be having a fun time guessing who everyone is dressed as."

"And who are you? I know Elaine is Lady Macbeth," Jules said.

"I'm Margaret Marmee March from *Little Women*," the bookseller said, fingering the cameo pendant around her neck.

"You both look lovely. Great costumes. Anything I should know about?" Jules asked.

"I hope I'm not jinxing it, but everything is running as planned tonight." Elaine peered over her shoulder. "We have to get through tonight and tomorrow. We're almost at the finish line," she whispered. "Oh, there's Windsor Abernathy. I gotta run. See you later."

Elizabeth and Jules watched the owner of Birds and Bees toddle off to the head table.

"Any word on Gigi?" Jules whispered.

Elizabeth pointed her French-manicured index finger at a table near the front. A pale Gigi sat bundled in an oversized sweater with her winter coat draped over her shoulders. "She's baaaack," Elizabeth whispered. "I don't know the details, but I'm sure they're juicy. I heard she was out of her gourd this morning. Let me know what you find out." The bookseller patted Jules's shoulder and gave her a nudge toward Gigi's table.

Jules approached the woman, whose right hand rested on a metal cane. "Hi, Gigi. You're looking so much better. How are you feeling?"

"I think I'm on the road to recovery. I don't know what hit me. I felt woozy, so I stepped out for some air, and the next thing I know, they're transporting me to the hospital. Look at me; I'm covered with bumps and bruises. Thankfully, my ankle is only sprained, but my shoes and skirt were ruined. Those nice EMTs took fabulous care of me." Gigi's smile looked like a grimace. She looked past Jules and waved half-heartedly at a group of women.

The trio, dressed as fairy godmothers, rushed over to the table and edged Jules to the side. *They looked like the characters from Disney's Sleeping Beauty cartoon.*

"Gigi, I'm so glad you're here. How are you?" the tall woman in the middle cooed. "We missed you today at the workshops. It wasn't the same without you."

"So sorry to have missed it. I stepped outside and couldn't get back in. I tried and tried to find an open door. I even climbed up a wall to an open window. I must have passed out. I don't know what hit me: chills, nausea, headache…I was so woozy. I think I fell while climbing. Thankfully, two really hunky EMTs came to my rescue and pumped me full of fluids. I'm feeling much better now, but I did a number on my ankle. I hope I don't have to have surgery. Hey, be a doll. One of you get me a ginger ale. The doctor told me to stay off of my ankle until it heals. It could be weeks."

"Of course," the woman in the blue chiffon dress said. "Be right back." She waved her silver wand and scurried to the bar.

"Gigi, are you sure you feel like being here tonight? You've been through some trauma," the woman in pink said. "Maybe you should head back to your room and get some rest."

"I'm fine. I'll push through this. I can't disappoint my fans. I'm sick that I missed the workshop today. Any idea how it went without me? I hope it wasn't a disaster. And I need to sell some books to make this worthwhile." Gigi rested her hand on the side of her head.

"It was very nice. Windsor, Allegra, and some woman with bright red hair pitched in to cover for you," the woman in pink said.

Gigi looked down her pointy nose. "I'm glad they were able to step in. I hope they did justice to my talk on how to cut the waste in your manuscript and in your professional lives."

The woman in pink looked a little puzzled. Her friend in blue returned with the drink and set it in front of Gigi. "Is there anything else I can get you?"

"I'm fine, dear. Thank you. My heart is full of joy to be surrounded by so many fans. I love being in my element. Make sure you tell all your friends to get my latest book. I think you'll like it." Gigi waved both hands and smiled at the trio.

"Well, we're so glad you're back. Come on, gals. It's time to make our rounds and see all the costumes. We'll stop back by a little later to check on you," the woman in green said. "I see Allegra Rhodes over there. Let's go get some autographs. She is so amazing." The three women drifted off toward the crowd, forming around Allegra.

Gigi made a harrumphing sound and looked around to see if anyone else was approaching her table. "I should have sat over there," she said under her breath. "That chubby woman told me to sit here. She always puts me at the wrong table."

"I'm curious," Jules said, stepping closer to Gigi. "You said that feeling came on you suddenly? Do you have any idea what happened?"

"I skipped breakfast. I had two coffees, a power bar, and a Diet Coke. Maybe my stomach was upset. I don't feel ill now. But after I drank the soft drink, I felt light-headed. You know, kinda tipsy. I drank some coffee after that, but it didn't help. That's why I think I went out for some air. I don't remember much after that except everyone asking me hundreds of questions at the hospital."

"Where did the drink come from?" Jules leaned closer to the woman and lowered her voice.

"I don't know. It was something they had in the green room. Echo and I both had one."

"Was it in a glass?"

"What? I don't know. No, wait. It was in a can, and I opened it and poured it into one of those Styrofoam coffee cups." Gigi waved her hand and looked around to see if anyone was approaching her table.

"So, who was in the room with you?" Jules asked.

"Echo and Phoenix. I don't know why any of this matters. Windsor and her toady little assistant kept popping in. Why the twenty questions?"

"Did the doctors give you the results of your tox screens?" Jules whispered.

"What?" Gigi said a bit too loudly, "No, I don't think so. Why would I have tox screens done? I'm not a junkie or anything. I'm glad I'm feeling slightly better. If you'll excuse me," Gigi leaned on her cane to stand. "I need to go mingle. I'm a pariah sitting over here by myself. I know my book sales will tank if I don't do something fast. I can't let them forget about me."

It took Gigi several times to get her balance, but she played it off like her injuries were painful. "Excuse me," she said, limping off toward Allegra. She approached two women in bathrobes and hair curlers. "Could one of you be a dear and get me a chair? I sustained some serious injuries today, and I'm exhausted. But I wouldn't have missed tonight's festivities for the world.

I'm a bestselling and award-nominated author, Gigi Jones."

Jules watched Gigi elbow her way into the center of Allegra's crowd. *She must be feeling better. She's back to her old self.*

Chapter Thirty

Friday Evening

Jules sampled some of the dainty desserts on the festive table. Her favorites were the book-cover cookies that were almost too pretty to eat. Finding a spot near the outer perimeter where she could lean on the wall, she watched the parade of costumes and the awards ceremony. She scanned the crowd for Jake and spotted him at a table with Echo, Gigi, and Allegra. He nodded occasionally as the authors held court. Gigi, still at Allegra's table, seemed to be inserting herself into every conversation.

I couldn't find any evidence of pills in her purse or her trailer. Someone must have spiked her drink.

Jules made a mental note to check with the sheriff again. With all the things going on around here lately, it wasn't that far of a stretch to think someone had slipped her something. The green room wasn't locked, and nobody there seemed to be paying much attention to security. And she did say she poured the canned drink into a cup. Anyone in the room could have tampered with it.

Jules shook off the icy sensation that slid down her spine. Someone was targeting the authors. Money and jealousy, both motivators for crime, but this seemed to be something deeper, something vicious. Maybe money was the root of all this.

Scanning the room, she located the handful of authors in a sea of costumed fans. Windsor sat at a nearby table with Tiffany several seats away. The assistant checked her phone slyly under the table every two or three minutes.

Windsor pounded her fist on the table, and Tiffany jumped to attention. The author's face contorted into a purple rage as she glared at her assistant.

Keeping her eyes on the pair, Jules moved through the crowd to get within eavesdropping distance of the table. As she approached, Tiffany stood up and bumped the table. Nearby guests reached to steady their drinks as the personal assistant flung her napkin on her plate and stormed off.

Jules followed the millennial out the door and across the hall to the restroom. Inside, Tiffany clutched both sides of the porcelain sink and stared into the mirror. Splashing water in her face, she dabbed off the dribbles with a brown paper towel. After balling the towel up and tossing it in the trash, she rummaged through her purse.

Jules turned on the water at a nearby sink and washed her hands. Hi, Tiffany. Is everything okay?"

"Just swell." The assistant puckered her mouth and applied cherry red lipstick. "I will probably lose my job. That old bat tears apart everything I do. She is never happy. Ever since her precious beauties were stolen, I can do nothing right in her eyes. I think, deep down, she thinks I'm the crook. I should quit and save myself all the worry and anxiety. It would serve her right. But mark my words, she won't fire me until we get back to the office. She needs me to be at her beck and call twenty-four-seven and to carry all of her crap around. This is not the dream job I thought it was. Who knew that being a personal assistant to a famous author would turn into being an indentured servant." The younger woman let out a heavy sigh and fluffed her hair with her fingers.

Before Jules could comment, Tiffany continued, "I mean. I'm twenty-seven years old, and I have no life. I tend to this biddy's every need. I even live in a room in the basement of her house. I never get a break. And to think I was so excited to go work for her. She is so self-centered. I can't remember the last time she asked me how I was doing. Sheesh."

"Sometimes, you have to do what's best and figure out a new plan," Jules said.

"Don't get me wrong," Tiffany said, louder than Jules expected. "I've learned stuff and made a ton of contacts. But the constant badgering and micromanaging are too much. She can kiss my…" She made a face in the mirror and didn't finish her sentence.

"It sounds like you've made up your mind," Jules said. "Make your plan and stick to your guns."

The young woman gripped both sides of the tiny sink again and took a deep breath that she exhaled like she was in yoga class. "I know what I have to do. Tonight was the final straw. She belittles me constantly, and now she's convinced that I'm trying to sabotage her. She thinks I'm telling her business to other authors and giving away her secrets."

"She said that?" Jules asked.

Tiffany nodded. "She's paranoid. She checks behind every single thing I do. I mean, why have an assistant if you spend all your time nitpicking and following up. Let me do my job. For Pete's sake, she should go finish her novel that her agent keeps hounding her about. She wants to know who I'm on the phone with and who I've talked to recently. She even wanted to see my texts. She always wants to know if I talked about her or if I tell my friends I work for an award-winning author. She gave me approved talking points on how to refer to her highness in public. It's too much. I want a normal job. There. I've decided. When I get back, I'll pack my things and give her my notice. And I will stand firm if she tries to bribe me with a raise or whine about how much she needs me."

"I wish you the best. You need to take care of you."

The younger woman smiled faintly. "Thanks. I have to stand my ground. I mean, she is so petty. She wants flattery constantly. If I'm not complimentary about what she does, she pouts for hours. And she is so afraid that some author will get something she doesn't have. She sticks her nose in everyone's business." She took another deep breath and closed her eyes. Her eyes fluttered open, and she smacked her palm with her fist. "I can tough it out until we get home, and then I'm dropping the bomb. That way, she can't lock me out of her house before I pack my stuff. Can't wait to see the old witch's face when I tell her." A cartoon villain grin crossed Tiffany's face, and she turned on her heels and stalked out.

Jules freshened her lipstick and washed her hands again to give the younger woman a head start. *My pool of suspects is getting smaller, but there's not one clear person at the top of my list. Based on my gut feeling, it's not Tiffany, and it probably isn't Allegra or Gigi because they were victims. That leaves Windsor, Echo, and Phoenix from the author side and Carrie and Lynnette from the publishing side.*

Determined to come up with a plausible hypothesis, Jules stared at her image in the mirror. Windsor had a deadly collection and a sharp tongue. Did someone steal her stuff to use as weapons or for the poisons? Gigi ingested something. Echo tended to fly under the radar, and Phoenix was no shrinking violet when it came to voicing her opinion and complaining about almost everything. Three pretty solid suspects. All had some sort of motive. The other two women were the agent and publicist for Echo, Cinnamon, and Allegra. It wouldn't make sense for them to kill off their golden-egg-laying geese. *So, I guess I can mark them off the list.*

Thoughts whirled around Jules's head as she made her way to the cafeteria foyer, where Jake stood against the tile wall next to the glass display case. He listened and nodded on cue as Phoenix ranted and waved her arms around.

As Jules approached to give Jake an escape route, Phoenix launched into another tirade. "I mean, really. Like, who goes around attacking romance writers? For the most part, we write happily ever after. We are all hugs and sexy stuff. This makes no sense. I hope they figure out who's doing this."

Jake nodded, and Phoenix, in her red silky kimono, waved her arms around again. "It is too crazy unless it's not about the writing. What if it's about money or prestige? I should have thought of that before. It's always about the money and the power." She extended the number of syllables in her final words for emphasis. "It's been nice talking to you. If you want to get a drink sometime, stop by my trailer. I mix a mean Long Island iced tea." She took a step closer to Jake.

Before he could reply, Jules strode over for Operation Rescue. "There you are," she said, scooting closer to Jake. "It's been fun, but I was going to see if you're about ready to head out. We need to get home and check on the baby." *The fuzzy baby.*

"Yep. Need to make sure she's okay." He draped his arm around Jules's shoulders. "And I still need to do some things at the resort. It was nice to meet you," he said to Phoenix.

"And don't forget to check out my books. I have male readers who like the spicy stuff," Phoenix said with a wink.

On the way out, Jules waved to Darlene and Kim, who mingled with a clutch of costumed folks.

Jules shivered in the night air as they hiked to Jake's Mustang. "Feels like snow," he said, holding the passenger door for her.

"I'm ready for spring. I like it when the mountains come alive with all the new leaves and buds." She snuggled into the soft leather seat and turned on the seat warmer.

"I could use a string of warmer days to get a jump on the tree house construction. This one is taking me longer since I can't do a lot of the work in the barn. Maybe I can make some progress this week and next. I got a text yesterday from Gabe at Red's. His buddy wants to put in an order for a tiny house for some land he has near the lake. I'll talk with him this weekend. So that might delay the tree house a bit."

"Not a problem. Paying clients come first," Jules said.

"I got another contact through the website recently. They're looking for something to be built this summer." Jake signaled and turned into the resort's main entrance. "I may have to start subbing out some of the work if the orders keep coming in."

"Good problem to have." Jules patted his shoulder as he stopped in her driveway. "You should be excited at how quickly your business has taken off."

"The baby's at the window," he said with a grin. He leaned over to kiss Jules, and the butterflies danced inside her. "Sweet dreams," he whispered when she climbed out of the car. He waited until she was inside with Bijou before he zoomed off to his cabin.

"Hey, puppy. I may have finally encountered a whodunnit that I can't figure out," Jules said with a heavy sigh.

Chapter Thirty-One

Early Saturday Morning

An extended shriek jolted Jules out of a deep sleep. Not sure if she heard it or dreamed it, Jules sat up in the bed on one elbow. The shadows from the nearby pine trees danced around her room. She blinked several times, straining to see in the dark and listening for any weird sounds. Bijou stirred in her bed, but she didn't seem too concerned about the noise. Three-twenty-three. Way too early to be awake. The dog didn't react. *Maybe it was a dream?*

At about the time Jules was about to roll over and go back to sleep, a crash echoed in the woods, and then she heard another scream. Bijou jumped up and growled at the window.

Jules bolted out of bed and slid into a hooded sweatshirt and jeans. Slipping on a pair of boots, she stumbled out to the living room and scooped up her phone and her keys. Pausing, she returned to the kitchen and slipped a utility knife and a can of pepper spray from the junk drawer into her hoodie's front pocket.

From inside her cabin, it sounded like the noises came from the woods behind her house. Outside, everything was eerily still. No people or animals in sight. Jules stopped near the lodge to listen for any noises. An occasional tree frog and the wind rustling through the branches broke the silence. Jules strained to hear anything that sounded human. Nothing seemed to be moving around. Where did the scream come from?

The dark village of vintage trailers looked peaceful in the blue-blackness of the early morning. No lights dotted any of the windows. Wondering if the screechy noise came from a fox or some kind of animal, Jules took several tentative steps toward her cabin.

A shuffling sound caused her to freeze in her tracks. *There it was again. It sounds like something is being drug across the grass.*

She hopped behind a nearby tree trunk and peered around as the sound got closer. A female voice carried on a one-sided conversation filled with exclamations, grunts, and panting.

Jules held her breath as the voice and the dragging sound got louder. Her heartbeat echoed in her ears. Taking a deep, cleansing breath, she tried to calm down as someone approached. Her hand darted to her front pocket and clutched the pepper spray and the knife.

A figure in a dark hood pulled something across the grass close to Jules's hiding place. She held her breath and watched. The hooded figure hunched over, and in the dimness created by the lodge's flood lights, it looked like the person had someone else by the arms, or maybe it was an arm and leg. It was hard to tell.

"Stop it, or I will hurt you," the standing figure yelled. "I've had enough of you. Stop being stupid."

The person on the ground reached up and slugged the attacker, who swore loudly and reeled back. Regaining her footing, the attacker backhanded the person on the ground. The person being dragged fell backward and lay sprawled on the grass. Jules leaned forward to get a better view.

The attacker smacked the person again, loud enough for the crack to echo through the trees. Before Jules could react, the attacker grabbed the person under the arms and started dragging her again toward the woods.

Jules let out a gasp and pulled out her phone. She tapped in a quick text to Sheriff Hobbs and Jake.

The attacker stopped suddenly, dumping the body in the grass. "What are you doing? Resisting will only make it that much worse. You shouldn't have done what you did. I told you you'd be sorry," she screeched.

"Shut up. I don't care what you do to me. When you're caught, your sorry butt will spend the rest of your days in jail. You can kiss your career and your contracts goodbye," the person on the ground croaked.

"Crap. You broke three of my nails. That freakin' hurts. You're making this harder on yourself. You never know when to quit, do you? Give up. It'll be less pain," the attacker hissed and kicked the prone figure.

Moans drifted Jules's way. The groans got louder. Jules pocketed her phone and fumbled around in her pocket for the pepper spray.

The attacker moved around the figure, still on the ground. The victim curled up in a tight ball while the attacker hunched over with her back to Jules and pulled on the other person's arm.

While the attacker continued to kick, tug, and berate the figure on the ground, Jules set her jaw. She had to do something before the attacker injured the woman further, and there was no sign of any help arriving anytime soon. Taking a deep breath, Jules charged the hooded figure. The attacker paused for a split second and turned toward Jules.

Jules flicked the cap on the canister open and aimed it at the attacker, who drew back. Trying not to squirt the woman on the ground, Jules sent a spray toward the attacker.

She doubled over, coughing and swearing. Jules tried to duck out of the cayenne cloud. Her nose twitched, and her eyes started watering. Trying not to rub her face, Jules put herself between the attacker and the victim. Her eyes and nose started to run. Using the back of her hand and her sleeve, she wiped away the streaming tears so she could see better. Both the victim and the attacker coughed until a cool breeze slowly dissipated the spray.

The attacker straightened from a coughing spell and clawed at her eyes. She turned and paused for a beat. The hooded woman looked like she was ready to pounce. Jules steeled herself. Then, the woman turned and sped off toward the woods, trailing her flowing cape behind her.

"I'll be back as soon as I can. I don't want her to get away," Jules yelled at the person on the ground.

"Get that witch," the injured woman said feebly.

Jules tore off after the ghostly-looking figure. The cape fluttered behind her as she picked up speed, running like she was dodging oncoming players on a football field. Turning right, she headed for the tree line. Jules knew she had to speed up before the woman had a chance to disappear in the dark woods. Low-hanging branches grabbed at Jules as she tried to keep her pace on the uneven ground. No time for a flashlight. Jules hoped she could keep her balance and not lose the fleeing figure in the darkness. She followed the woman's noisy footfalls and the sounds of her heavy breathing.

Then, for no obvious reason, the figure turned and ran the way she came. Jules stumbled, landing on one knee. She tried to break her fall with her hand, but her wrist bent backwards. White stars shot through her line of vision. Sucking in cold air, she stood and ran despite the pain in her knee and wrist. The throbbing matched the pounding of the heartbeat in Jules's temples.

Once the pair reached the grassy area, the figure ran back toward the woman on the ground. The caped figure screeched and squealed as she approached. The other woman tried to crawl away, but the attacker approached too quickly.

It's now or never. You've got this. You're the only chance to stop the attack until the sheriff arrives.

Pouring on the steam, Jules lunged for the cape. Grabbing the hem with both hands, she pulled as hard as she could, jarring the woman and jerking her shoulders. Her head snapped backward, and she pulled forward, trying to escape. The caped woman stumbled before face-planting in the soft grass.

Ignoring the pain in her knee and wrist, Jules sprang forward and landed on the woman's back. The pair rolled around in the dirt and grass. Biting back the hot pain that zinged through her body, Jules gulped in the air and tried her best to subdue the flailing figure, who bucked like a bronco. Jules and the attacker traded places on top of the pile several times in a jumble of arms and legs. Wiggling one arm free, the hooded woman slammed her fist into the side of Jules's head. The pain from the contact shot through Jules's system. The attacker took advantage of the situation and slid out from under Jules.

The attacker crawled toward the woman on the ground. Jules reached up and grabbed the back of the hood and the woman's hair. She slammed the woman's head onto the frozen ground. Feral-sounding grunts seeped from the attacker. Jules slammed the woman's shoulders down and managed to flip the prone figure over.

Turning on her phone's flashlight, Jules shouted, "Echo! Phoenix!"

Chapter Thirty-Two

Early Saturday Morning

"What?" asked the groggy voice, curled up on the ground.

"What are you doing here with her?" Jules asked, putting her knee in the back of the attacker.

"She tricked me," Phoenix slurred from where she lay in the grass. "Echo said she wanted to talk to me about collaborating, and then she hit me in the back of the head and drug me out here in the dark. She's nuts."

"It'll be okay. Help will be here soon." Jules pulled out her phone and tapped 9-1-1 while using her knee to keep Echo from escaping. When the call connected, she said, "This is Jules Keene. I'm outside at the Fern Valley Luxury Camping Resort. There's been another attack. I need an ambulance and the police."

"Is everyone safe?" the dispatcher asked.

"Yes. But I have two injured women who were in a fight. I think they're both conscious, but they're both lying on the ground."

"Any bleeding? Obvious injuries?" The dispatcher asked.

"It's hard to tell. It's dark. Please tell the police to come up the maintenance road from the main gate. We're in the field near the large lodge on the back of the property."

"A deputy and an ambulance are on their way. Stay with me until they get there. I need to know you're safe."

The breeze picked up again as Echo arched her back and tried to knock

Jules off of her. Caught off guard, Jules had to steady herself. The phone flew out of her hand. She grabbed a hunk of Echo's hair to keep from falling off the woman's back.

"Ouch! Let go of me," Echo bellowed. "I'll ruin you like I did the others. People who get in my way have to pay. Cinnamon was the worst person ever. She had to go. Too bad my plans didn't turn out for Allegra and Gigi. They are despicable and needed to be taught a lesson," the author shrieked. She writhed on the ground, trying to shake Jules off. "This is not how this was supposed to turn out."

Echo managed to flip over. Her flailing fists swatted at Jules. Trying to dodge Echo's arms, Jules bobbed and ducked. One of Echo's hits connected with the side of Jules's head, and she toppled off of the author. A shockwave of pain seared through Jules, and red flashed in front of her eyes. She shook off the dizzy feeling, determined to detain Echo until the police arrived.

The author crawled toward her, scrabbling to get a grip on Jules and clutching at her ankles. Flipping on her side, Jules mule kicked as hard as she could. Her boot connected with Echo's head, and the author landed on her back with a loud thud and a grunt.

Not waiting to see what happened, Jules pounced on her and punched the author in the face. The woman struggled meekly and then twitched.

Jules balled her fist and readied herself if Echo attacked again. Her heartbeat pounded like a bass drum in her ears and head.

Two hands encircled Jules and pulled her up. "What are you doing? Get off of her!"

"Jake! It's me," she said as he lifted her to her feet.

"Jules? What are you doing out here? Are you okay?"

"I guess I'm okay," she said, shaking her sore hand.

"Sorry it took so long. I didn't hear your text come in, and then I couldn't find you. What happened?" Jake asked.

"Echo tried to kidnap Phoenix. She was attacking her. I heard the screams. Police and an ambulance are on their way. May I see your flashlight?"

Jake handed her his flashlight. She swooshed the beam around the ground and located her phone. Pocketing it, she hurried to Phoenix to check on her injuries. "Make sure she doesn't get up," Jules said, pointing to Echo, who moaned and braced her head with her hands.

Leaning over Phoenix, Jules shone the light to see if there was any bleeding.

"Hey, that's bright." Phoenix shaded her eyes with her arm.

"What hurts?" Jules asked.

"Everything," Phoenix replied. The rest of what she said was drowned out by the wail of sirens approaching.

Within minutes, Sheriff Hobbs and Deputy Mario Caswell jogged over to the group, adding their powerful flashlights to the dark corner near the forest. Phoenix looked small, curled up on the ground, and Echo didn't look that threatening, sprawled out in the loose dirt, surrounded by her cape.

"Jules, Jake. What's going on?" Sheriff Hobbs said, shining his light on the two women on the ground.

"Some noise woke me up, and I found Echo dragging Phoenix across the field to the woods." Jules pointed toward Echo.

"Looks like you all had a little altercation," he said. His lip twitched into a bit of a smile.

Jules, suddenly conscious of how she must look, tried to pat down her hair and dust off her sweatshirt. The mud and grass stains, along with what looked like blood on her jeans, made her realize the attempts were futile. Plus, the pain from her head, knee, and wrist reminded her to find an icepack soon. The swelling had already started.

Another siren interrupted their conversation, and they turned and watched the ambulance bounce over the field, slowing as it approached where they huddled. Three EMTs hopped out, dragging armloads of equipment with them.

"So, what happened?" Sheriff Hobbs asked as the others tended to Phoenix and Echo.

"I thought I heard a scream. Then I heard another, so I went outside to see what was happening. A hooded figure was dragging something toward the woods. It turned out to be Phoenix."

"I was not." Echo leaned around the deputy and snapped back. "You can't prove it. I am the victim here."

"Shut up," Phoenix moaned. "You said you wanted to talk to me about a project, and stupid me blindly met you outside. You hit me in the head and kidnapped me."

"That's your story. I came outside to talk to you, and you tried to extort money from me. I don't know who you think you are," Echo squawked. "Then you both attacked me and held me against my will. I want to call my lawyer. I will sue all of you and make sure you pay. I'll ruin you both."

"We'll get your statements in a minute," Sheriff Hobbs said over his shoulder. He nodded to the deputy, who moved closer to Echo.

"She attacked Phoenix, and I jumped in to help," Jules said. "I had no idea why she was dragging her into the woods. I had to stop her."

"She saved me," Phoenix added. "Who knows what this beast had in mind for me. I know she planned to leave me for dead. The whole thing is chilling. She's a psycho. She killed Cinnamon and attacked Allegra and Gigi, and then she came for me."

"You can't prove anything," Echo hissed. "You're the money-grubbing so-called writer who jumps on every get-rich-quick scheme. You're known as a cheat and a charlatan! I was trying to stop you. To prevent you from scamming people."

"But at least I'm not a killer," Phoenix croaked.

"See, she admits to cheating people," Echo said.

"Are you done with her?" Deputy Caswell asked the EMT who stood next to Echo.

"Her wrist is swelling. We should transport her. The head injury needs to be checked on, too," the EMT said, rising and draping his stethoscope around his neck.

"I'll call for another ambulance for transport. These two shouldn't be in the same wagon." The deputy reached for his shoulder microphone.

"Go ahead," Sheriff Hobbs said to Jules.

"That's about it. We separated them until you all arrived," she said.

"That's not true. She chased me down and through the woods. That's how I got all these scratches on me. I'm gonna sue. This is a dangerous place with all kinds of evil people running around. I was just trying to stop them. And then the owner of the place attacked me. Just wait until I tell my TikTok followers. You will be so sorry that you messed with me," Echo said with an ugly sneer.

Jules clamped her lips shut before a sharp retort escaped.

Sheriff Hobbs interrupted, "Deputy Caswell, please go with Ms. Aames to the hospital, but first make sure she understands her rights. Ms. Abbott will follow in the next ambulance."

The EMTs eased Echo on the gurney as she resisted the assistance. Her arms flailed, and she tried to shake off the two men.

"Ma'am, calm down. You'll hurt yourself," the taller medic said. "If you don't, we'll have to restrain you for your safety and ours."

"I'll take care of it." Deputy Caswell recited her Miranda rights as he handcuffed her wrists to the gurney."

When the ambulance's back door finally closed. Deputy Caswell nodded to the sheriff and sent some unsaid, telepathic message before he jogged toward his cruiser.

"Thanks, Jules," Sheriff Hobbs said. Turning toward Phoenix. "Start at the beginning and tell me what happened." He leaned down on one knee near her.

Phoenix started at the author costume party and described the events up until moments ago in colorful detail and a lot of side commentary. Sheriff Hobbs listened attentively and jotted notes.

"Thank you," he said when she finally took a breath. "That's good timing." He looked over his shoulder as the second ambulance approached and stopped several feet away. "Go ahead and transport her. I'll meet you all over at the hospital in a little while," the sheriff said to the medic who had stayed with Phoenix from the first ambulance crew.

The EMT nodded. He walked over and huddled with the new arrivals. Within minutes, they loaded Phoenix on a gurney and wheeled her over the bumpy ground.

"You sure you don't want to get checked out before they leave?" The sheriff nodded his head toward the ambulance.

"It's nothing that a couple of icepacks can't fix. I'll be fine."

He raised one eyebrow and gave her his best sheriffy look.

"I'll be fine," she repeated.

"State police and forensics will be here shortly. I need the key to Echo's accommodations," Sheriff Hobbs said.

"Do you want to come back to the office to warm up and get some coffee?" Jules asked.

"I need to stay here until they get here."

"I'll go get the key and coffee," Jake said.

"Anything else that stands out about these two?" Sheriff said.

The early morning air sent a shiver down Jules's spine. Hugging her sweatshirt closer to her, she said, "Echo and Cinnamon had a long-standing feud. Echo seemed jealous of anyone who did better than she did. She also accused Cinnamon of stealing her idea for a western romance that was sold recently for a movie. I have no idea what provoked the attack on Phoenix, but they argued a lot, too."

The sheriff shifted his weight from one leg to another. "I'm waiting on the tox screens to come back on Gigi Jones. The doc thought she had been drugged, so he ordered some screens that aren't part of the normal process. Echo's list of offenses keeps getting longer, and so does the pile of charges."

"Any news about Allegra's attack?"

"Not sure yet. Playing with some possible theories. I think the pieces will fall into place when we question Phoenix and Echo further today."

As the pair stood in silence, waiting for forensics, Jake drove the golf cart across the field and stopped nearby. "Here ya go," he said, handing the sheriff the key and coffee.

"We're going to be here a while. We've got multiple crime scenes to work," Sheriff Hobbs said, taking a swig from the to-go cup.

Chapter Thirty-Three

Saturday Afternoon

After a hot shower and toast with jam and tea, Jules was too amped up to return to bed. She and Bijou headed to the office to catch up on email. She laughed when she read Elaine's latest missive about plans for the Spring Fling activities. *We haven't even put the "Love is in the Air" festival to bed yet, and she's ready for the next one.*

The police activity in the back field kept drawing Jules to the window like a magnet.

"Whatcha peeking at?" Roxanne asked, stopping next to her.

Her aunt's voice made her jump and squeal. "I didn't hear you come in. Thanks, Bijou. You're slacking on the guard duties in your job description." On cue, the little dog rolled over and did her best puppy eyes.

"You must have been lost in thought," Roxanne said, picking up Bijou for a cuddle. "It looks like it's been hopping out there. I'm sure Lester doesn't know whether to peep out the window or stay plugged into his scanner. Wonder if the chord to his headphones reaches all the way to the window."

Jules snickered. "He's in his element. I haven't heard anything from him today, so he must be glued to his scanner."

"So, what's shaking around here? With all that police presence, it doesn't look like a boring Saturday. I want details." Her aunt cracked a smile and pulled a mug down from the nearby cabinet. "And what's that on your cheek?"

Jules's hand touched a bruise under her eye. "My day started with a scream in the woods. Echo abducted Phoenix and dragged her across the field. I kinda got caught up in a tussle. I ended up with a bunch of bruises and scratches."

Roxanne's eyes widened. "So, the killer was Echo Aames? She seemed so together and so professional. Of all the high-maintenance divas who descended on us, she was one I never suspected. Why? And do you want me to get you some ice? That shiner's already blue and purple."

"My face is okay. A little sore. I'll put some concealer on it. My wrist is throbbing a bit. I twisted it in the tussle with Echo."

"Sit still. I'll get you some ice." Roxanne wrapped several handfuls from the icemaker in a dishtowel and handed it to her niece. "I think you should get checked out."

"Thanks." Jules rested it on her wrist and sank into her chair. "Maybe later when things calm down here. With Cinnamon, it was a festering fight over a story idea that Echo claimed Cinnamon stole and made a fortune with. It dated back to their critique group days. She felt she didn't get what she deserved, and the other authors did her wrong. She called them sinful and said they had to be stopped."

Roxanne let out a whistle and whirled her index finger next to her temple. "Money and power and a lot of crazy," Roxanne muttered as the coffee maker sputtered to life.

A knock at the back door sent the brown and white Jack Russell terrier into Rambo mode. The sheriff stepped inside the doorway and took off his Smokey Bear hat. "Hey, Jules and Rox. Hey, pup. It's going to take longer than I thought out there. You okay if I give you the key to Echo's trailer later? There's a bunch of stuff for the forensic folks to process, and I've got to head over to the office. The questioning will take a chunk of time, too."

"That's no problem. If it goes past Sunday, I'll let Crystal and Mel know to delay our normal, after check-out cleaning."

"Leave Echo's stuff where it is for now. Phoenix should be released from the hospital either today or tomorrow, so she'll be able to collect her belongings then," he said.

"So, Sheriff Matt, I guess this means I won't be seeing much of you in the near future." She handed him the mug of coffee and popped a pod in for another cup for herself.

"Not sure what this week will bring, but my guess is a ton of late nights. The paperwork alone is going to take me at least a week." He let out a slight sigh under his breath.

"Fill us in. Echo killed Cinnamon and attacked Allegra," Roxanne said.

He nodded. "And Gigi and Phoenix. Deputy Caswell said she vacillated between ranting about being the victim and then boasting about her clever means of getting rid of the annoying competition and those who she felt had harmed her."

Roxanne's eyebrows shot up under her platinum bangs. "She's a piece of work."

"In her twisted mind, she justified what she did because she felt she was wronged and preventing them from hurting others," Jules added.

"Maybe. When she realized we were taking her to jail for processing, she lay on the moans and complained about the pain. Who knows when the docs will release her. I've got a deputy stationed outside of her door. She tried to slip out once already. And she said she's planning a press conference."

"What about the other things…the trashed worksite at the tree house, Windsor's missing items, and Gigi's escapade?"

"She was scoping out the tiny houses and the vintage trailers, and she tried to throw the suspicion off herself with the vandalism to the tree house. The stolen items could have been for multiple reasons. It seems her grand plan was to have murder weapons from the dead author's stories. Hence the knitting needle we found with Cinnamon's body. But she didn't continue with her original plan, and thankfully, for the victims, she was only successful with one murder. She was interested in Windsor's deadly antiques," the sheriff said.

"She wasn't very consistent. It almost feels like the Allegra, Gigi, and Phoenix attacks were kind of random or at least not well planned," Jules said.

"I think some of it was a spur-of-the-moment thing. She took advantage of what was happening around her. Echo admitted to Deputy Caswell that Gigi was the most annoying person on earth, and she was doing everyone a favor by getting rid of her. Thankfully, her other attacks weren't successful."

"A lot of her ramblings don't make much sense. She hinted that she was righting wrongs that had been done to her and getting what she always deserved," Jules said.

"But Allegra was everyone's darling. She's been a fan favorite for decades. What could the royalty of romance do to Echo?" Roxanne asked.

"She told the deputy in no uncertain terms that she was sick and tired of Allegra being everyone's favorite. It was time for the old guard to step aside. Echo claimed Allegra's sweet persona was a front for a sadistic hack. Her words, not mine. It seems early on in Echo's career, she had asked Allegra for a favor. She wanted an in with Allegra's publisher. She asked the seasoned author to recommend her and her book. Echo didn't get the book contract, and she blamed Allegra for bad-mouthing her to the publisher and cheating her out of a lucrative deal."

"She holds a grudge for a long time," Jules said.

"Like I said before, money and power and a twisted little mind." Roxanne raised one eyebrow.

"Thanks for the coffee. I need to get back. Rox, I'll call ya when I can. It may be late." He kissed Jules's aunt on the cheek and waved as he headed for the door.

"It was Echo Aames all along." Roxanne made a tsking sound. "When the press gets hold of this story, I'm sure you'll have some media inquiries and enough material for a true crime documentary."

"Free publicity, I guess," Jules said, scanning through several news and gossip sites. "So far, nothing has broken yet. I don't see anything online about it. Let's see how long that lasts."

"You'll hear from Jane the Pain before the day's out," her aunt said with a wink. "I'll bet money she's already heard about all the activity on her own police scanner. It's a matter of time. I can hold them off here and keep an eye on things. You need to go see a doctor. I've texted Jake to bring the car around."

Jules frowned slightly. "I'm fine. I'll be good as new tomorrow."

"Pick up that laptop." Her aunt pointed to the desk.

When Jules winced, Roxanne said, "See. I'm right. Don't argue. Jake will be here in a minute. Bijou and I will keep things humming here."

Jake slipped in the back door and sent Bijou on a barking jag.

"See. Even Bijou insists. Go. Get your coat." She gave her niece a side-eye until she slipped on the coat that Jake held and followed him out the door.

"You won't miss anything here," Roxanne yelled after them.

Chapter Thirty-Four

Sunday Morning

Roxanne breezed into the office a little before nine with a to-go carton from the lodge's brunch. "Good morning. How are things?"

"Fine. Thanks for locking up and taking Bijou to my cabin. It took longer at the emergency room than I anticipated. Jake stopped for dinner, and it was after seven before we were back." Jules held up her wrist brace.

"No headaches or dizziness this morning?"

"It's fading. At least it wasn't a concussion. I'm glad to be back to normal. Any scuttlebutt on Echo's arrest?"

"No, not really. It's been steady with checkouts since I opened the doors a little after eight. We also have ten couples checking in this afternoon around four for a winter bird-watching excursion."

Jules nodded. "Elaine sent me the lead for the guy who owned the tour company. If it goes well, he may bring back more groups."

"That's always good. I remember when the campground closed at the end of summer. I'm glad you can keep it open year-round. You've put the resort on the map as a tourist attraction. Let me throw these on my desk, and I'll be back to help you in a bit."

The bell rang, and Jules greeted Windsor and Tiffany. "Hello, ladies. Ready to check out?"

"It's been a whirlwind," Windsor said, leaning on her elbow on the front counter. "I'm exhausted. I'll need at least a week to recover, but it's always wonderful to have an opportunity to mingle with fans."

Jules printed out the paperwork and handed it to Windsor to review. She fished around in her purse and pulled out the key. Then she snapped her fingers at Tiffany. "Hurry up. Where's your key? I don't want to get charged for a missing one."

Tiffany slid the key across the counter as she glared at Windsor.

Oblivious to her assistant's feelings, Windsor continued, "I heard from the gals that the police arrested Echo. Who knew we had a killer in our midst? I was sure that it was some crazed fan. I've been looking over my shoulder the entire time I've been here. I guess you never know. I'm wondering if the police will link the theft of my property to her, too. That'll get you off the hook," Windsor said, peering down her pointed nose at Tiffany.

"I hope they catch the thief. It's time to shake things up," Tiffany said in a small voice. "It's about time we right some wrongs around here." She winked at Jules and followed Windsor out the front.

Roxanne slid behind the counter next to Jules. "What was that all about?" she asked as Tiffany closed the door.

"I think Windsor will be in the market for a new personal assistant soon. Tiffany's ready to explore new opportunities," Jules said.

Roxanne raised an eyebrow. "She can do better than that cantankerous woman."

No sooner had quiet returned to the office than the door flung open and bounced off the hinges. Gigi, dragging a rolling suitcase and juggling her cane, oversized bag, and purse, dropped everything on the wooden floor with a clatter. She pulled off her tortoise-shell sunglasses and stared at Roxanne and Jules.

"Would you like to check out, Ms. Jones," Roxanne said in her sacchariney tone reserved for her favorite guests.

"That's why I'm here. It's been a wild ride, but thankfully, it's time to head home. It's a little too quaint here if you ask me. Time to get back to the nightlife and my life. And I've got a deadline, so it's back to the grind. I've always got something in the hopper." She waved her hand and looked down her nose.

"I hope your accommodations met your standards," Roxanne said with a toothy grin.

"Well, mostly. The bed was lumpy. I can't believe y'all don't have a turn-down service. This town needs Uber and more places to dine. But I guess it was okay for a back-woodsy sort of place. No offense, but it's not somewhere I'd go on purpose. I'd never be able to write here. The woodland country noises are too loud and creepy. I need to be around people."

Jules hoped her smile wasn't too much like a grimace. "Well, we're glad you came for a visit. I'm sure your fans enjoyed seeing you up close and personal."

"It was good for that. But I told that pushy lady in my survey about the issues with the festival and what she could do to improve. If you ask me, I think she played favorites with the authors. My comments were quite detailed, and I provided lots of examples." She tapped her bottom lip with her index finger. "Oh, but if you do a book festival next year, make sure to let me know."

"She will appreciate all the feedback," Jules added, hoping no sarcasm seeped out. "How are you feeling after your ordeal?"

"Oh, I'm fine. My appetite's still not back to normal, but I should be okay after I get home and settled. The water and the food are different here, so I'm sure that's the reason. Your sheriff said that I may get called to testify when Echo's case goes to court. Can you believe she tried to drug me?" Gigi's hand fluttered to her forehead. "I guess that's to be expected when one is famous. I may have to think about hiring security. Who knows what lengths angry, jealous people will go to."

Jules handed Gigi the paperwork, and the author signed with a flourish of John Hancock. "Thank you," Jules said. "Have a safe trip home."

"I'm glad to be heading out." Gigi shoved the receipt in her oversized bag and strode out the door, dragging her suitcase and cane behind her.

"Can't wait to see what she puts on our comment card," Roxanne said. "Though, we've already heard most of it already. She doesn't sugarcoat her words. We won't miss that one. I hope Elaine and Elizabeth are keeping a list of the drama llamas."

"But she did say to let her know if we have another book festival. Not sure if Elaine and Elizabeth will be ready to do one of these anytime soon. I think we all have scars and bruises from this event." Jules winked at her aunt.

The door opened, and Lynnette D'Angelo dropped her suitcase and carry-on at the door. "Morning, ladies. This has been fun, but I need to hurry back home and get caught up on stuff I missed while I was here."

"You'll be busy with all that's going on with Echo right now," Roxanne said as she printed the publicist's receipt.

Lynnette paused and stared at Roxanne and Jules. Her dark eyebrows formed a "V" as she continued to stare.

"You did hear about Echo's arrest this morning," Jules added.

Lynnette reached for her receipt and nodded. "She brought this all on herself. I have no sympathy and no time to help her resurrect her career after all the damage she's caused. Carrie and I talked at length and decided that we could no longer represent her. She'll have to look elsewhere for a support team. We need to focus on our other authors and not clean up her mess. Thanks again. You have a lovely resort." Lynnette picked up her bags and hurried out.

"Well, for the fans, 'Love was in the Air' was a huge success. I know the business council folks all need a break." Before Roxanne could continue her thought, the door opened a crack, and Sheriff Hobbs strode in.

"Hi, Jules. Hi, Rox. How're things?" he asked.

"Life is good. I didn't expect to see much of you. I thought you were tied up with your investigation," Roxanne said.

"Thankfully, we're wrapping up the big stuff. Just wanted to check in with Jules. I want forensics to go over the campers one more time before you all start cleaning and returning them to service. It shouldn't take all that long, especially if today is change-over day."

"You want the keys now? Phoenix, Allegra, and Carrie are the only ones who haven't checked out yet," Jules said.

"I'll get the keys for the empty ones for you and make you a list of the others. The rest of the folks should be out by noon," Roxanne said, pulling out a legal pad. "We got a little tidbit of interesting information from the publicist."

"Do tell," he said.

"According to Lynnette, she and Carrie Shultz have decided to no longer represent Echo."

"Hummm-huh. Everything else back to normal here?" he asked Jules.

Jules nodded. "I've got a group of bird watchers coming to town. And there's a wedding and some folks coming in for a wine tasting. I'm ready for spring." She glanced at her aunt, researching accommodation information of their recent check-outs. "Hey, I'm curious about some of the unrelated stuff like the vandalism at Jake's job site, Windsor's missing items, and the weird stuff under Cinnamon's camper."

"Echo said they were supposed to be clues to the author's deeds. Everything with her was about retribution, and then in her next breath, she asked for a psych evaluation because she claimed to have blacked out like some kind of Dr. Jekyll and Mr. Hyde thing," Sheriff Hobbs said.

Roxanne's stylized eyebrows shot up as her eyes widened, but she continued to make the list for the sheriff.

"She was on a walk and saw Jake's stuff. I guess in her jumbled mind, it made sense to try to throw suspicion in another direction. Though she did return to the scene when she dumped Allegra Rhodes at the tree house. I'm still not sure why she dragged her up to the platform. She could have easily dumped her nearby."

The resort's phone jangled, and Jules answered, "Welcome to the Fern Valley Luxury Camping Resort. How may I help you?"

"Good morning. I'm looking for some accommodations for a group at the end of March or maybe later in the spring. I know it's short notice, but I was hoping you could help me."

"How many in your party? We can accommodate groups and special occasions. Let me pull up the calendar of availability," Jules said.

"I was wondering if I could get you to hold a block of rooms, and then all the participants could make their own reservations," the caller said.

"That is fine. We can work out pricing for your event." Jules reached for the mouse, and Roxanne pushed it closer to her niece. "Let's see. Starting on February 22, I have fifteen trailers that could accommodate two adults comfortably. I also have two tiny houses that are available."

"Sounds perfect. We'd need the rooms for at least two weeks for a paranormal investigation we're doing in the area."

"Interesting. They say that there are lots of haunted places along the Blue Ridge Parkway. What's the name of your group?"

"ECP, East Coast Paranormal. I'm Eliot Kellogg. I'm the president of the chapter."

Jules explained the hold system for the accommodations and recorded all the details for the group's two-week stay. "I'll send you an email confirmation with the details and reservation code for your group. What is your email address?" Jules jotted down the information. "Thanks. I'll get this out to you for East Coast Paranormal today."

When she disconnected, Roxanne and the sheriff stared at her. "Well, that should be something new," her aunt said. "Not sure if I want to summon up any ghosts and demons, but it should give us something to talk about besides murder and romance novels."

The sheriff cracked a smile and picked up the list and keys Roxanne offered.

Roxanne's Spicy Fudge

Ingredients:

3 cups milk chocolate chips

14 ounces of sweetened, condensed milk

1 teaspoon vanilla extract

1 teaspoon cinnamon

¼ teaspoon of cayenne pepper

Directions:

1. Line an 8-inch square baking pan with aluminum foil or parchment paper.
2. In a small pot, heat the chocolate and sweetened condensed milk over medium-low. Make sure all the chocolate melts. Stir constantly.
3. Add the vanilla, cinnamon, and cayenne pepper. (If you are concerned about the spiciness, add the cayenne pepper slowly and taste the sample.)
4. Pour the fudge in the baking pan. Refrigerate for four hours to allow the fudge to set.
5. Remove the fudge from the pan and cut into small squares.

Mel's Chocolate Popcorn Surprise

Ingredients:

2 ounces of unsalted butter

1 ¾ ounces (about 7 cups) popped popcorn

3 ounces of water

4 ounces of light corn syrup

9 ounces of sugar

3 ounces of dark chocolate (chopped)

¾ teaspoon baking soda

¼ teaspoon kosher salt

Tools:

Candy thermometer

Directions:

1. Pop your popcorn. Lightly grease a large bowl. In a saucepan, mix the water, corn syrup, butter, and sugar over a medium heat. Stir continuously for about four minutes.
2. Increase the temperature to medium-high. Use your candy thermometer to heat the mixture until it reaches 340 degrees F.
3. Lightly grease a baking pan/sheet. Mix the remaining ingredients in a bowl. Remove the heated syrup when it reaches the correct temperature. Stir in the chocolate, baking soda, and salt. Mix thoroughly and pour over the popcorn. Thoroughly coat the popcorn.
4. Put the popcorn on the baking sheet. Divide the popcorn into bite-sized clusters. Cool until the candy shell is hard. Store the candied

popcorn in an air-tight container.

Crystal's Milk Chocolatey Skillet Cake

Ingredients:

For the Cake:
- 6 ounces of unsalted butter
- 6 ounces of black coffee
- 1 ½ ounces of Dutch cocoa (Don't substitute natural cocoa)
- 3 ounces of dark chocolate (finely chopped)
- 8 ounces of light brown sugar
- ¼ ounce of vanilla extract
- ¾ teaspoon of kosher salt
- 4 large eggs
- 4 ½ ounces of all-purpose flour
- 1 ½ teaspoons of baking soda

For the Icing:
- 6 ounces of milk chocolate (finely chopped)
- 8 ounces of heavy cream
- Salt

Directions:

The Icing

1. Put milk chocolate in a medium mixing bowl. In a 10-inch cast iron skillet, bring the cream to simmer over medium heat. When it bubbles, pour over the milk chocolate and whisk until smooth. Add salt to taste.

When it has cooled, cover and refrigerate until needed.

The Cake

1. Preheat your oven to 350 degrees F. Combine the butter and coffee in the cast iron skilled. Warm over low heat until the butter has melted. Remove from heat and mix in the cocoa and dark chocolate. Then add the brown sugar, vanilla, and salt. Mix in the eggs, flour, and baking soda. Continue to stir until the batter is smooth.
2. Put the skillet in the oven and bake until the cake is firm (about 30 minutes). Remove the cake from the oven and let it completely cool.
3. Stir your icing mix until it has thickened. Ice the cake completely. You can garnish the icing with sprinkles or candy, if desired.

Gooey S'mores Bites

Ingredients:

9 full-sized (rectangular) graham crackers

¼ cup unsalted butter (cut into cubes)

1 ¾ cups of sugar

3 tablespoons of sugar

4 ounces of semisweet chocolate

4 ounces of unsweetened chocolate

1 cup of heavy cream

8 large eggs (egg whites only)

¼ teaspoon cream of tartar

¼ teaspoon kosher salt

1 teaspoon vanilla extract

Tools:

Candy thermometer

Directions:

1. Preheat your oven to 325 degrees F. Line a square baking pan with foil. Mix the crackers, butter, and 3 tablespoons of sugar thoroughly. Pat the mixture into the bottom of the lined pan. Bake this for fifteen minutes. Then cool the mixture on a wire rack.
2. Break up the semisweet and unsweetened chocolate in a microwave-safe bowl. Melt in the microwave. Heat for 30-second intervals until the chocolate is melted. Make sure that you stir after each heating.
3. Whip the heavy cream. Chill in the refrigerator.

4. Mix the egg whites, 1 ¾ cups of sugar, the cream of tartar, and the salt. Simmer a pan of water on the stove. Put the bowl over the simmering water. Whisk the mixture until the temperature reaches 165 degrees F. Remove the bowl from the water and whisk the mixture until it has stiff peaks. It may take about 4-5 minutes. Add the vanilla and beat for an additional minute.

5. Set aside half of the meringue. Fold the cooled chocolate mixture into the remaining egg white mixture. Spread this mixture on top of the cooled crust. Then ice the dessert with the remaining meringue.

6. Preheat your oven for broil. Broil the dessert for about 30-60 seconds. *Make sure that it doesn't burn.* Chill the entire dessert for about 2 hours.

7. Slice the s'mores into smaller squares and serve.

Crystal's Chocolate Volcano Lava Cake

Ingredients:

2 teaspoons butter

8 ounces of bittersweet chocolate (chopped)

¾ cup butter

3 eggs

3 egg yolks

1/3 cup granulated sugar

1 teaspoon vanilla

1 tablespoon all-purpose flour

Powdered sugar

Directions:

1. Use the butter to grease six 8-10 ounce ramekins or custard dishes. Put the smaller dishes on a large, baking pan.
2. In a saucepan, combine the chocolate and ¾ cup of butter. Cook on a low heat until all the chocolate melts. Make sure to stir constantly. Remove the pan from the heat.
3. In a large mixing bowl, beat the full eggs, egg yolks, sugar, and vanilla with an electric mixer on high for about 10 minutes. Fold 1/3 of the chocolate mixture into the egg mixture.
4. Then mix in the remaining chocolate and flour. Spoon about 2/3 cup of the batter into each ramekin or custard dish.
5. Bake at 425 degrees F for 12 minutes. Cool the containers on a wire rack. Use a knife to loosen the edges of the cake from each dish. Invert each onto a dessert plate. Cover each cake with powdered sugar.

6. Garnish with raspberries, candy, or other fruit.

Jules's Jammin' Chocolate Banana Smoothie

Ingredients:

- ¾ cup milk or almond milk
- 1 teaspoon of cocoa powder (Add more if you like it chocolatey.)
- 2 teaspoons or honey or maple syrup
- ¼ cup ice cubes (about 6-7)
- 1 large, frozen banana

Instructions:

1. Put the milk, cocoa powder, honey, ice and banana in your blender. Blend on high until all ingredients are smooth. Enjoy!

Mel's Decadent Strawberry Brioche

Ingredients:

¼ cup softened butter (unsalted)
3 tablespoons of sweetened, condensed milk
2 tablespoons of honey
1 large egg yolk
1 teaspoon of vanilla extract
¼ teaspoon of salt
12 slices of brioche
1 pound of strawberries (chopped)
Juice from a ½ of lemon
1 teaspoon of sugar
3 cups of whipped cream
Coconut flakes (optional for topping)

Instructions:

1. Preheat the oven to 350 degrees F.
2. Mix butter, milk, and honey. Whisk until fully mixed. Add the egg yolk, vanilla, and salt. Mix thoroughly and set aside.
3. Using a knife, cut a diamond-pattern in each slice of toast (about an inch apart). Don't cut through the bread completely.
4. Spread about 3 tablespoons of the batter over each slice. Make sure that each is fully covered.
5. Line a baking sheet with parchment paper. Put the bread on the baking

sheet. Let the honey mix settle on the bread for about 10 minutes. Then bake for about 16 minutes until the toast is golden brown.

6. Mix the strawberries, lemon juice, and sugar.
7. Cool the bread for about 10 minutes. Add several spoons of the strawberry mixture to each piece of toast and top with whipped cream. Drizzle honey over each. You can add toppings like coconut flakes for more flavor.

Acknowledgements

I want to thank my family and friends who provided all the wonderful support for me and this book: Stan Weidner, thanks for traveling on this writing journey with me, my parents who instilled in me a lifelong love of reading, Cortney Cain for being my texting buddy at five a.m., Meagan Van Laeken and Jocelyn Cain, my social media subject matter experts, and Bill Cain for always keeping everyone entertained. And I appreciate all the encouragement from my Bethia UMC family.

A huge thank you to Shawn Reilly Simmons and everyone at Level Best Books for letting me share the fun of the glamping mysteries and the mayhem in Fern Valley.

I treasure my talented Sisters in Crime, Guppy, Writers Who Kill, and James River Writer friends. Your support is invaluable! Mary Burton, Tracey Livesay, Avery Flynn, and Lisa Dyson, thank you for all the great ideas and being great panelists for our "Spice up Your Writing" presentation. Many thanks to Leah Price, K. L. Murphy, and Judy Chalkley. It has been an honor to serve with you ladies.

To all the readers, podcasters, bloggers, and reviewers. Thank you for making all of this possible and letting me share Jules, Bijou, Roxanne, Jake, and the rest of the gang with you.

And tearfully, thanks to Dawn Dowdle for all her help, encouragement, and hard work. I miss you.

About the Author

Through the years, Heather Weidner has been a cop's kid, technical writer, editor, college professor, software tester, and IT manager. She writes the Jules Keene Glamping Mysteries, the Mermaid Bay Christmas Shoppe Mysteries, the Delanie Fitzgerald Mysteries, and the Pearly Girls Mysteries.

Her short stories appear in the *Virginia is for Mysteries* series, *50 Shades of Cabernet, Deadly Southern Charm,* and *Murder by the* Glass, and she has non-fiction pieces in *Promophobia* and *The Secret Ingredient: A Mystery Writers' Cookbook.*

She is a member of Sisters in Crime: National, Central Virginia, Chessie, Guppies, and Grand Canyon Writers, International Thriller Writers, and James River Writers, and she blogs regularly with the Writers Who Kill.

Originally from Virginia Beach, Heather has been a mystery fan since Scooby-Doo and Nancy Drew. She lives in Central Virginia with her husband and a pair of Jack Russell terriers.

AUTHOR WEBSITE:

http://HeatherWeidner.com

SOCIAL MEDIA HANDLES:

Website and Blog: http://www.heatherweidner.com

BlueSky: https://bsky.app/profile/heatherweidner.bsky.social

Twitter/X: https://twitter.com/HeatherWeidner1

Facebook: https://www.facebook.com/HeatherWeidnerAuthor

Instagram: https://www.instagram.com/heather_mystery_writer/

Goodreads: https://www.goodreads.com/author/show/8121854.Heath
er_Weidner

Amazon Authors: http://www.amazon.com/-/e/B00HOYR0MQ

Pinterest: https://www.pinterest.com/HeatherBWeidner/

LinkedIn: https://www.linkedin.com/in/heather-weidner-0064b233?
trk=hp-identity-name

BookBub: https://www.bookbub.com/authors/heather-weidner-d6430
278-c5c9-4b10-b911-340828fc7003

Threads: https://www.threads.net/@heather_mystery_writer

TikTok: https://www.tiktok.com/@heather_weidner_author

YouTube: https://www.youtube.com/channel/UCyBjyB0zz-M1DaM-r
U1bXGA?view_as=subscriber

LinkTree: https://linktr.ee/heatherweidner

Also by Heather Weidner

The Jules Keene Glamping Mysteries:
Vintage Trailers and Blackmailers
Film Crews and Rendezvous
Christmas Lights and Cat Fights
Deadlines and Valentines

The Mermaid Bay Christmas Shoppe Mysteries:
Sticks and Stones and a Bag of Bones
Twinkle Twinkle Au Revoir

The Delanie Fitzgerald Mysteries:
Secret Lives and Private Eyes
The Tulip Shirt Murders
Glitter, Glam, and Contraband
Male Revues and Subterfuge

Non-fiction:
Promophobia
The Secret Ingredient

Short Stories: The *Virginia is for Mysteries* series, *50 Shades of Cabernet,*
Murder by the Glass, and *Deadly Southern Charm*